PERFORMANCE
ANOMALIES

PERFORMANCE ANOMALIES

ANOMALIES

VICTOR ROBERT LEE

PERFORMANCE ANOMALIES

Published by Perimeter Six
Email: info@perimeter-six.com

www.perimeter-six.com

Perimeter Six is an imprint of The Pacific Media Trust.

ISBN 978-1-938409-22-6

Library of Congress Control Number: 2012937262

First published in the United States of America

Printed in the United States of America

Cover design by Ervin Serrano

"Human performance anomalies arising from extremely rare genetic variations will be exploited for strategic and tactical purposes."

— *"Capabilities for a New Millennium," U.S. Defense Advanced Research Projects Agency classified document, serial no. 55-89-144, p. 87.*

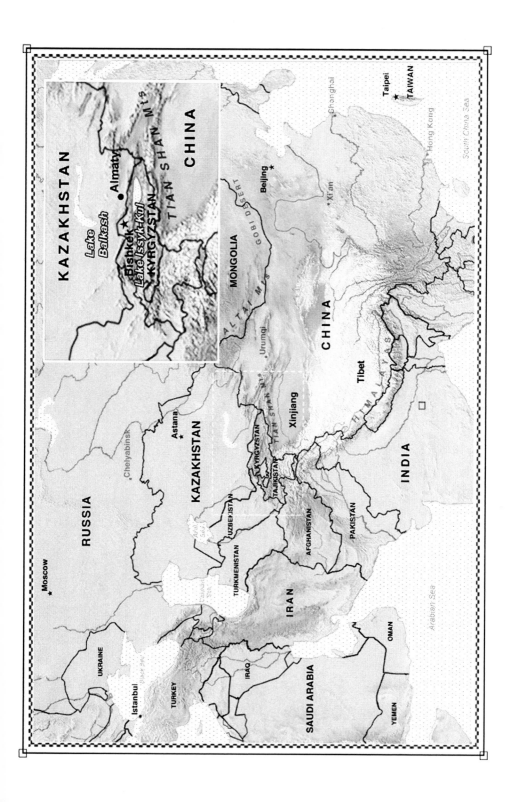

PERFORMANCE ANOMALIES

1

His sun-bleached hair floats in the breeze. The wave lifts him, the spray is warm. He rides the board as if airborne like the gulls, torques and glides up to skim the crest the way the big boys do, sweeps down again to the hollow of the water, faster, faster.

In the final curling of the sea he drops to hug the plank and rolls onto the sand, soaking in its heat as the waves dash themselves around him. Mama leans down and takes him by the hand. How can you surf on just a piece of broken wood? she laughs. Come dance with me, filho. Papa's favorite song is on the radio.

Beads of sweat on Mama's brown skin sparkle before his eyes. Her body takes the shape of the music. Like this, she says, like this. Her bronzed legs move faster. He feels the acceleration through her clasping hands and molds his steps to match every one of hers. Yes, filho! she says. Meu Deus, how fast you catch on!

Gostosa! Mais cerveja! A fat man with red eyes is pounding one of Mama's tables on the beach. Yes, yes, Mama says, more beer, only a minute. My little boy is learning to dance. See how quick he is! The man pounds again. Other men look over.

Cerveja, puta! Mama's legs slow down. Her hips stop, her shoulders go limp. Her fingers peel away from his in a thousand miniature steps that seem to have no end. The fat man stands and stumbles toward them. His arm begins to swing. It seems to stand still, and yet it is moving fast, toward Mama's head. Fear flickers across her face. With the speed of a hummingbird, a small fist hits the fat man hard between his legs. The man bellows and lunges.

Mama cries out.

Cono woke up suddenly. His mother was gone. The window of colored glass above his head was glowing as if it were too hot to touch. Sunlight pierced the holes in the sheet hung over the other window in the bare room where he lay. He was sweating. He was in Istanbul. A phone was buzzing.

He rose and pulled aside the sheet, squinting out at nearby Galata Tower. Beyond, he could see the ferries of Eminönü criss-crossing in the softly glittering waters of the Bosporus, and farther still, the hovering dome of Hagia Sophia and the sharp minarets of the Sultanahmet, like upright javelins in the haze. He picked up the mobile phone. The woman on the static-filled line was speaking rapidly in Mandarin, one of Cono's mother tongues. Finally Cono could make out a few words. "It's Xiao Li, your Xiao Li."

"Xiao Li who sings and likes to be held in the air from a balcony eight stories up?" Cono said in Mandarin. He knew exactly who it was. For a few years now their telephone conversations had always ended with her saying, "I remember you holding me there ..."

"I'm in trouble, Cono." The line became clearer. "No time. They cut my hand."

"Where are you?"

"I'm locked in. It'll get worse."

"*Where are you?*"

"Here." Her voice cracked. "Almaty."

Almaty. Kazakhstan. In late summer the city would be overgrown with green, its streets running in tunnels through the trees. Kazak girls in sunflower dresses. Russian men in fake Nikes huddling on street corners. Chinese traders in wrinkled suits. A hungry city with one foot in its herdsmen past and the other in its oil-rich future.

"Who and where exactly? And numbers."

"Hotel Svezda, Room 217. They killed my customer. Beijing men. Three of them. I think they want to kill me, too," she said, her voice rising. In Xiao Li's way of life there were countless dangers, but she had never before phoned Cono in distress. Her call had been forwarded via one of a dozen lines that tied him to the workaday world.

"Phone number, Xiao Li. There's no caller ID showing."

"I don't know! They took my phone!"

"What's the number you're calling from, Xiao Li? Concentrate."

There was a moment of semi-silence, with only the sound of Xiao Li's uneven breathing rising above the static on the line. "Here, here it is, I got it to come up." She repeated the number. "Cono, I'm the baby mouse in the three-scream meal. Baby mouse screams when the chopsticks pick her up. I have one more scream before …"

"I'll try to get you out. But I'm far away."

He heard a muffled sound.

"No crying, Xiao Li. Stay alert."

"Cono, I'm afraid." The panic in her voice was unbearable.

"Cono, I need to tell you. I love you. Promise me …" The phone beeped and the line went dead.

Xiao Li. She called herself Julie in English, Yulia in Russian. She had been twenty years old and a newcomer to her trade when he'd met her, another keen-eyed arrival from Xinjiang, the Chinese province hugging the country of Kazakhstan for a thousand miles along a border that obeys no natural features of the earth. The one night Cono spent with her had turned into weeks of sex and breakfasts, of laughing and walking and afternoons singing at an outdoor karaoke box in the center of Almaty, a capital of post-Soviet dislocation.

With three phone calls Cono got the number for the Svezda and rang it. In slow and precise Russian, he told the receptionist that there was a bomb in the hotel, set to explode quite soon. "You have unwelcome guests," he said. "I have given you time to open all the rooms and let them leave. Begin on the second floor, in the wing toward Karl Marx Street." He hung up.

Cono gazed across the rooftops toward the waters of the Bosporus, thinking. At this distance the ships looked immobilized, but indeed they were moving, more than a hundred of them a day, in long, silent processions—either north to the Black Sea or south to the Mediterranean. Most were cargo ships that appeared to be enormous until they were dwarfed by the mammoth tankers squeezing through the twisting channel that was now a major conduit for the planet's oil supply, carrying exports from the former Soviet republics to a world that demanded more and more. To the east, beyond the Bosporus and the Black Sea, beyond the Caucasus and the Caspian, were the deserts, the steppes, and then the mountains of Kazakhstan.

Cono turned away from the window and slung on his undervest, buttoned a shirt over it, and stuffed some toiletries into a small travel bag. After locking the apartment door and activating two alarms, he ran down the spiral staircase of centuries-old wood. He was tallish and muscular without being bulky, but he carried himself with the tensile swiftness of someone small and compact, like an acrobat or gymnast. If an observer stopped to think about it, he might be puzzled by the way such long limbs moved so quickly and efficiently. Watching Cono move was pleasing and yet slightly unsettling.

The cobblestone square around Galata Tower was bright with sunshine. A young man carrying a load of sesame-covered *simit* on his head recognized Cono and waved, as did the vegetable vendor next door. Cono smiled at both, nodded back, and instantly ducked. A soccer ball sailed over his shoulder and bounced against the wall behind him. Cono twirled and met it with his chest. He bounced the ball off his knees, keeping it in the air as he turned and faced the five boys and lone girl who were shouting at him. Cono caught the ball on the top of his foot and popped it up to his head, then let it dribble down his face, his chest, and the length of his right leg until it rested once again on his raised foot.

The ball wiggled on his suspended toe as the kids hollered and clapped. Cono glanced at the stone façade behind him, gauging its distance, then propelled the ball backward over his head. It rebounded off the wall and flew in a gentle arc straight into the arms of the laughing girl.

Cono sprinted across the square with the kids running after him, and the soccer ball hit him in the back of the head just as he dodged into a taxi. For several blocks the kids chased the cab, until they could no longer keep up, the sounds of their shouting and laughter quickly fading away.

Four minutes later, after several failed attempts, Cono reached Timur by phone.

"How is my spy-not-spy friend?" Timur asked.

"In a hurry. How's my pimp?" Timur had taught him the word.

"Pimp is *much* bigger pimp now. Maybe a little thanks to you. Come to Almaty and you will see."

"Good idea. I'll be there in six hours." Cono's gaze was directed out the window, but it was the face of Xiao Li he was seeing. "In the meantime, some foreigners are being unpleasant to a friend of mine at the Hotel Svezda. Room 217. They need some company. Now."

"My rich friend will need help at the airport."

"Your friend has full pockets. Here's the number to call. Tell them the lady they're holding has a price. It's almost as big as yours," Cono said, reciting from memory the phone number Xiao Li had given him.

"I will make the call. You remember Gula? She still asks about you."

"Lilia and Petra, too, don't forget."

"Okay, funny man. We'll have a party. And good fuckeen. Which flight?"

"The one from Istanbul. And bring Muktar to the party."

"Muktar ..." Timur's voice trailed off. "I'll tell you about him when I see you."

The taxi sped along the coastal boulevard, around the thumb-shaped center of old Istanbul, the girding walls of Topkapi Palace on the right, the ship-studded flat blue of the Sea of Marmara on the left, stretching to the shores of Asia. Cono thought how strange it was that this seaside avenue, encircling the heart of the ancient capital, was named Kennedy. "He paid to get his name on it," a taxi driver had told him. Sometimes it seemed to Cono that there was nothing in this world that wasn't for sale.

He called Annika, the economics attaché at the Swedish consulate in Istanbul, his skydiving partner. They made their jumps from 10,000 feet or higher, with their feet bound to skyboards, which allowed them to ride the air as if it were one constant wave, a wave that permitted inversions and spirals and somersaults. They'd had a date set for weeks, after cajoling a Turkish air force pilot whose under-the-table tariff, Cono knew, was below market rates because it guaranteed the pilot a chance to again shine his charms on the lithe Swede. Annika and Cono were planning to jump from 12,000 and do their stunts to 4,000, when they would invert themselves, embrace, and kiss until the altimeters on their wrists vibrated with alarm.

Their landings were always followed by elongated lovemaking in a field beneath the parachutes.

"Halloah," she said.

"Annika, I have to postpone."

She didn't respond.

"Annika, are you there?"

"You know what?"

"What?"

"I think you're scared."

"Of course I'm scared," Cono said. "That's the point. But it's not the reason I have to postpone."

"So who am I going to kiss upside down today?"

"It's just a delay. We'll fix it for another day."

"A man with your reflexes should never be delayed, but it seems to happen all the time."

"Annika." Cono tried to clear his throat. He was worried

that she would write him off altogether, because he had already cancelled or postponed so many outings with her, always with trepidation. "It's important. An emergency."

"Another one of your mysterious jobs?"

"No. It's personal."

The line was quiet for a few seconds, then Annika said tersely: "Just be sure to rip the cord in time and come back in one piece. I want us to jump from fourteen next time. Bring your oxygen—you'll need it."

She clicked off.

Cono took in a deep breath and exhaled slowly. He didn't want to lose her. And it wasn't just because of the jumping and the celebration under the parachutes. She was the only person he had ever been close to who had a normal life, and the only one with a normal life who had ever liked him and treated him, to his surprise, normally. He supposed it was normal for her to be mad.

The taxi veered between the construction pylons at Ataturk Airport and deposited Cono at the bustling curb. He bought his ticket, got a boarding pass, and again called the number Xiao Li had given him. No answer. Cono thought it was lucky that he'd gotten Xiao Li's call when he was in Istanbul, rather than in one of his other roosts farther afield—Barcelona or Hong Kong or Rio. But the truth was, Almaty was far from anywhere, and the chances were small that he would be able to help at all. And yet he had never asked himself whether he should go to her. He hadn't thought twice about it. He hadn't even thought once.

Cono had thirty minutes before boarding. He took off his shoes in an empty corner of the departure hall next to an airbrushed portrait of Ataturk, closed his eyes, and started his daily ritual of tensed body postures and stretching. He guessed that Istanbul's airport was the last one in Europe where something as innocent as exercising didn't result in encirclement by an antiterrorist squad.

Memories of Xiao Li appeared and receded with the rhythms of his breath and movement. At first it was her singing that had captivated him, even more than her tantalizingly proportioned body or her face, which in one moment could be the Han version of Aphrodite, and in the next a distorted devil's mask, depending on her mood. Xiao Li had been sitting on the low wall in front of the Arasan Baths, the massive multi-domed relic of Soviet times, selling the bundles of myrtle leaves with which the sauna customers would thrash themselves inside the labyrinth of superheated chambers. With no customers passing by, she was singing a Chinese pop song and Cono had joined in. She took it naturally and the two sang louder and louder, finally waving their arms in the air for the last exuberant refrain. Orchids leaped out of the summer dress that hung loosely from narrow straps on her shoulders.

Although she claimed she had a mother somewhere back in China, Xiao Li had grown up mostly without parents, as had Cono. Maybe that was part of their bond. Yes, it was. But they had never sulked about it—that wasn't in either of their natures.

Xiao Li amateurishly asked him for money that first night after they made love, and Cono obliged. Then she had second thoughts and handed back the overly generous wad of bills, but Cono refused to take it. They made love again. Her smile was giddy as her sweaty body descended on his once more, taking him into her. She stayed the night with him there at the Hotel Svezda, and Cono stayed in Almaty much longer than his assignment, his *tontería*, required. That was years ago, during his second sojourn in Kazakhstan.

Cono was now standing on his hands in the airport lounge, toes pointing toward the ceiling, eyes closed; he heard soft steps nearby, followed by a tentative touch on his back. He opened his upside-down eyes and saw a toddler next to him and the boy's mother pulling the child away. Cono lowered his feet to the ground and his exercises were over.

He stood up, his shirt patched with perspiration. He put on his shoes, hoisted his bag onto his shoulder, and ambled toward the boarding gate, singing a song about a beach town called Itapuã as his eyes followed a seam in the polished floor. His voice was strong, almost loud, and caused other travelers to look at him. He didn't notice, though, and if he had, he wouldn't have cared. When he finally looked up, he marveled at the somberness on all the faces he saw, with no hint of vitality or wonder—no savoring of the hot taste of life, nor even simple amusement at being alive on this day while others were dying, or about to die.

He stopped at a newsstand to glance at the headlines of the papers he could read—*Corriere della Sera*, *Le Figaro*, the *Financial Times*. At this moment he would have preferred something in Chinese or Portuguese, but there was nothing. Then he noticed a Russian paper—*Moscow Express*. Above its masthead were several frames with small pictures, directing readers to articles in a travel insert. The frame that caught Cono's attention was for a new attraction, the Republic of Kazakhstan. He picked the paper off the rack and turned to the travel section. A sidebar accompanied a full-page spread dedicated to the destination for "adventurous vacationers."

Kazakhstan in Perspective:

It's bigger than all of Western Europe, spanning from China on the east to the fringe of Europe on the west, with Russia hovering across its entire northern border. Kazakhstan is a land of bounding steppes and desolate deserts, as well as majestic mountains to the south—a snow-capped wall that has so far protected it from fundamentalist influences in the neighboring "stan" countries.

In the aftermath of the Soviet rupture, its people have proudly renewed their lineage from the conquering hordes of Genghis Khan, whose nomadic lifestyle is maintained even today in the circular yurt dwellings and livestock herds that are hallmarks of the lives of the country folk. The noble, roaming spirit of these people is evoked by the very word *Kazak*, whose original meaning was "free warrior."

You will find in Kazakhstan a melting pot of other peoples as well—Russians, certainly, and Volga Germans, Ukrainians, Tatars, and Koreans relocated during the Stalin years. Other neighboring countries have contributed their kind: Tajiks, Uzbeks, Kyrgyz, Uyghurs. You will even find Pakistanis and, of course, Chinese, the last group having for some time recognized the commercial attractions of this vast territory.

The remoteness of this country unfortunately made it convenient ground for slave camps and forced labor during the Second World War. Kazakhstan also served as a home of exile to such celebrated figures as Dostoyevsky and Shevchenko, who wrote of their adopted land with affection. Trotsky and Solzhenitsyn, also former residents, had less favorable camp experiences there.

In more recent decades Kazakhstan served as the major Soviet source of uranium, as well as the venue for nuclear weapons testing at the renowned Polygon complex. It also serves as home to the Cosmodrome at Baikonur, from which even today multinational teams of cosmonauts are launched toward the International Space Station.

The sixteen-million-strong population of Kazakhstan may be facing a brighter future, thanks to recent discoveries of extensive oil and gas fields. Multiple countries seeking access to these resources have contributed to a Kazak economy that now shows signs of rebounding from its post-Soviet decline.

Cono chortled as he read these last sentences. He'd had enough personal experience with the "countries seeking access" to Kazakhstan's resources to know the wealth they were spreading around went mostly into a few pockets. He lowered his eyes and read the editor's postscript.

Note to travelers:

As in all of the former Soviet Republics, petty extortion, especially by local authorities in the largest city, Almaty (population one million), should be mitigated by avoiding encounters with police or other employees of the government. It should also be noted that recent arrests of Islamic terrorists operating in the country have led to increased security measures, which may cause inconveniences for the traveler.

"Perfect for a vacation," Cono muttered as he folded the newspaper and put it back on the rack. He heard his flight being called.

Before handing his boarding pass to the attendant at the gate, Cono again called the mobile number Xiao Li had given him; a hoarse male voice responded unintelligibly after the first ring. In the background an alarm was clanging, then there was shouting. Cono could make out the yelling in Mandarin: "Quick. Get the body down to the car. And take the whore!" He also heard orders barked in Russian. One of the voices was Timur's. There was a clapping sound as if the phone had fallen to the floor, and then the signal was dead.

So Timur had put himself into the fray, Cono thought. He hadn't just sent his minions. Even so, it was clear from the noise that Timur didn't have things under control. And Xiao Li was still like the baby mouse, about to be eaten. Cono felt a flushing sensation run up the back of his neck. He was suddenly sweating, unbearably hot. It wasn't like him; he never worried like this. *It's just another tontería, another mission,* Cono told himself. But the flushing continued and turned into a wave of prickly irritation across his entire body. It was going to be a very long flight.

2

"You really must get on now," said the attendant, reaching for Cono's boarding pass.

The plane was nearly full, with portly white men in front, Asian faces in back, and a smattering of Turks in both sections. The majority of the men in front, Cono knew, were Brits and Americans and other Westerners in the oil business, soldiers in the corporate armies that were tapping into Kazakhstan's newly proven Caspian fields. Most of the other white faces would be Canadians who would transit at Almaty and go on to Kyrgyzstan for its gold and silver mines. As Cono walked through business class he casually let his knee bump an aluminum case held by a bulky man with a shaved head standing in the aisle in front of him. The man turned and glared, and Cono saw the individual pulsations of blood filling the tiny vessels in the man's bulbous cheeks. Cono smiled and said in Portuguese, "My, what a heavy load of greenbacks you carry." The beefy man didn't understand, and twisted to confront Cono directly, but he was put off-guard by Cono's beaming smile with its rows of white teeth. He was a bag man, Cono knew, one of the frequent pigeons on these flights, carrying hard-cash payroll for oil company employees—never more than a million at a go, so the deliveries were frequent. Cono smiled again and the bag man took his seat, planting the case upright on the floor behind his thick calves.

Cono walked on to the back, amid the central Asians, most of whom he guessed worked the oil fields and the mines; others had somehow gotten enough money to leave the country and were returning to visit their kin, loaded with gifts and electronics to sell or barter. Cono took his aisle seat, next to a stout man with thick palms. The man was surprised when Cono said hello to him in Russian.

"You don't … look Russian," he said with a puzzled smile.

"Nor do you. What *is* a Russian, after all?" replied Cono with an easy laugh that brought the startled man's eyes directly into Cono's gaze, where the man found himself lost for a moment.

He was Kazak, he told Cono. He had a broad face and tilted dark eyes and full cheeks pinched close around his fleshy nose. A handsome, robust man with jet-black hair.

They spoke for a few minutes before the plane took off. Cono learned that his name was Anvar and that he worked for the Finance Ministry. As he said those words, Cono saw the fleeting tension at the corners of his mouth that betrayed something amiss—probably just the slight discomfort of having an undeserved job that entitled him to off-the-books income.

"A small, small job," Anvar said, putting his thumb and forefinger together to show something the size of a pea.

Anvar seemed relieved when Cono said he wasn't a businessman, and was only going to Almaty to visit distant relatives. He relaxed even more when Cono spoke of the pretty women who went every night to the Cactus bar at the Hotel Ratar.

16

"So you know Almaty?"

"A beautiful town of overgrown trees, the whole place flat like a tabletop, but tilted—upward toward the shining Tian Shan Mountains," Cono said as the plane rumbled off the runway. "And on the other side, downward, toward the steppes, the desert, the oil."

The two were silent until the jet had leveled off. Cono proposed that he should take Anvar's number in case there was a night free for an outing at the Cactus. "Some of the girls there even know how to dance salsa," he said, moving his hips in his seat and raising his arms to show a dancing embrace.

"Yes, yes," Anvar said with hesitant enthusiasm as he wrote his number on a napkin. Cono took it and slipped it into his undervest. Made from a lightweight synthetic fabric, the vest was crafted with pockets and sheaths, some concealed, that contained bank account and telephone numbers in code, identity cards in separate sealed envelopes, several mobile phones, a stack of untraceable SIM cards, three passports, antibiotics, a wafer-thin alarm clock, credit cards and stashes of various currencies.

The dark-haired woman serving the first round of refreshments paused as she reached to give Cono his orange juice. She appeared mildly disturbed by the large and placid blue-green eyes she had just seen. The eyes didn't match his slightly Asiatic, slightly bronze-colored visage. He'd spoken to her in English, but with an accent that was as hard to place as his face.

Half an hour later, as she served him a glass of water, she made a point of asking him what country he was from.

"I am from … Where am I from?" he replied, his eyes fixed on hers. "I am from where these two feet meet the ground." He circled his scuffed shoes with a pointed finger, smiling.

"But we are flying," she declared.

"It's a winged country then!" Freed momentarily from his worries about Xiao Li, Cono laughed deeply, openly.

The flight attendant's impatience with the remark was tranquilized by Cono's broad grin.

"Your accent hints of Spanish," Cono said. "Where are *you* from?"

"You're right, I'm from Granada. Are you familiar with it?"

"I know an old woman there who sells flowers in Plaza Santa Ana. She mostly complains about the Gypsies, but once in a while she claims to see the ghost of a dead local poet stealing her red zinnias. She's nearly blind, but she told me where to find the music academy, a fine place to sit on a hot afternoon. Her name is Concepción. Maybe you know her?"

The young woman standing with the tray in her hand seemed amused by the non-sequitur, and by Cono's manner; perhaps she had never seen a person talk while staring directly at her. Not exactly staring, but gazing without blinking, and without the murky boundary that usually separates strangers, and even friends. She struggled to release her eyes from Cono's, saying, "No, I don't know Concepción."

The plane dipped suddenly and the water pitcher lurched off the flight attendant's tray. Before she could even gasp, Cono had caught it.

She stared at him in disbelief. "How … ?"

The young man grinned. "Practice," he said, handing the still-full pitcher back to her, along with three packets of peanuts she hadn't seen slide off the tray. "Lots of practice."

She looked at him again, uncertain what to make of him. Finally she nodded slowly, thanked him, and moved on.

Cono's practice had originally taken the form of stealing pieces of meat or bread or fish or fruit when he was a child in Fortaleza, a poor town in the far northeast of Brazil. He had preferred to hunt octopus on the reefs, but he could not always fill his belly that way, or the bellies of his mother and father.

It was through these minor thefts of food that he first became aware of a peculiar ability of his mind and muscles that his mother had noted much earlier as she taught him to dance. Any movement he chose to learn took only one viewing to register in his mind, captured as if it were presented in slow motion and then replayed through his body at normal speed.

He could perceive motion in infinitesimal detail, as if he were looking at the world through a high-speed camera, and could direct his body movements with a corresponding swiftness. It was a simple matter to snatch an orange from a display crate in the moment the shopkeeper was distracted, even as he and Cono stood facing each other. From Cono's perspective, the movement— the reach of his arm, the extension of his fingers, the grasping of the orange, the retraction of his arm—proceeded in minutely segmented stages. But others would see only the beginning of his movement, and the end, as if he had merely adjusted his stance; the rest of his motion was as imperceptible as a single missing frame in a film reel, or the flick of a frog's tongue when it seizes a damselfly.

During a private walk with his mother when he was seven, hand in hand beneath clacking palm trees, she had told him that his father was afraid of him, afraid of how quickly a child with almost no schooling could absorb languages, even those of passing foreigners; of how he could recite, syllable by syllable, long pieces of overheard conversation; of how casually he learned to write the

Chinese characters his father laid before him; of how effortlessly he could catch a coffee cup falling from a table.

Cono's father, a math teacher who was occasionally forced during his itinerant career to also teach reading, had his own theory to explain the strangeness in Cono. He had encountered children who had great difficulty learning to read and who pushed his impatience into a rage of disgust. "Their brain clock is too slow!" he told his wife and son as they sat in plastic chairs around a rickety table. He was drinking *cachaça* heavily and pounding the table. "And your damn brain clock is too fast!" He leered at Cono, his eyes wet and bloodshot. He grabbed a pen and scribbled mathematical formulas on a paper napkin to explain, jabbing his finger into each line, saying, "This is the slow ones! This is us! This is you!" Cono's eyes met his mother's in the light of the hanging bulb surrounded by fluttering moths; he could see the insects' swishing woolly wings as if they weren't moving at all. And he saw his mother's almond-shaped eyes lower themselves in segmented steps, each one a separate snapshot of her guarded pride.

The flight attendant from Granada smiled at Cono as she passed by his seat; his eyes were closed, almost, and his breathing was slow and deep. He was sunk in meditation, hands loose in his lap, spine erect. Xiao Li was there with him, kicking with delight as he held her supple body, suspending her in the air beyond the railing of the balcony. He heard her giggling and could feel the weight of her in his outstretched arms, with eight stories of open air between her and the ground. She fluttered her legs with abandon toward the night sky. "See the moon? Do you see the moon, Cono?" Just as Xiao Li turned her body and reached toward the moon as if trying to cuddle it, Cono lifted her back to the safety of the balcony, where they spent the night—Xiao Li wanted to see the moon while they climaxed together.

She was like him, trying to embrace the moon while making her way in the world through instinct and drive that came only from within, because she had only herself. Yes, she had spoken of a mother. A mother who, when Xiao Li was thirteen, had thrown her out of their home with the words: "My man looks at you too much. I'm saving you from him. Now get out and make some money, get your own life. I'm sure men will pay you plenty." And yet Xiao Li always spoke of her mother as if her image were mounted in a red-and-gold picture frame resting on a shrine in the corner of a tidy house, to be venerated and pleased at all times, like a deceased ancestor ever-present and scrutinizing her progeny.

Xiao Li's rough life had made her prickly, an eye-catching rose with not a single thorn missing. Her goodness showed itself rarely, and usually by accident. But no matter how long the passage of time since they had last seen each other, Cono felt a pull toward her. He could call it duty, or honor, or affection; he preferred not to put a word on it. Worrying for her, setting out in this way to try to ensure that she saw this round of life a little longer, was strange to him. Personal. It was a world apart from the trips he made for others who needed his talents. He did *their* bidding by impersonal choice, and for his own amusement and occasional gratification, for he had no need of the money they gave him for his trouble.

Xiao Li was unique. But there were many other unique women in his nomadic life, who together formed a network of sorts. It wasn't a formal network; it had just emerged and grown and changed over time. And it wasn't fashionable in the Western world—a man at the center of a web of women. They lived in varied spots around a shrunken globe, in cities or towns or villages. Some traveled, and some were trapped in place by poverty or tradition or family or men, or even by wealth and position.

At times Cono thought it was he who was trapped by this carousel of women, despite his freedom to go anywhere on the planet he chose. Trapped by his desire for them, his admiration of them, his adoration of their strength and beauty. And they in turn persisted in their allegiance to him, an allegiance of spirit that was hardened by the intensity of their encounters with Cono, who offered each a different relief from her circumstances.

Cono's meditation faltered. Rather than going deeper, as if tied to a heavy stone sinking into a dark river, it leveled out, then began to bob and rise, tugged toward the surface by his aching worry for Xiao Li.

3

Cono's seatmate, Anvar, was still asleep, his hands resting palms-up on his crotch, when Cono pressed a finger into one of the palms to wake him and tell him the plane was at the gate.

As Cono walked briskly among the passengers in the dim airport corridor, he spotted his friend Timur in wraparound sunglasses at the side of the brand-new immigration booths. The two did not greet each other, but Timur signaled to the official to let Cono pass. "It's the gray Mercedes, to the right," Timur said softly without looking at Cono. As Cono passed the customs desk he glanced behind him at the bag man, the pigeon, next to Timur, still standing beside the immigration stall. The bald man holding the case passed through, leaving the other passengers in a jostling crowd. Timur was always doing double duty.

Cono got into the back seat of the Mercedes. In less than a minute, Timur opened the car door and climbed in next to him. Without instruction the driver pulled into the trickle of cars and vans exiting the airport. When they were on the lightless road heading into the city, with whitewashed tree trunks flashing by in the headlights, Cono looked at Timur's face, still concealed by his wraparound shades. Timur extended his hand to the seatback in front of him, where the driver couldn't see it through the rear-view mirror. He made a thumbs-up. Xiao Li had been spared.

It would be at least another half hour before they got to the center of the city. There would be no conversation during this time—no further information about Xiao Li, no news of their friend Muktar, no details shared about the twists and turns of their lives since last they had last seen each other. Four years. Had it been that long already? And before that, another four years since their first meeting. Cono was startled by the realization that Timur was one of his oldest friends.

Timur had grown into a big-time player, but when they first met he'd been just a soldier on furlough, singing his own form of Tupac-inspired rap in mangled English, drunk on warm afternoon beers.

It was a week after two of Timur's buddies had been shot through the head next to him on night patrol at a southwest border. "Wahhabis," he'd explained to Cono. "They take Afghanistan, then they move into Uzbekistan, now they want Kyrgyzstan and Kazakhstan." Timur had had to give the bad news to the mother of one of the dead comrades. "She cried. She screamed, 'Why did he die and not you?' Fuckeen good question. She'd begged Zaman to stay out of the service, just like my mother begged me. But I say only a man who has been in the military and seen the worst is a man. Really lived. Just like the prostitutes," he said. "They have nothing except their bodies. Their bodies are money. They know like a soldier knows." Timur turned away, and then abruptly looked back at Cono. "Okay! Now we talk no more military. We talk women! And rap! And next bar!"

Back then, when they'd first met, Cono had been an even freer bird, not yet swept up by one tontería, one foolish mission, after another, and another. He was already a rich young man, but keeping to his simple ways. Hitchhiking down to Almaty from Russia, he had noted in some of the women shades of the Slavic features of Antonina, his mother's mother. Those hints of her face brought her voice to his mind, her precise speech in Russian and French and late-acquired Portuguese. Through her meticulous care with words she preserved the elegance and dignity of her childhood in Russia, before her family was obliterated in the Bolshevik uprisings, before poverty became her new way of life and the path to her early death.

Cono loved the hitchhiking—the open roads, the expanse of countryside in summertime as he walked beneath lost white clouds drifting across high blue skies. Often he wouldn't bother to wave down a car or truck when he heard it approaching, preferring instead to walk, to feel the strength in his legs and the tranquility in his mind. He would sleep in fields of hay or barley or sugar beets, clearing a spot for himself so he could see the stars, which he knew by heart in both hemispheres. He would talk to Antares and Alrisha and Denebola as if they were friends until his unnatural need for sleep began to sweep over him. No matter what dew or dust or insects of the field made his body their home, he slept like a buried stone, and was replenished when morning came.

Before that first visit to Almaty eight years ago, Cono had walked from the Russian town of Chelyabinsk all the way to the Kazak frontier, where three border guards were surprised to see a traveler on foot. After many rounds of vodka, a show of juggling skills, and several wads of cash delivered in enthusiastic handshakes, Cono won a visa stamp to enter the vast, infant nation of Kazakhstan.

25

It was much farther south, on his first day in Almaty, that Cono met Timur, and that same evening he met Timur's friend Muktar, the painter. Despite being several years younger than the two Kazaks, Cono was adopted as an equal. The three caroused together for weeks, bedding girls, exchanging them, drinking a lot.

Then Timur got called back to duty, and Cono fell into the arms of a young woman named Irina. Muktar was left to find his own amusement, and returned to his old ways of brooding in his tiny apartment filled with pencil drawings, solvent fumes and half-finished oil canvases.

The Mercedes cruised past the hardscrabble shanty flats at the edge of the city and started to rise on the constant incline of the Almaty grid. The driver stopped the car a block down from the Hotel Ratar, leaving Timur and Cono to walk in the darkness of Panfilov Park. When they reached the festooned and dilapidated Zenkov Cathedral in the center of the park grounds, they stepped into the moonlight shadow of the church. The trees were musty, hinting of approaching autumn.

"Cono, my brother!" Timur exclaimed. The two embraced and slammed their hands against each other's shoulders. Cono felt the pistol sheath beneath Timur's expensive leather coat, at his left armpit, and his hand lightly grazed the bulge of another gun wedged into the belt at Timur's spine.

"Such a good-news friend," Cono said in Russian as they pushed each other apart, smiling. Timur took off his shades.

"She's safe, a little cut up. And still beautiful, your tart friend. How could she bring you all the way to Almaty? There must be more—some unfinished business."

"Ah, Timur, there is always unfinished business, and tides are always turning. Where is she?"

"Right there." Timur pointed at the bright block of lights spelling the name of the Ratar through the branches. The "T" was burned out.

"And the Chinese, the Kitais?"

"All happy, gone away. I made them take their dead friend with them, in a bag." The slight change in the timbre of Timur's voice told Cono it was a half-truth. "So, Cono, why the trouble of flying to Almaty on such short notice, a man with so many women? Didn't think I could spring your girl?"

"I came to say thanks, and to show the flag."

"The flag of which country? Hah! I know," Timur rolled his eyes. "The country around your own two feet." Timur looked Cono up and down, searching for changes in his appearance since last time; there weren't many. "And by the way, the bomb scare wasn't necessary."

"Just a little insurance, in case you had been tied up. Busy guy like you, chief of the whole damn National Security Bureau, keeping the entire country safe."

The pleasant scent of mulch was suddenly poisoned by a stench like that of burning hair. A few trees away, five figures were squatting around an open fire. They were roasting pigeons on sticks, and the feathers were crackling in the flames; filaments of singed plumage floated up through the branches.

Cono and Timur walked in a loop past the World War II monument of elephant-size bronze faces lit by an eternal kerosene flame. When they were beyond the glow of the war memorial, Timur broke the silence.

"Your friend, she's going to be in trouble."

Cono cocked his head. Again, the timbre of Timur's voice had shifted. "What do you mean?"

"She saw too much. Maybe heard too much, too."

"Traders disappear all the time in this town, part of the business risk. She's smart enough not to say anything," Cono said. He knew the murder of Xiao Li's client wasn't the problem; it was something else.

"Her customer was in a delicate position." Timur cleared his throat. "He had a heap of cash, probably working as a carrier, just meant to give and go. Apparently he didn't make the delivery on time and was dipping into the purse to pay for his pleasures. Unfortunately, he had no idea who he was working for."

"Ah," Cono murmured. "So the dead man's comrades weren't just doing business. They were Beijing boys, working for their government. Probably aiming to buy off somebody high up. Maybe even a minister or two." In the faint light Cono saw the clenching of Timur's jaw muscles, the pulsing of his temporal artery.

"Probably."

Cono pulled a thick envelope from his back pocket and with a whip of his hand lodged it in Timur's armpit, next to his gun strap. Timur jolted as he stabbed his right hand into his jacket, reaching for the handgun. The envelope dropped with his movement. He picked it up and handed it back to Cono.

"Thanks, swifty. Those gifts aren't necessary anymore. The girl's for free. But you owe me."

Cono slid the envelope into his vest, keeping his surprise to himself; this was a generosity Cono had never seen in his friend. "Very charitable of you, brother."

"I'll get her down from the hotel now," Timur said. "Then I'll meet you around back at the Cactus." Timur snapped open his phone to dismiss his driver for the time being, and the two men waited among the trees to see that the car had driven off.

One of the Pakistani doorkeepers at the Cactus stifled a fleeting sense of recognition as Cono walked in, his bag on his shoulder and a two-day growth on his face. The Cactus was done up like a ranch from America's Wild West, with yellow pine posts and hip-high railings dividing the dark, low-ceilinged space into little corrals with benches and wooden chairs. Here the Russian and Kazak and Uzbek and Kyrgyz working girls would gossip until the men arrived—the Turkish entrepreneurs, the mafia thugs, both Russian and Kazak, the oilmen from Europe and America, and the embassy functionaries from all corners of the world. The atmosphere was lightened by the trickle of college students who loved to dance—many of them sons and daughters of the regime, who were occasionally surprised and embarrassed by the presence of their fathers.

It was a place where the Chinese merchants never came. They always met their women in more private settings.

Cono asked the Pakistani bartender to put on the old salsa and Brazilian music he knew they had. As he turned away from the bar, a Tsingtao in hand, a Kazak girl flashed her smile of silver front teeth and asked him to dance. It was a custom in this part of the world for women to cast their teeth in gold or silver, a remnant of the need for portable wealth. Cono admired the broad, angular structure of her youthful face. "Not now, bright flower," he replied in Russian, and went to a seat in a corner that was darker than most. It was early, but there was already an intermittent stream of men stepping through the doorway onto the creaky floorboards. Timur came in alone and went to the bar. He'd seen Cono, but ordered a vodka and drank it all before coming to sit at Cono's table.

"They're bringing her," Timur said.

Cono heard the voice of the doorman snapping in English, telling a woman she would have to pay to get in, like all the other girls. Then Cono was startled to hear Xiao Li's voice, arguing back in ferociously vulgar Mandarin before adding sweetly in English: "Here just friends. No business." Cono heard the clack of her stiletto heels as she stepped in; it was a full minute before her head, elevated with haughtiness, turned toward Cono. His heart lost its rhythm when he finally saw all of her, now even more breathtaking than before, but his elation was checked by the momentary alarm in her eyes as she spotted Timur. Yet she kept her composure and stepped toward them briskly and sat next to Cono.

Cono pressed her good hand in his. Her other hand was bandaged, and at the edge of a light sweater she had wrapped around her neck like a makeshift scarf, Cono could see a small flap of white gauze. They greeted each other with their eyes. When little glistening crescents appeared on Xiao Li's lower lashes, she looked down abruptly to search her purse. Cono lit her cigarette and she tapped his forearm with two fingers to say thank you, as she had always done.

"Your friend saved me, but ..." Xiao Li spoke in Mandarin before Cono cut her off. He looked at Timur, who was eyeing the dance floor and taking another hit of vodka.

"She says you saved her. Let's speak in English so Timur understands. Timur, she says thank you for keeping her alive."

Timur raised his glass in a silent toast, still looking toward the dance floor, and downed the drink.

Xiao Li's palm was moist in Cono's hand.

"Mister, you good man. So good. So powerful." Xiao Li reached across Cono to touch Timur's arm with her bandaged hand. He withdrew his arm and said, "All for my friend." Xiao Li pulled Cono's hand into her lap; with her finger she drew in his palm the Chinese character 蛇. It meant *snake*.

Timur waved the waitress over for another vodka and leaned closer to Cono. "I never should have been seen head-to-head in public with the Chinese at the Svezda." His voice was low and tense. He switched to Russian, which he knew Xiao Li wouldn't grasp. "I could have just sent my toads. I went myself. All for a tart. All for you."

Xiao Li had lit another cigarette by herself, with a huff and a twist of Cono's thumb, but she was listening intently, trying to recognize a word or two in what they said.

"Here's how you pay me back," Timur said. "We're taking bids from the oil companies for the readjustment of the contracts that you helped with four years ago. I need a go-between I can trust. You did such a good job last time. No leaks."

Cono leaned closer.

"This time you'll get the numbers from the Chinese, too, and an advance gift in cash, a show of goodwill. Then you can make the rounds of the other guys you know so well from last time—the Anglos, the French, the Italians—and see what their numbers are, how much goodwill they are offering. Then I'll give the numbers to Kurgat, our esteemed minister of the interior, and he and the premier can decide how to reallocate my country's resources in the most advantageous way. The minister hates the Chinese, but they're pushing hard and hinting big numbers so they can finally get in.

"And then you go back to wherever your two feet want to be," Timur concluded. "And everyone will be happy."

"The Chinese you packed off are no doubt already happy," Cono said, his mind racing to understand what Timur was really asking of him. "By killing their own delivery man they showed the minister they're not like their competitors. These guys are working for Beijing after all, not just another oil company. It will be hard for Kurgat to say no to them."

"It's lucky for him that you're in town," Timur said, smiling. "Even a minister needs help sometimes."

"Poor Minister Kurgat."

"You *will* help."

"Do I have a choice?"

The club was now crowded and beginning to seethe. The Brazilian music had given way to Celia Cruz roaring "Azúcar!" through the speakers. Cono pushed back the table and leaned toward Timur. "Can't resist this. Just a quick dance before we go." He stood and grinned at the scowl on his friend's face. "Not with you, brother—not your kind of music. I meant with her." Cono pulled Xiao Li up and joined the rhythm with his hips well before the two reached the dance floor. He saw a pair of Timur's men glancing toward their master as he guided Xiao Li along the railing, and recognized the tall one with the thin white face as the brute who had nearly beaten to death two of Xiao Li's working girlfriends the last time Cono was in town.

Timur watched closely from the shadows, but the couple were not talking, only lost in their swirling embraces.

The music climaxed and Xiao Li arched backward toward the floor as Cono held her head and the small of her back. He made her rise in a sweeping spiral, and as his body blocked

32

Timur's view he slid one of his cell phones under the sash around her waist.

"It'll be as hot as July for a few weeks," Cono said as he kissed her sweaty temple. "Keep the baby mouse out of the chopsticks. Get out of Almaty. I put five thousand in your purse. My cell number is under the address Sleeper."

Xiao Li wrapped her arms around Cono and pressed her cheek to his chest. She squeezed him lightly at first, then harder and harder, until Cono saw Timur approaching.

They bumped through the crowd back toward the table. Xiao Li took her purse. Cono lifted his traveling bag. "I think we'll take a room at the Hotel Tsarina," Cono said. "A high room with one of those broad balconies and a view of the premier's palace."

Timur shrugged. "Sure."

He led the way as they pressed through the odors of perfume and sweaty groins toward the door. The two toads in black leather jackets hustled in behind them. There were two more guards waiting for them as the group exited onto the veranda and down the steps to a patch of trees lit by the sparks of a shashlik brazier. Cono saw the shashlik man glance up and then quickly look down again to be sure he saw nothing. There were two cars waiting, neither one the gray Mercedes that had driven them from the airport, and more toads.

Timur flashed a lighter, but was holding no cigarette. At the signal, two of his men grabbed Xiao Li and thrust her into one of the cars. She cried out for Cono as they closed the door on her kicking legs. A high-heeled shoe fell to the ground before they managed to slam the door shut.

Xiao Li was pressing her face against the inside of the window, panic in her eyes. "Just a little insurance, to make sure you don't change your mind about being my helper," Timur said. "She'll be at a good hotel, good service." He bent down to pick up the fallen shoe and gave it to Cono. Cono was dazzled by the sharpness of the spike he held in his hand. In the fraction of a second in which he glimpsed Timur's face and measured the distance of the men around him, Cono swung the point of the heel into the neck of the tall guard he'd recognized, the thug who had brutalized Xiao Li's friends. Cono's own awareness of his action, the idea of it, appeared in his mind only after it was done. He had pulled out the stiletto before the others could see the sweep of his arm, and they had noticed no more than a quick change in his posture. The man crumpled to the asphalt, clutching his neck, blood seeping out in a dark stream. Only Timur took a step backward from Cono and pulled the gun from his armpit. The others quickly crouched against the cars, looking for snipers as their injured comrade lost consciousness.

"I'll keep the shoe until I see her again," Cono said. "And if she's touched by anyone, they'll go down like the toad who swallowed this." Cono rotated the shoe so the dagger-like heel was pointing up.

"Cinderella will be safe as long as you do your job," Timur said, putting his gun away. He screamed at his men in a mixture of Kazak and Russian, and the car holding Xiao Li sped off. Cono got into the other car with Timur and two of his men. As the Mercedes accelerated, Cono's head was thrown back against the seat.

"Not so fast, slow it down," Timur barked to the driver. To his right Cono saw the raised eyes of the shashlik cook shaking his head. The bloodied thin-faced man was left for others to pick up.

Cono mentally replayed the scene in the Cactus, and the earlier one in the park. Timur's discomfort, his agitation, had been obvious, but his duplicity—Cono couldn't fathom how he'd missed that. Feelings of guilt and incompetence made the small shoe in his hand seem heavy. Cono wiped the shoe's heel on the carpeted floor of the car. He'd been blind to the truth on Timur's face, but his reflexes were intact. He wondered, in fact, if his reflexes were leaving his thoughts behind. And yet the attack couldn't be just a reflex—he had struck the brute he recognized, no one else. Maybe the thinking had been done long before, and the reaction was already primed. What other thoughts had already taken hold without his awareness, and had already primed a reflexive trigger?

And Timur? He could have shot Cono right there, because he knew the blow came from Cono, with his strange quickness— Timur had experienced it first-hand more than once. There must be desperation in Timur's need for Cono. And maybe Timur, too, was happy to see the thin-faced man taken down, for different reasons.

They pulled into the shimmering driveway of the Hotel Tsarina. Cono and Timur got out and stood next to the car.

"Don't worry about your little china doll," Timur said. "Do you really think I would return her to you compromised?" He shook his head with a laugh. "I know you better than that, brother. You would hunt me down and find a way to make me pay. No." He shook his head again. "She'll be well taken care of. You have my word.

"But I need your help. And I need to make sure you stay here to give it to me. You got me into this stinking mess. If the premier or Minister Kurgat thinks I was at the Svezda to work my own deal with Beijing ... you can see where that might lead."

Cono remained silent.

"Hey," Timur said, clapping him on the shoulder. "I had the hotel bump out an American so you could have your favorite room, with the view. Want me to call a companion for you? Help you forget your friend?"

"Another time, brother. I'm a working man. Working for you."

"Suit yourself." Timur climbed into the idling Mercedes. "We'll get started in the morning."

Upstairs, Cono yanked back the curtains and opened the sliding doors. The nearby amusement park was still lit up, the rides spinning with primary colors but no passengers. As he watched, the rides gradually slowed and stopped. The tinny recordings of calliope music were switched off one by one. With rhythmic precision, the garish lights went out in stages, as if a giant were squashing each ride with his steps until only a skeleton of pale lampposts was left. Farther to the east was the great bland square, illuminated with floodlights that made the government buildings glow. At the top of a rising lawn littered with shadowed monuments was the flat-faced Stalinist palace. It leaned forward in the stark white glow of the lights as if it were about to slide down the whole tilting mantle of Almaty.

Cono stripped off his clothes, stretched out on the balcony and began his exercises. The fatigue crept away from him and was replaced by a fresh rush of the joy he'd felt when Xiao Li walked into the Cactus, alive and stunning. Then he was swamped by imaginings of how Timur's men might treat her. In his mind, hundreds of minutely differentiated images of Xiao Li's panicked face began to flash, like freeze-frames taken milliseconds apart. In each, she was calling to him from behind the car window.

He looked out toward the city lights to stop the flashing pictures plaguing his brain and concentrated on his rhythmic breathing. It was over the railing of this balcony or one near it that

36

he had held Xiao Li in midair; they had left the stodginess of the Hotel Svezda for the glossy newness of the Tsarina on that second stay in Almaty, when he'd recklessly given himself over to her even though it had been a working visit.

It was a working visit that had begun with a phone call from a woman who said she and Cono had a friend in common, Irina. The woman spoke in Russian, but with a Ukrainian accent like Irina's. Cono was surprised to hear that Irina had friends at all, but in fact he knew little about her life. "Why ruin the present by talking about the past?" Irina had said. On the other hand, she knew perhaps too much about Cono's tonterías; when he occasionally saw her on layovers in Berlin, he diverted her from her studies by recounting vignettes from his exploits. Names and locations obscured, to be sure, but all the same, he had not been terribly discreet.

The friend of Irina's said she was merely a messenger for a large company that needed his help to make things right.

"What for you is right?" Cono asked. He heard the pursing and unpursing of her lips as she weighed her answer over the phone.

"It is better that we meet in person," she said.

Two days later they sat in the sun with their feet dangling in a seafront swimming pool in Barcelona, where Cono kept one of his austere apartments. He had suggested they swim and have their conversation in the water. It was mid-afternoon at the tail end of the season, and the pool was mostly empty, as was the adjacent beach. The sunlight skittering on the surface of the water was mildly unpleasant to Cono. They slid into the water.

She called herself Katerina. It was a simple matter, she explained as they stood in the shallow end. A couple of offices needed to be entered, a few electronic taps placed, a few friends newly made, certain documents stolen or copied … originals would be better. An American oil company felt too hemmed in by its country's laws against bribing for business overseas, and wanted to level the playing field by threatening to expose its European competitors' generosity toward Kazak officials. The companies were all hungry for a piece of the giant oil reserves under and around Kazakhstan's portion of the Caspian Sea.

Cono interlaced his fingers and put his hands into the pool, pulling water into the space between his sealed palms. He lifted his hands and squeezed a stream of water into Katerina's face. She laughed and splashed back.

"You mean the other companies give gifts to the top men?" Cono said.

Katerina cocked her head and smiled. She knew he must be joking, but he sounded so very sincere. "Well, only the top part counts in some countries."

"Like asparagus, then."

"Yes."

"Not like an iceberg, where what counts is below."

She grinned. "No."

"So you need a faceless man who knows some languages," Cono said after a moment.

"And who is free and fearless and trustworthy. Irina said those things about you. And that you are addicted to the thrill of your work."

"Irina is free and fearless and trustworthy."

"She is free, thanks to you. She will always be grateful for how you helped her."

"And you? Are you free?" Cono lowered himself into the water except for his head so that the sun would be blocked by

Katerina, allowing him to clearly see her face. Her eyes twitched only so slightly left and right, then met Cono's. The sun's shielded light made a corona around her head.

"Not free," she said. She lowered her head, tipping the sun's glare into Cono's eyes, and making him squint. "Not yet."

Cono stood up and clapped his hands on the surface, sending a spray onto Katerina's face. He took her hand. "Water is a great freedom. You can glide wherever you want through it, bury yourself in it, and come out alive, as long as you know which way is up." Cono took her under and they swam beneath the surface until Katerina came up for air. Kicking like a dolphin, Cono made a complete underwater circuit of the edges of the pool before rejoining Katerina in the center.

His head rose and he exhaled slowly. "How do you know Irina?"

"From Almaty."

Cono didn't ask more, but she went on.

"We had the same … client. He liked to have two girls at the same time. He had favorites. But, then, after a while, he wasn't nice." Katerina tentatively reached upward, paused, and finally scooped her hair off her back, showing Cono a scar the length of a finger at the base of her neck. She turned slightly. On her right shoulder there was another scar—a double band of teeth marks. Cono had seen that type of mark only once before, on Irina. He had traced his fingers over it and wondered without asking.

"And your work for the Americans?" Cono said.

"It's my chance to be free. I'm just a go-between, a scout. They hired me because of my client. Mr. K, Minister Kurgat, runs most of Kazakhstan."

Cono breathed deeply now as he stood on his left leg on the balcony, extending the other leg straight out in front of him, with a finger hooked around his big toe. Even the lights marking the skeleton of the amusement park were now extinguished. He finished his exercises and went to bed, where he tried to fight his restlessness by chiding himself for his sentimentality. It didn't work.

Xiao Li's call came an hour later. She was whispering, her voice hard to make out.

"Where are you?" Cono interrupted.

"They put a bag over my head in the car. We made lots of turns. I don't know where I am. No windows. It's very noisy below."

"Xiao Li, tell me details, what you hear, any smells, any …"

"Cono, I dream about you. I want to make love on a balcony again …"

"Xiao Li, don't worry. We will dance again and sing together." Cono told her to do what the thugs said, not to fight or they would beat her, or worse, and to call him only when she found out her location. "It's safer that way."

"Cono, the Beijing men wanted to kill me too," Xiao Li whispered. "I heard them say they were worried about what my client might have told me. The dead man, he had a lot of money." Xiao Li's voice became shaky. "Cono, they came in … they came in and pulled him off me, then broke his neck."

"What did the client tell you, Xiao Li?"

"He said China wanted to get something more than oil. He was bragging. He laughed about how easy it was to buy top military men in this country. I didn't want to listen. He wasn't a nice man."

"Better not to speak any more right now. Dream of me tonight, Xiao Li. I will dream of you."

"Cono, listen. Our son is strong and smart. He has your eyes and your lips. Mother takes good care of him. You never believed he was yours. When you see you will believe."

"We will talk about that later, when you are free," Cono said.

"You have my shoe?"

"I have your shoe." The phone clicked off.

Cono did dream of Xiao Li that night, and of the smell of a warm evening ocean, and of streaks of moonlight swallowed by the waves as they crashed and receded, pulling him, sweeping him, into the sea.

His bare feet patter on the red dirt road. They are big for a boy of five. Slap-slap, go the plastic thongs on his mother's feet. Her hand is tight on his, too tight, and he tries to shake free. She squeezes harder and marches faster, lifting red dust with every slap. There's a tug of his arm and a turn into a big white room full of rows of people, with words painted on the walls. They sit on a bench next to a fat lady who answers the questions of the angry man in front. His mother says she must leave him there, to talk to a man about a dancing job. The family needs money. His father will be happy. Stay, listen to the preacher, I'll be back in an hour. She is wearing her only dress. The flowery fabric brushes his bare knees as she leaves. He looks over his shoulder but his mother does not turn her head.

The angry man in front shouts and waves his arms in the air. The fat lady and the other people make noises, sounds he cannot understand. It is another language, or no language. The people stand up and more strange sounds come from their mouths. He stands up, too. The fat lady shakes and shouts, and he makes the same sounds come out of his mouth as soon as they come out of hers. Her brown head looks down at him. Maybe she, too, is angry.

People stumble up to the man in front, like a magnet is pulling them. They shout the sounds that make no sense and the man hits them on the head, but they do not fight back. They shout and cry and shake and move away to make room for the next person.

His hand feels the dampness of the lady's big fingers as her flesh wraps his wrist. He is dragged by her to the front, to the angry preacher man swaying like the trees do in the big storms. He looks up to the shouting man and repeats the sounds as they emerge from the man's mouth, an instantaneous echo. The preacher stops swaying, bends down, staring. The noise of the people gets softer, then there is silence. He looks up to the eyes of the preacher; the man seems afraid, like an octopus making itself big before the hunting wire snags it.

He is back on the bench and his hand is free of the wet-liver grip. The preacher is shouting again, but now the sounds are words, real words. The fat lady is holding a book and starting to sing. All the different voices make his ears sting.

He leaves the singing, and the light outside hurts his eyes. Blinking, blinking against the brightness. His mother. She is standing across the big open square, standing next to a man in a brown jacket, the same color as his pants. There is money in his hand as it comes out of his pocket. The other hand tries to touch his mother's face. She takes the money quickly from his hand and pushes him away. The man's moustache lifts up to show white teeth.

His mother turns away. Little red clouds follow her feet.

Back inside the hall, darkness. He sits still, waiting for his eyes to work again. His mother sits down next to him. His hand feels the trembling of her palm. She has a smell he has never smelled before.

4

"Cono, you're a wreck." Timur was at the door of the hotel room, trim and tall, wearing the same jacket he'd worn the night before, with two of his men behind him. Cono was dressed but hadn't shaved or showered.

"Embarrassed to be seen with me?"

Timur snorted. "I've put up with worse."

They drove in a zigzag course, up toward the mountains, then down through scarred and decrepit apartment blocks with kids kicking balls on broken sidewalks, and then west to the outer edge of Almaty, where the driver had to steer around several cows searching for grass. They passed a row of scarfed women seated on the edge of the road, each with a pyramid of apples for sale, each pyramid a different color, running from shades of red to burnished gold, amber and on to bright yellow. Ahead was a roadblock, with two cars stopped, trunks open, their drivers waving papers at the policemen. Timur's driver slowed to let an officer approach. Timur rolled down the window. Seeing his face, the officer saluted and frantically waved at another policeman to let the car proceed.

"There have been some incidents," Timur said, not looking at Cono. "The fundamentalist wave has landed on my country."

Finally the car pulled into the courtyard of a gray complex of apartment buildings, the city's last reach of Soviet-era construction, and stopped alongside a fence formed by tractor tires half-buried in the dirt. Timur got out and opened a steel door covered with graffiti. There were beer cans in the stairwell. Timur kicked them aside as he and Cono climbed the stairs and unlocked the door of a second-floor apartment. The driver and the other guard were left outside.

"It's not luxurious, but it's clean of all sorts of insects, including the kind that have ears," Timur said as he switched on the light. "Welcome to my home away from home." The windows were covered with sheets of black plastic and the corner of a mattress was visible on the floor of an adjoining room. Timur grabbed a chair and shoved it toward Cono, then sat down across from his friend. Between them was a large brown folding table on which rested a solitary bottle of vodka.

Cono whistled. "So life has been good to you. With a view like this we could be in Paris." He nodded at molasses-colored marks on the wall behind Timur. "But you really should tell the maid to clean up the blood stains."

"*You* should tell *me* about blood. I'd offer you a drink but I know ..."

"I'm a hops and grapes pussy wimp from the West."

Timur chuckled. "You don't forget a thing, Cono." He took a quick swig from the bottle. "No glass for you here anyway." His face became serious again, his eyebrows drawn together in a single line of black fur.

The lay of the land had changed, Timur explained. The Tengiz field that had had the oil companies salivating during Cono's last

Kazak enterprise had proved out well. Too well, in fact, for the government, particularly for Kurgat, the interior minister, who was dissatisfied with the price of the stakes they had sold to the oil companies—the "sows," as Timur called them. And now the exploration of the new Kashagan field showed reserves of such magnitude that the companies and the top officials were giddy with greed, and its handmaiden, suspicion. The Kashagan held the largest reserves found in the world in a generation, and was expected to be the second-largest source of oil on the planet, after the Ghawar field in Saudi Arabia. Now it wasn't only Kazak officials who were forecasting the country's momentous daily output; petroleum experts around the world had joined the chorus as well.

The newfound reserves gave the government leverage to renegotiate the old Tengiz allotments while extracting higher prices for further exploration agreements, with another round of commissions flowing to the top of the government. The sows at the trough this time around were mostly the same, although a few had merged, or sold their stakes to others. And there was a new one, from Beijing.

"They grow them big there in China, you know," Timur said, taking another gulp from the bottle. "They get bigger by the day. Very hungry." Despite the periodic sloshes of vodka, Timur's speech never slurred.

"In Suriname I saw an angry sow crush a man," Cono said. "He lived, but afterwards he couldn't walk."

"Better to keep the big ones happy. And at a distance."

"And the distance is for me to provide." Cono fixed his eyes on Timur's. He saw the minuscule squeeze of the aperture of his pupils before Timur tilted back his head to gaze at the water-stained ceiling.

"Look, brother," Timur said. "Last time I helped you and you helped me. We can do it again."

"Maybe with more help you will have your own oil empire," Cono said. "I already gave you ammunition for it, last time I was here. It seems you've sat on the fact that your leaders like the Alps. I even gave you the paper trail that proved they've been stashing hundreds of millions in Zurich." Cono was reading every minute twitch of Timur's body across the table.

Timur placed his hand around the bottle and gripped it tightly. "Paper trails are made of paper. It was nice work, even if it was just a lucky extra take from your job for the Americans and the Ukrainian bitch. Thanks for the reminder. You're just angling for the girl."

"A maiden for a kingdom. A small price."

"Brother, you are a strange man."

"And you, brother, breathe ambition. Let's call you Genghis." Cono smiled.

"You're all the more strange because you are still friendly even while I've got your girl locked up. Maybe she's not such a big deal, after all."

"You and I go way back, Timur, my friend. I know the forces that twist you. I'd help you anyway, and that's why," Cono softened his voice and slowed his cadence. "That's why you should let her go."

Timur caught himself being lulled by Cono's open gaze and the rhythm of his speech, which kept tempo with Timur's breathing. He unlatched his eyes from Cono's and looked up at the ceiling again.

"Besides," Cono continued, "no person is just one person. Everyone is a crate of fruits, a crate of mixed fruits. The apple in there may have worms, a peach may be mildewed, a banana may be too green, a pear may be in perfect ripeness, and a melon may have the sweetest smell. And do you know, Timur," Cono's voice slowed again, almost imperceptibly, "do you know, the expression the Kitais have for friends? They say, to make a friend you must close one eye. And to keep a friend, you must close both eyes. And so, Timur." The huskiness of Cono's voice was soothing, melodic. "I will close both eyes, for you, for now, because … we are friends."

Timur's eyes were back on Cono's, suddenly glazed and droopy. Cono raised his right hand and rubbed his ear, breaking the dull, hypnotic stare. Timur blinked and was reaching for another drink when the stillness was cracked open by a moaning muezzin's call to midday prayer. The powerful loudspeakers of the mosque wailed on for minutes.

Finally it was quiet. Timur's body had tensed with the sound of the muezzin, and now it relaxed. "Our friend …" he said. "Muktar, our painter friend—he went that way. I should tell you. You asked me on the phone." He was wistful, as if he had lost a real brother, but slight asymmetries in the ripples of his facial muscles caught Cono's eye.

"From painting to Islam?" Cono thought of the grotesquely fascinating painting of deformed faces he had bought from Muktar back then, and that now hung on an otherwise blank wall in Cono's terrace apartment at Repulse Bay, Hong Kong.

"You know how lost he was," Timur said. "That's how it happens. Unsettled, aimless, alone, so you make some visits to the mosque, find a new and better family, a family of believers. All the questions answered. All those words fill the vacuum. Imagine—he doesn't even take women anymore."

"Where is he?"

"I don't know. He's lost to me. Gone to the other side. It's better I don't know." There it was again: a slight unevenness in the modulation of Timur's voice. He was not telling the truth.

Timur lifted the bottle. "He liked you. Strange guy. He was a good friend."

"How far has he gone?"

"All the way. Fanatic, with all the jihad blabber of a central-Asian caliphate. He's on the Bureau's terrorist watch list." Timur shook his head. "His mother thinks her boy might as well be dead. If he has to be a fanatic I wish he would be just a freelance one like you."

"Ah, Timur, if it's not one god it's another. Allah or oil. Jesus or Jewels. Lenin or lust."

"Nice lines, Tupac. I know you've got no religion."

Cono looked at Timur with a wide-open face. "Oh, but I do."

Timur was puzzled.

"I believe in the goddess of mystery. And she's always pregnant," Cono laughed.

"Fuck religion. Let's get on with it," Timur said, scowling. "These will be busy days for you. Some of the dogs are the same, some are different from last time." He ran through the list of the dogs—what he called the official and unofficial go-betweens employed by the oil companies, the sows. *Dogs and sows*, Cono thought. *What does that make me?*

"And why the gifts in cash instead of bank wires?"

"The Americans have a saying: 'Cash is king.'"

"And what do the Kitais say?"

"Back off. It's a simple auction. And you are the auctioneer," Timur said.

"No, *you* are the auctioneer, and I am the bag boy."

"No one better, brother."

Timur handed Cono a restaurant receipt. The first names of the go-betweens, phone numbers, and a password for each one, in English, were written on the back. There were four names on the list.

"It's short."

"The two American sows don't want to play this way anymore—they're counting on their government to provide the grease. And the Russians aren't going to pay enough because they're drowning in Siberian oil. Besides, they still think they own my country. The dogs on the list work for the Italians, the French, the Anglos, the Dutch. I've stepped up the schedule to take advantage of your presence."

"It looks like a busy week's work." Cono held up the list so he could view Timur's face at the same time. "I hope I don't have to take each of these distinguished men to dinner."

"We don't have that much time. You want to spring the girl, after all."

Timur plucked the restaurant receipt out of Cono's hand. "Before we get to these old reliables, you have to tend to the new bidders, from Beijing. They'll be less predictable—better to take them on first. Here." Timur handed Cono a 100-tenge note with writing along one edge, a number, and a pass phrase.

Cono nodded, studying Timur's face carefully. "And after all the bids are in, the girl is freed."

"The girl is freed," Timur echoed as his cell phone started vibrating in a jacket pocket. "Yes." Timur listened for a moment. "Then get some cuffs on her. Send him on the holiday. Yeah, that holiday. He knew the rules." Timur snapped the phone into his jacket.

"Your tart is a wildcat. Nearly scratched the eyes out of one of my employees who tried to misbehave. You seem to like them like that." Timur smiled.

"She's stronger than either of us."

Timur took another swig and went into the bathroom to piss. Cono studied the only decoration in the room, a frameless canvas of rough brush strokes propped up against the wall. The tortured faces, harshly rendered, had to be the work of Muktar.

While Cono listened to Timur's drizzle, he wondered what prank he could pull—a jest like those they used to play on each other years ago, usually followed by a bout of brotherly wrestling. In the early days, Timur *had* treated him as a brother, helping him navigate rough-and-tumble Almaty with hard advice and sharp humor, supplying a little piece of family that Cono hadn't known since childhood, rescuing his spirits and bringing him out of one of the deepest troughs of his aloneness. Cono suddenly felt embarrassed—embarrassed by the thought that he might have been just another pitiful orphan trying to turn friends into family, and that he might still be blinded by his need, a need that colored his whole life, that ache to offer worth to someone. Wasn't that the constant engine for his bizarre career, servicing the ambitions of the reputable and disreputable—all the same to him as long as they acknowledged the necessity of having him and only him do the job?

Cono spotted an electrical box on the wall of the main room and lifted its lid, then twisted out two fuses. The apartment went pitch black. As Timur hurried back into the room, Cono ripped down the plastic from one window, letting the daylight stream in. Timur's pants were still undone, urine dripping on his leg. And a pistol was staring at Cono from the end of Timur's arm. Pranks were a thing of the past.

"Timur, friend, you were made for Paris, where they pee in the streets."

Timur's arm gradually lowered. The gun went back to his armpit. He zipped his pants and fumbled for the key to the lock he had secured from the inside. "If you weren't a friend, I'd kill you now," Timur said as they went into the stairwell. He kicked a beer can and sent it flying ahead of them.

Cono stepped out of the building first, with Timur close by. The black Mercedes was in the same place to the left, with the driver and the other toad standing in front of it. Cono glimpsed a momentary tautness in their faces as they watched their boss emerge on the crumbling concrete steps. The scene was the same as when they had arrived—the row of green and russet trees, the kids chasing one another in the gravel enclosure formed by the looming buildings. It was all the same except for the shadows Cono saw cast by two trees to the right, shadows with irregularities that weren't there before. Cono slammed his shoulder into Timur and the two crashed off the steps into a garbage pile. Automatic gunfire sprayed the face of the building. As Cono and Timur dug themselves frantically into the rubbish, Cono counted the rounds. Eventually he heard a voice shout *"Khvatit!"*—"Enough." He also heard the individual steps of two pairs of feet running until they were lost. Then a distant sound of wheels scratching gravel and fading away. Timur had his pistol in hand, but there was nothing to shoot.

"They're gone," Cono said. "But your friends' faces showed they knew the future."

They rose from the trash pile as Timur's two comrades slowly stood up behind the Mercedes. Cono took note of the calmness of Timur's body as he shook off the fetid debris of kitchen remains.

Timur didn't scream at his men. He simply got into the car, followed by Cono, and told the driver to go to the lookout point called Koktyube, on the southern fringe of the city, where the mountains started their rugged rise to snow-fed streams and the simpler lives of nomads.

"I guess they didn't like our visitor," Timur said to the driver, letting out a deep burp. "Anyone you recognized, or just the usual thugs dressed like you?"

"No sir. They came out of nowhere, from behind the trees." The driver's reply was slightly rushed.

"And you, Mazhit, proud father of little six-year-old Amira?"

"Nothing to see, sir. It was so quick," said the other guard.

The car stopped at the top of a long rising road with a concrete barrier on one side that held the foothills at bay. Timur and Cono got out and walked to the edge of a broad terrace rimmed by a stone wall overlooking Almaty. It was a strikingly clear day, with a sky of such bright blueness that it hurt the eyes. The overgrown greenness of the city grid was splotched here and there with yellow and orange. In the distance the vegetation and low buildings gave way to a flat grayness that met the blue sky in a sharp line. Just below the terrace was a small café with red parasols. It was empty.

Timur spoke first. "There are not so many clear days like this. Usually the haze cuts off the view."

"A good clean day for an assassination."

"Assassination? You make me out as some government prince." Timur lit a cigarette.

"Someone thinks you are." Cono stood so he could glance at the car as they spoke. "You can't blame them. You carry yourself so nobly, with that ambition in your eyes. If only they could see you grovel at the feet of pretty women like I have!" Cono laughed, and as he did so he saw the driver through the car window, speaking on a cell phone.

Timur ignored the humor. "There may be a split, Cono. Between the premier and Minister Kurgat."

"Which one is your boss?"

"I could say I'm a patriotic employee of the republic, but you would laugh."

"How could I laugh when your patriotism almost got you killed?"

"Almost. Only almost. Thanks to you. A second time. Thanks, brother." Timur took a long drag on his cigarette.

"Don't thank me now," Cono said. "It depends on whether future life makes you happy you didn't die."

"That's the question every day, I suppose." Timur flicked his cigarette ash over the edge of the wall.

"And, every day, *you* have to wonder who you work for, poor bastard," Cono said, laughing. "Okay, enough philosophy!" He spanked his knee in self-amusement. The men in the car were looking at them.

Timur breathed out a stream of smoke. "Why the fuck are you so happy all the time?"

"Life and death—doesn't the sharp edge between them make you happy?" Cono asked. "It makes me ecstatic. Only sex can give as much pleasure. I nearly came when they nicked my shoulder."

Timur was startled. He looked closely at Cono for the first time since the shooting and saw the stained rip in his shirt, on the bulge of his deltoid.

"It's only a cut," Cono said, "a reminder of this day. A reminder to ask every day, Why am I doing this?"

"Cono, you *are* a fanatic. Sometimes I think you'd make a

great terrorist." Timur raised his hand to examine the wound, but Cono waved him away.

"It's a tiny problem. We have bigger ones." Cono shifted his eyes toward the car, then back to the panoramic view.

Timur tapped his fingers on the stone wall. "Are you sure the two in the car were part of it? The shots that got you off?"

"If they hadn't ducked just before the others started firing I wouldn't have been sure. I see things a little differently. Time. It separates itself." Cono nodded. "I am sure."

"And I'm sure you're a freak of nature."

"That's the same word the doctors used. Freak."

Timur was gazing far away. "Look down there, Cono—all green except for a few trees that have already turned. You never know which ones will turn yellow or orange first. It seems to happen overnight, with no warning. There's a forest of green and then one day the first one changes color. No fuckeen warning. Another one turns, then another, but you never know which one is next.

"There's a tree down there on Gogol Street, a big one." Timur pointed with certainty at the middle of the city below. "I walked by it for years when I was a kid. Climbed it often, to take a look around, to get higher than everybody else. It made me late for school, so they whacked me. It was worth it. Sometimes that tree was first to turn, sometimes it was last, sometimes it was somewhere in between. But always, by the end of October, it and all the others were yellow or naked. I suppose the unnatural one that didn't lose its leaves wouldn't survive for the next season's go-around." Timur turned toward Cono.

"It all depends on the climate," Cono said with a smile. "In Brazil the trees never lose their green. You should see Brazil, after you've had your pee in Paris." Cono paused. "What about your two dedicated employees?"

"It's tempting. They both deserve a nine-miller to the head. But if I start with them, it won't finish. Better to know where they stand and use it later. Their leaves have just started to turn, not yellow or red yet. And next season they might remember I didn't put a bullet in them. Changing sides—it's the custom here. You live with it. You try to live with it." Timur looked at the rip in Cono's shirt. "I'll tell you where the china doll is, but I can't be there to help you spring her. Politically unwise. And if I do tell you, you'll still have to help me get through the forest."

"Agreed. As long as all three of us get through the forest."

"More of a jungle than a forest. You know that." Timur was tapping his fingers again. "But I won't tell you where she is until after you get the gift money and the bid from the Beijing sow. They are the tough ones, and you speak Chinese, you get the nuances. No need for a troublesome talkative translator. It really would be such a waste if you skipped out before collecting from them. You're even part Kitai. Maybe that's what makes you chase around the world for her."

"Right, brother, don't trust me with those fellow Kitais who kill their own countrymen. Italian in me too, so I'll play for them as well. Don't forget the Russian genes and whatever the rest was. Do I care who sucks the oil out of the Caspian?"

Timur was taken aback by Cono's sharpness. "Sounds like you're applying for the job."

"For a government employee you're pretty quick," Cono said. "But I saw that from the first day. No wonder you can shoot to the top and shake off your assassins."

"Would-be assassins."

"Them too."

As they turned toward the cool air oozing down from the mountains and walked toward the Mercedes, the driver and the other guard scrambled into the car.

The ride down from Koktyube was long and silent until Cono began fiddling with the hinged metal cover of the ashtray next to his arm. It made a clinking sound as he opened and closed it, slowly at first, then faster and faster until it resembled chattering teeth. Timur looked at Cono with annoyance. The chattering slowed and stopped.

Even from a foot away, Cono could sense the tension in his companion's muscles. He started to lean back in his seat but something clinging to Timur's lower pant leg caught his eye. It was a long shred of gristle, a reminder of the pile of garbage that had saved their lives. He leaned forward and plucked it off, then handed it to Timur, who frowned at it for a moment before lowering the window and flicking it outside. The window whirred shut again, sealing the car in a silence that stretched out until they glided onto the city streets below.

5

Timur instructed the driver to stop in front of the Arasan Baths. He and Cono got out on the sidewalk where vendors watched over their stacks of cut-and-bound branches—myrtle, linden, oak, birch. The vendors were barking their wares to the trickle of men in search of their favorite branches with which to beat themselves in the steam rooms. Cono smiled at his nostalgia for this stretch of sidewalk, where he had met Xiao Li, but he pushed the feeling away.

Timur was the first to break the silence. "Call the Chinese now. Tell them your meeting has to be within two hours. In back of the musical-instruments museum—the old officers' hall—all the way up the driveway, where it ends in the park. Use this. It's clean." He handed Cono a cell phone. "I'll leave these two idiots back at the garage. Later I'll be following you in something beat-up, maybe a Toyota. Luxury has its downsides."

Cono tapped in the numbers written on the tenge note Timur had given him. The phone rang several times. Then there was an answer. "*Wei?*"

Cono conversed in Mandarin while Timur stood next to a big oak rooted in concrete and turned slowly right and left, glancing at Cono and the waiting car. At last Cono laughed and flipped the phone shut.

"He was telling me the old joke about the Dalai Lama coming to visit the Forbidden City. Sounds like a charming thug."

"Are we on?"

"In two hours—ten after five. He says the gift will be in four cases."

A tottering Russian who had just bought his bundle of myrtle leaves bumped into Timur. Timur jabbed an elbow into the man's ribs. "We have manners here in Kazakhstan! Fuck off."

The old man shuffled on. "And you learned them from us Russians," he muttered, the myrtle in one hand and a colorless frayed towel in the other.

"Four cases," Timur mused. "It's a good sign, maybe three, maybe five million. Good for starters."

"I hope the cases have labels, to make it easier. 'For Mr. K, For Mr. Premier, For Mr. Timur.' Each with 'Greetings from the Forbidden City' on a postcard inside."

Timur ignored Cono's remark and rapped on the darkened window of the Mercedes. He took a cell phone from each of the employees inside. "These little things are dangerous," he said to Cono. "More dangerous than guns. And a little hard to get in my dear country. Losing one is like having your dick cut off."

Timur stuffed the phones into his coat. He pointed his dark eyes at Cono's. "The Kitais know that if they help me they can play both sides. The minister and the premier, split or no split. Isn't that worth a little compensation?"

"A man of your talents—why would the Kitais pay anyone but

you? The trouble is, one side or the other, either the minister or the premier, is trying to rub you out. And I hope they don't succeed, at least not until the wildcat princess is free from your safe-keeping."

Timur walked over to the beige stone wall encircling the monumental baths and sat on it. He lit a cigarette as Cono sat next to him. More old men sauntered past, Kazaks and Russians, to climb the broad steps nearby. Timur took a hip flask from his coat and quickly jerked it to his lips; then it disappeared again.

"It's a delicate situation, Cono. Minister Kurgat is grabbing more and more power, and tightening his grip on the oil contracts; he's become too powerful for the premier's comfort. And there's a court case in the U.S. that is complicating things here. A longtime American adviser to our government has been indicted for corrupt operations, or whatever they call it—just normal grease for oil contracts. The case could bring out a few details that reflect poorly on our fine leaders. This will hurt bidding prices, both the ones on the record and the ones off the record, because the sows are following the story every day and they don't want to end up in court in their own countries. That's why we've gone back to the Stone Age, like apes, carrying money in suitcases and trucks. It all has to be untraceable."

"And the unflattering details, like the American grease case, get no play in the papers here at home, I guess."

Timur snorted. "Little brother, sometimes I think you'll never learn. All the press is under the regime's thumb. There won't be any coverage of it here. And if it did somehow get out, the people would just write it off as an American scheme to insult all Kazaks. *So what* if the chief is taking his cut, and is a tyrant, and plenty brutal? The people need a strong leader. They feel insecure if they don't know who to fear. Isn't that why god was invented?"

Cono laughed at his friend's distillation of human nature.

"The premier wants to deal with the Americans through diplomacy," Timur said, "which means buying as many politicians in Washington as he can. Getting the American oil companies to crank up the pressure at home on his behalf. And maybe leasing some land to their air force. Then there's Minister Kurgat."

Timur sucked his cigarette again and exhaled the smoke slowly. "Kurgat has other ideas. He wants to box, to stick it to the Americans. And with help from Beijing, he might just be able to knock our premier out of the ring. How convenient for him."

"If he clears away a few obstacles—like you—in advance?"

"I've got you to thank for that, Cono. The run-in at the Svezda to save your tart, with my squad and the Chinese Embassy team all together like we're having some fuckeen Politburo meeting, and the hotel staff swarming around? Fuckeen mess. No way Kurgat wouldn't know about it and suspect I'm trying to cut my own deal with Beijing."

"Aren't you?"

Timur ignored the comment and stepped toward the waiting car. "You'll have to walk to your date with the Kitais, Cono. Take a roundabout way, and try not to get robbed. Almaty is a dangerous place—nothing's nailed down in my country. I'll be waiting nearby, not too close. I would send someone else to pick you up, but they might take the money themselves and dump your corpse on the side of the road. Both results would be unpleasant. Put the cases under the trees by the drive-up to the museum and tell the Kitais to go away. Then wait. No one's ever there, except for the old guy who sweeps the place. He's my uncle—worse scum than my old man."

Timur got into the Mercedes and drove off.

Cono looked south and upward, toward the Tian Shan range, the mountains catching the afternoon sun on their iced and glowing edges. He turned and walked north, down sloping Karl Marx Street, then east beyond the central avenues where the high-end-business fronts behind the trees wore new façades of fake marble and chrome. Each was lettered with big Cyrillic signs—banks and medical suppliers, apparel shops and travel agents, followed by more modest stores selling industrial pumps, electrical fixtures, and spooled cables.

With almost two hours on his hands, Cono found himself wandering without direction, replaying the events of the day in his head—his old friend's request for help with the bribes; the assassination attempt; the promise that Xiao Li's whereabouts would be revealed; the bullet wound that caused less discomfort than being called a freak.

Freak. Cono had been trying to get used to that word ever since the doctors had first spoken it a decade ago.

The clinic physician in São Paulo who had started it all had no idea what he had set into motion. He had been treating Cono for recurring headaches, and was intrigued by the results of the neurological exams he performed on the unusual, ragtag young man who had just returned to Brazil after years of roaming alone across several continents.

In order to satisfy his own curiosity, and to get his name on a case report in a prestigious medical journal, the Brazilian doctor offered, at his own expense, to send Cono to a medical-research lab at Stanford University, in Palo Alto, California. The intention was for Cono to spend a few days there to determine which rare syndrome he exhibited, then return to Brazil. But the stay in California dragged on and on.

It was in the first battery of tests that Cono learned of his susceptibility to certain types of lights. The scientists asked him to give the exact count of rapid flickers he was being exposed to, in intervals as infinitesimal as hundredths of a second. Cono's count was always accurate. They tested the flashing lights over a wide range of frequencies, and at different distances. Once, when a high-frequency light was positioned an arm's length away from Cono's face, it had thrown him into a seizure. Afterward, when he had regained consciousness and was connected to an intravenous line, Cono was told by two of the self-assured doctors that they had predicted this response.

They tested reaction times—visual, motor, auditory, even tactile and gustatory. There were endless variations of tests employing video screens, but the videos' standard scanning speed of thirty images per second was too easy—Cono could pick out variations in each individual frame, even though it gave him a dull pain deep in his brain. They brought in faster equipment, which flashed visual scenes at forty, fifty, sixty images per second and more. The machines hit their limit, and Cono suggested to the frustrated scientists that they give him a glass of water and an aspirin and then show him a real situation, like a falling orange that he could catch and stuff into his pocket before anyone saw. Or a bird he could snatch with his hand as it flew by.

One of the doctors, a patient older man, asked Cono how well he slept at night, and what his dreams were like. The doctor explained why he was asking: dreaming was the brain's way of re-equilibrating after a day of sensory inputs; the sensory overload of Cono's hyper-fast perception might require longer and deeper dreaming in order to re-equilibrate his cortex at night. And the dreams might be different in character than those of a normal person—more intense, more vivid, faster, or the opposite of all of these; he didn't know. Of course Cono also couldn't know, because he had no way to compare his dreams to the dreams of others. But the older doctor's questioning brought out several findings. Cono's dreams often replayed real events with high fidelity to all the senses, not just the visual. He needed much more sleep than the average person, and a shortfall in sleep over a few days could cripple him, distorting his perceptions and clouding his thoughts. Cono told the doctor he had discovered that he could temper this need for long sleep by falling into deep meditation for short intervals; there had been times during his years of traveling when the technique had been necessary for survival. Out of desperation he had tried amphetamines, too, but they had a paradoxical effect and made him even more stuporous.

Geneticists were brought in to evaluate the strange young man. They spoke of genes called *timeless*, *FoxP2*, *STX1A* and others—genes they thought controlled the cycle times of the brains of various animal species unfamiliar to Cono. They were eager to know if these genes exerted the same control in humans. The geneticists analyzed Cono's blood; later they could say only that they'd found a mutation they'd never seen, in a yet unnamed gene that they proudly asserted must be the regulator of sequential awareness. One of the geneticists speculated that Cono might have a version of this gene similar to that of a shark or a falcon or a reptile, a version that had been lost somewhere along the march into mammalian evolution.

This theory was immediately contested by another geneticist, who said it was likely that one or more of Cono's brain-regulating genes located on the long arm of the seventh chromosome had undergone spontaneous mutations that somehow resulted in "this freakishly faster cycling." The scientists argued over the competing theories, but finally agreed that regardless of the source of the genetic aberration, the result was analogous to the evolutionary progression of computers—new machines steadily came out in faster and faster models, doubling their cycle-times every year or two. But so far among humans, there were only two models—Cono and everyone else.

"It's inevitable that new genetic anomalies like this will crop up as we get better at detecting them," explained a bearded doctor in horn-rimmed glasses and a bow tie. "A lab in Europe just worked out the reason for a Finnish sports hero being unbeatable in cross-country skiing back in the '60s. He has a mutation in a gene that controls red-blood-cell production. His body cranks out red blood cells in overdrive—very handy when your muscles are aching for more oxygen. And recently there was a baby born in Germany who looks like a body builder. The kid's myostatin gene is mutated so that it doesn't restrain muscle growth like it should. No doubt he'll grow up to be abnormally strong. There are a handful of people in the world who cannot feel pain because of a defect in a single one of their genes. And you've probably heard of perfect pitch—I'm betting it's the result of a genetic alteration we haven't pinned down yet. You, Cono, are part of a new trend of uncovering the genetic basis of human performance anomalies."

Cono was concentrating hard to understand all the English words, sometimes stopping the doctor for clarification. "Other person, someone, fast, making time slow down like me?" he asked.

"We've had a few cases of abnormally fast reaction times in patients with a disease called Tourette's, but at most we see a doubling of speed of movement. You are way beyond that. And in you, both motion and perception are accelerated." The doctor paused in thought. "Some, but not all, of your reaction times suggest that your brain is routing signals through a shorter pathway for sensation and response, via the amygdala. *Amygdala* means 'almond' in Latin, and that's what this part of the brain looks like." Cono was frowning as he tried to comprehend all the words. "There are two amygdalae," the doctor continued, "deep in your brain, above the roof of your mouth, one on each side. They play a role in emotions and aggression. Signals routed through them can be so fast that they are complete even before you have any conscious awareness of them. It's analogous to me tapping on your knee. Your quadriceps contract and your leg kicks out before you have any knowledge of the action. But I must say, your case is considerably more complex."

After three weeks of examining Cono, the doctors sat down and gave him an overview of their findings. Cono had already soaked up a great deal more English. Following their summary, he recalled the seizure that had been provoked by the flickering lights and said, "Well, so, that explain why hard it is to watch TV for me." The doctors all laughed, guardedly. They looked around the room at one another; too much, Cono thought. They were unusually gracious toward him, and he noted minuscule, fleeting contractions around their eyes and instantaneous shivers near their lips when they gave bland answers to his questions.

The scientists wanted more. They wanted to test Cono's biological relatives and their genes, and to study Cono's physiology in much greater detail. "After all, who knows the bodily consequences of a brain ticking so fast," one of them said. "Maybe it shortens life expectancy." A woman wearing a pinstriped dress said it was essential that they test the effect of Cono's mutations on language acquisition, because of the probability that an increased cycle time would facilitate linguistic processing. Another specialist in the room said they had prepared a laboratory to study his dream patterns. Cono laughed at these proposals as he reached across the table to place his hand near the chief doctor's ear, and plucked a Brazilian real coin from it. He flipped it into the air with his thumb, observing their faces and the tumbling coin at the same time. The coin was gone with a swipe of his arm that the scientists never saw. "The Freakish say no thanks."

Cono made that his last day with the doctors. He had to change motels twice to evade their aggressive pursuit. But he didn't leave Palo Alto immediately. He had agreed to meet a young oddball video technician named Todd who had slipped him a note on that last day. Todd had run the machines for most of the perceptual tests that Cono had endured, and he wrote in the note that he had important things to discuss with Cono.

When the goateed young man wasn't running the visual equipment at the medical labs, he was working on his doctorate in mathematics. He wanted to put Cono's way of seeing things into equations. "I'm into data compression," he explained. That seemed to be the only thing Todd was into. He had no interest in women or men, and was barely sociable. He was neuter, it seemed, except for the near-orgasmic pleasure he took from his formulas. Cono guessed that only a person who didn't really care for people could find personalities in equations, and friends in matrices. Todd spoke of datasets as if they were current or future lovers. Cono admired him for his ability to find joy beyond the secretory impulses that controlled most humans.

The two developed a friendship of sorts and worked together each night for weeks at sandwich shops and a joint called Michael's Café. Cono had no money left, so Todd let him sleep on the floor of his flimsy-walled apartment, between stacks of computer magazines.

Todd asked in a dozen ways exactly what Cono saw in the split-second images that appeared in his mind as he watched something moving. Cono explained that the stationary objects would melt into the background, and he would actively perceive only what was moving, the edges especially. The rest could be black, or empty; it didn't matter, because, "If I see that part once and it makes no move, I don't need to see it again. I have it."

Todd's eyes pointed upward into his lids, so that Cono saw only the white sclera. When his pupils returned, Todd grinned and licked his lips. He started writing furiously on a notepad. Finally he spoke. "Stationary image fields are condensed, pocketed away by the math, so more strenuous formulas can work on the moving parts. Just think of a movie, Cono." Cono replied that he didn't watch movies; they gave him a headache. "Well, in movies, most of what you see is not moving much, but those pixels still choke up the data stream. So we'll carve them out and stuff them away temporarily, and give them five-hertz updates. It frees up gobs of processing muscle."

"Gobs?" Cono said.

"You know, lots, big amount, truckloads. Got it?"

"Got it. I learn gobs of English from my friend Todd."

Todd smiled, briefly. "What about color? D'you see everything in color?" He thumped his bright-yellow pencil on the table. Then he twirled it around his thumb repeatedly—a little acrobatic trick he did when he was impatient, which was often.

Cono stared at the twirling pencil against the background of the green napkin Todd's hand rested on.

"I know the pencil is yellow, but when it moves fast like that, it's just gray. The napkin stays green."

Todd picked up the napkin and waved it quickly back and forth. "Green?"

"Gray."

"And now?" Todd stopped his waving.

"Now it's green."

Todd bit the eraser end of the pencil. "Maybe normal humans are just like you, Seven Q. The color disappears when something moves fast, and they just don't notice the color's gone. But you, you can see the change because, well, you know …"

"Normal? What is normal, Todd? Are you normal? And what is Seven Q?"

"I guess the docs didn't tell you. They nicknamed you Seven Q because they think your mutations are on the long arm of your seventh chromosome. Chromosomes have a long arm and a short arm. The long one is called Q. They write it like this …"

Todd wrote "7q" on his notepad. "Kinda funny, huh?"

"My name is Cono, not Seven Q."

Cono's comment was lost on his friend, who was back to scribbling equations.

Todd looked up. "If it's true and we can cut color from any fast movement in the display, that's a 66 percent bit reduction, limited of course to the moving parts of the field, but those are the processor hogs anyway."

"Hogs?"

"Pigs. Eat a lot. We'll have to see if it pans out in normals, but if it does, it'll be a great data stuffer, and easy to deal with—just some eigenvector transformations."

Todd was immersed in his formulas again when Cono reached beneath the table, pulled a box out of a sack and placed it next to the notepad. It was a mini Sony video camera, the latest. Cono nudged it forward to get Todd's attention.

"What's this?"

"For you. To say thanks for letting me stay at your place."

"Hey, man, it's too much. You don't have the money for this."

"I didn't pay money for it." Cono looked at Todd in amazement. "Of course I didn't."

"Some girl give it to you? The one at Michael's who keeps giving you the eye?"

"No."

"No, what?"

"I took it."

"You *stole* it?"

"I feel a little guilty, because it was so easy. The man at the store left it there."

"On the counter top, you mean."

"Yes," Cono said, "then he went to help someone else."

"And you helped yourself." Todd rubbed his fingers across his forehead, hard.

"Too easy, you're right," Cono said. "Didn't have to use any tricks."

Todd scolded Cono. It was the only time Cono had seen Todd's eyes get lit up by anything other than their discoveries.

"Cono, I don't want to commute all the way to San Quentin to continue our collaboration. You have to get a job. No more stealing."

Cono got a day job, "serving petrol," as he put it, at a station on the other side of the highway that kept the blacks and Latinos a safe distance from the mandarins of the university. Todd and Cono continued their evening sessions.

"Cono, when you hear things, *how* do you hear things?" And on and on.

Three months later they knocked on the door of a patent lawyer down the street from Todd's apartment. The next day the attorney said he was so interested in their data compression techniques that he would work for them for no fee and wait to get paid out of downstream licensing fees. To Cono's eye, the creases above the attorney's mouth seemed to quiver too much, and there was a lack of smoothness as ripples of expression flowed across his face; Cono told Todd the guy couldn't be trusted. Todd disagreed. A month later Todd said, "He's a schmuck."

"Schmuck?"

"Like you noticed the first time. What the hell did you see, anyway? Maybe there's another algorithm there ..."

On a Sunday morning at Michael's Café a man with thick, white hair overheard one of their bizarre conversations and approached them. Jim became their Silicon Valley godfather. He was a lawyer, a local figure with a storied past who seemed to know everyone. He set up a company to hold the patents for them, and soon everyone, it seemed, was interested in their data-compression algorithms: a chip company that wanted to provide video on demand; a consortium that intended to leap-frog videotape technology; a company hoping to send pictures using a new fad called the Internet.

Try as he might, Cono couldn't perceive any telltale shimmying of facial muscles that would signal him not to trust Jim.

"Jim, what do you want?" Cono asked him square on.

"I want you to succeed!"

They did succeed, but neither Todd nor Cono was interested in business. Cono was restless and had had enough of California; his hands still smelled of gasoline because he hadn't given up his day job, despite the mounting income from numerous technology firms. "Jim," he said, "I want to move on. Change the business papers so Todd gets more of the money. He did all the work."

Todd stopped chewing his pencil and threw it like a dart across the room. "No way, Jim," he said. "I'm not a schmuck. Don't change anything. Cono and I did it together."

Cono did move on, though, and in time their algorithms for manipulating and compressing images became more than popular; they became essential. The mathematical inventions soon crept into countless devices, including something called Digital Versatile Disc. It also turned out that a system named MPEG worked best when using their methods. The patent royalties made the two young men rich, in a recurring fashion. In Chinese, Cono called this compounding windfall his *"zìyóu lǐwù."* His freedom gift.

The wealth meant nothing to Cono, except that he decided to resist the urge to steal, and he felt freer to travel. And he could help friends when he wanted to. Friends like Xiao Li, and Irina, and a schoolteacher named Dimira.

Cono looked up and searched for a familiar landmark. He smiled when he realized that he had gradually made his way toward Zelyony, the sprawling bazaar. It was in this neighborhood that Dimira had lived, in one of the squat rows of apartments on the fringe of the vast open market. It must be why he had thought of her. He walked in a zigzag path through streets lined with uneven concrete sidewalks and finally found the mottled amber-colored building that had been her home. He recognized it by a tree whose roots had cracked the bottom of the front wall.

He walked up the stairwell to the second-floor door, pressed an ear against it, then knocked. No answer. He searched for signs of a change in the flaking paint, the three locks, the doorjamb marred by grooves of forced entry. They were all the same as before. Cono sat on the stairs above the landing and looked at his watch.

He had met Dimira four years earlier, on his second stay in Almaty, before encountering Xiao Li outside the Arasan Baths, and before starting his job for Katerina and the Americans who used her. He'd given Dimira a "Hi" and a smile as they passed each other on Avenue Abay in the screeching sunlight. Only when they sat down for beers at a cottage pub did he notice the deformed, miniature ears that had been hidden beneath her long, black hair. They were like the ears of a wrestler or boxer who had been smacked or squeezed with too much force.

Dimira was happy to meet a foreigner, and proudly told Cono she had a young daughter, beautiful, smart and perfect, but too dark to be accepted by the people of her country. She always referred to it that way—"*my* country," with the word *my* stressed and elongated. Dimira came from near Balkhash, in the flat rural middle of the country, and had fallen in love with an Ethiopian man who was studying there in the last days of Soviet-sponsored educational exchange. Dimira's family threw her out when she became pregnant. The Ethiopian was threatened with death and fled. Dimira gave birth, alone, in a nearby small town. She and the baby rode the train to Almaty and lived on the floor of the railway station for months as the Soviet Union collapsed and chaos reigned.

Somehow Dimira pulled herself out of this despair. She got a job teaching the Kazak language, newly required in all the country's schools, and was brimming with happiness that summer when she and Cono met.

They had kissed once, and nothing more.

The door at the bottom of the stairwell creaked open and banged shut. Cono went up the next flight of stairs and looked down at the door of the apartment. A woman with wide hips and slender legs appeared. She had twisted a key in the third lock when Cono whispered her name, leaning over the railing, behind and above her. As she turned, she held out a canister of pepper spray and fired it.

"You missed," Cono said, still whispering.

Dimira dropped the pepper spray and put her hand on her mouth. She dropped her purse, too, and leaped to hug Cono on the staircase.

She took him into the apartment without speaking. When the door was shut and triple-locked, Dimira disappeared into the kitchen without meeting Cono's gaze. "I'll make some tea," she called from the other room. A few moments later there was a crashing sound of falling plates and utensils.

"Is that another Almaty earthquake?" Cono joked.

"It's okay. Just a minute."

Cono sat down on one of the carpets in the single room that was her living space. The apartment was largely as he remembered it. There were two small mattresses covered by hand-woven blankets, a chest of drawers, two lamps, and a rod suspended from the ceiling that was hung with clothes. The wall around the chest of drawers was a patchwork of photos of Asel, Dimira's daughter, from her toddler days up to when she was gangly with beginning puberty. Cono got up to look at the pictures and saw only two photos that included Dimira, beaming, standing next to her child. He recognized those pictures because he had taken them years ago, after insisting over Dimira's protests. On the other walls were paintings drawn by a child's hand, some in simple frames, some tacked directly into the plaster.

The home was the same, except that it seemed too tidy.

Dimira emerged from the kitchen with a tin tray in her hands. As she approached, the tray shook and two spoons clattered to the floor. She stood before Cono, the teacups rattling, her head lowered.

"Let me help you," Cono said. He placed the tray on the floor and turned back to Dimira. With two hands, he raised her head so he could see her face. She was crying.

She fell against him, pressed her head to his chest and dissolved into violent sobbing. Cono held her for long minutes, lightly swaying from side to side, until her gasping and crying gradually subsided.

"Cono, she's gone. Asel is dead." Dimira let out one long, piercing cry. Suddenly it stopped. She hugged Cono and stepped back. She looked at him, her face streaked with tears. "Asel was murdered on the street, stabbed, two blocks from here. Six months ago. I wanted you to know but I had no way to contact you. She …" Dimira's voice caught and she bowed her head.

Cono pressed his lips against Dimira's hair and held her until she slipped away to wipe her face. They sat down next to the tray, Dimira folding her legs to one side. Cono righted the cups and poured tea. He grasped Dimira's hand.

"At least they didn't rape her," she said. "I don't think so. That's what the doctor told me."

Asel had come home from school at this same hour of the day. Her mother had been delayed at work because of an argument with another teacher who accused Dimira of being too easy on the students, for why else would she be so popular with them? It was Dimira herself who found the child, still just barely alive as her liver bled inside.

Dimira collapsed onto Cono's knee. "She was all I have. She was all I am." Cono put his hand in her hair and stroked it as her tears dripped onto his thigh. He considered the chances of finding Asel's murderer in this city where murders were commonplace, a city full of motives and random nonmotives. Murders here were like waves slapping at a shore. He could offer nothing more than his stroking hand.

Dimira sat up and wiped the wetness from her face with delicate fingers. "Cono, you helped us so much. I thank you."

"Dimira, it was only money."

"No, no, no! Cono, she adored you. You drew puppets on your hands for her. You showed her how to paint with her fingers. You taught her how to juggle. She always asked when you were coming back." Dimira covered her face and began to cry again, slumped on Cono's leg. He lightly twirled a finger in her thick black hair and began to sing in a soft, clear voice that came from deep in his chest. The words and the tones emerged immediately, coming to him from a place beyond his awareness.

Even now, I feel your arms around me
My breath is your breath and yours mine
Even now, I hear you laughing like bells ...
You sing to me and I sing to you
Dear child of my womb, my love,
Time has left us, left us forever together.

The two of them were silent for several moments, Dimira's head resting heavily on Cono's thigh. "She still lives in our memories," Cono said. "She told me that she wanted to grow up to be like you and to teach, that she was lucky to have you as her mother."

They sat quietly for a long time, occasionally sipping the tea, until there was no more water in the pot.

Cono unbent his legs and stood up. They hugged at the door. When he was outside and the last lock had clicked, he heard a muffled shriek of grief.

6

Less than an hour remained before the meeting with the Beijing men. Cono made his way to Zelyony Bazaar and entered between tables laden with audiocassettes and CDs. Rows of boomboxes were blaring out the wares simultaneously—Russian pop and American hip-hop competed with nostalgic strains from a Kazak zither. Farther down, a Turkish crooner was drowned out by a Hong Kong diva who had been all the rage during Cono's last trek in the People's Republic.

The path narrowed as he approached the heart of the bazaar. Canvasses stretched between low poles were protecting stacks of socks and baby clothes from the sun, as narrow-faced Tajik women watched over them. He turned a corner and collided with the breasts of a rotund Russian shopper carrying several heavy plastic bags. He apologized in Russian as she laughed flirtatiously and ambled on. In the next aisle, two angular tea-colored men barked at Cono in Pakistani-accented Russian, coaxing him to have a look at the shirts and jeans hanging like rows of curtains. Cono ducked his head to avoid raking off a T-shirt featuring

Madonna's gap-toothed face and the words "Material Girl"; just behind it he brushed against a shirt emblazoned with the bearded muzzle of bin Laden.

The next intersection of aisles was partly blocked by an old Russian man singing and holding a cup, his eyes vacant with blindness. The stooped woman at his elbow accompanied him with an accordion. Cono recognized the tune, and after listening for a minute, sang along until the couple finished. Quietly, he put a 50-tenge note in the cup. The blind man reached forward until Cono clasped the knotty hand.

"Your voice paints the air with beautiful colors," Cono said.

"Young man, you sing well," said the blind man. "Sing! Sing! That's all there is!"

Cono squeezed the old man's hand, contemplating the truth of his words. Singing gave him slowness, a gift that little else was able to confer. As his body vibrated with sound, the world gradually receded until it almost disappeared, and Cono felt that he himself almost slipped away into nothingness. *The old man is right—when singing, that's all there is.*

Cono entered the market's food hall and strolled past the mounds of dates, open sacks of spices and dried beans, and pyramids of fruit watched over by plump Kazak and Korean women waving away the flies and flashing silver teeth as they chattered. Cono smelled the meat stalls before he reached them. The lateness of the day had released the iron-tinged odors of entrails and hanging shanks. Pink rabbit carcasses, with the fur still on their feet, shined beneath the overhanging fluorescent lights. Whole cows' tongues, still attached to the larynx, wagged from hooks. Bowls of rippled intestines jiggled to the pounding of a nearby cleaver. Suspended goat carcasses extended their limbs as if leaping up to the skylights. A woman with her hair tied in a kerchief was stuffing meat into a glistening arc of fresh horse rectum to make *kazy*. A row of skinned sheep heads stared at the dwindling number of shoppers.

It was here, four years before, that Cono had caught a knife an instant before it would have entered Timur's abdomen. A diminutive Uzbek man in a rectangular skullcap had approached, saying he had an important confidential message for Mr. Betov. As the man moved close to whisper in Timur's ear, Cono saw the motion of his arm and caught the knife by the blade in a movement that was completed before any thought of the action could appear in his mind.

A surprised Timur saw the knife in Cono's hand and quickly grabbed the man in a chokehold and lifted him, kicking, down the steps to the urinals behind the beef tongues. Timur smashed the man's head once into a sink and pressed him face down on the grimy floor tiles. He barked at him in Russian and in Kazak, demanding to know who he was and whom he worked for. The man coughed and spit blood and yelled: "Allahu Akbar! Allahu Akbar!"

Timur planted his knee in the man's back and pushed his arms upward until one shoulder dislocated with a pop, and then the other one. "Who?"

"Allahu Akbar ..." The man's response was muted by the crush of his mouth against the floor. Timur heaved him, his head landing in the urinal.

"One more time. *Who?*"

"Yes," the man gurgled. "Allahu ..."

Timur stomped his foot on the back of the man's neck until Cono stopped him.

"Cono, your hand is bleeding." Timur reached down and ripped off the tail of the dead man's shirt. "Wrap this around it. Thanks, brother, thanks a lot."

That was on Cono's second stay in Almaty. Timur Betov was already an important man.

Cono glanced at the doorway to the toilets, then at the scars on his fingers, and exited the food hall. He wove a different route through the tin pots and hardware until he emerged from the sprawling network of tents onto a dusty road, full of people going home, that pointed him toward the clapboard building with the peaked copper roof that housed the Museum of Musical Instruments.

The road veered to connect with the pavement of Kaldayakov Street. Cono followed the rising sidewalk, lowering his head to avoid the tree branches. Two boys were collecting fallen chestnuts and competing to toss them into a metal pail.

"Throw one to me!" Cono called.

The younger one lobbed a nut, which Cono caught in his mouth. Just as quickly, he blew it out and kicked it with his instep like a hacky sack, aiming it directly into the pail. The boys came nearer, tossing more chestnuts toward him. Cono caught three of them and started juggling. And a fourth, and a fifth. The boys were now pulling chestnuts out of the pail and throwing them. He caught two more for the whirling circle. Then, as the boys watched, all the chestnuts disappeared. Cono leaned down, put his finger in the older boy's ear, and pulled out a chestnut, which he tossed into the pail. The smaller boy pushed his brother away and looked up at Cono expectantly. Cono knelt and took the boy's hand. When he released it the boy held a chestnut and a blue button.

The boy reminded him of the one he and Xiao Li encountered years before at the amusement park in Almaty, during their first few days together. They were eating ice cream near the rollercoaster, and Xiao Li drifted closer to watch. A little boy, maybe six years old and looking like a street urchin who had snuck in, saw a popsicle fall from one of the cars high on a curve. He began to run across a stretch of ground-level track to grab his good fortune. But the coaster cars were swooping down the same rails. Xiao Li leaped and snatched the boy into her arms. The two of them would have been hit but for inches. Xiao Li shouted at the boy and slapped him hard and kissed him on the cheek. Then she bought him an ice cream cone. And all the while she was wearing her high heels.

The brothers were fighting over the button as Cono continued up the sidewalk, the bright mountain peaks etched with shadows high in the distance. When he reached the corner of Panfilov Park nearest the museum, he made a wide loop, just close enough to watch the building and its driveway between the tree trunks. Halfway through his return on the same loop, he saw a silver Mercedes slowly gliding up. It came to a stop close to the pine trees, where the final curve rose to the steps of the wood-gabled museum.

A Chinese man in a shiny gray suit that almost matched the color of the car emerged from the front passenger seat. His coat was buttoned and the stiff white edge of a handkerchief in his breast pocket caught the sunlight before he stepped into the shade.

Cono began whistling the national anthem of the People's Republic as he walked across the mulch. The man in the suit turned his trim body, scanning the darkness beneath the trees. He had a square, handsome face, and although he was squinting, his features showed no perturbation. Cono appeared, still whistling, and tossed a chestnut toward the man. He snatched it with a downward flick of his hand and threw it in a high arc back to Cono, who caught it with the top of his foot and let it drop. The Chinese man nodded his head slightly at Cono.

"Too bad we don't have a soccer ball," he said in English.

Cono responded in Mandarin. "And who would keep score?"

"The game's the thing, after all." The Chinese man stuck to English.

"Ah, the game. Let's begin with tennis in Tulufan." The obtuse pass-phrase that Timur had chosen caused the man to smile in a quick, well-practiced motion. His teeth seemed to be newly polished. He held out his hand and Cono shook it. Cono felt no faint twitches of trepidation in the man's grip. He was a man at ease.

"Let's sit down," Cono said. They sat cross-legged on the carpet of pine needles a few paces away from the car. The Chinese man unbuttoned his suit coat and pulled out a pack of cigarettes. Cono declined his offer of a smoke, and the man lit a Dunhill, dragging on it deeply.

"My friend," he said in Mandarin, "you have dirt on your face."

Cono wiped the specks of dirt left on his lips by the chestnut husk he had caught in his mouth. "The measure of a true friend …"

"… is whether he will tell you when your face is dirty," said the Chinese man. "Well, we are not friends. There is too much business in front of us. And your boss has given us such short notice—I was supposed to have this pleasure weeks from now. I wonder why the rush. No time for niceties before getting to the details."

"The details. How many flowers are you offering?"

"The gift is six million. Dollars, I should say. And, for the oil contract when it's done, ten times that, on top of the first six. Even though you look like a strong young man, you will have a hard time carrying the flowers through the park, especially with that wound on your shoulder." The man held the cigarette to his mouth but did not inhale. He was waiting for Cono to speak.

"And that is your final number?" Cono stroked his cheek with a pine needle and held it to his nose to enjoy the scent.

"Yes, but the gift comes in halves. Half now and—there is a little bump in the road."

"A bump?"

"They have a Chinese girl who could make everything slightly dirty, like your face. Just a whore who knows too much and needs to be returned to her homeland, where she belongs, where she will be safe. The other half of the gift, three million, comes when we have her." The Chinese man settled his hands on his knees and looked at Cono.

"Sounds like a high-priced whore. You've lost your business sense for a pretty face. She must be quite appealing."

"I've never seen her. Those are just my orders." He sighed. "Otherwise you would be right—there are many more just like her, at bargain rates."

Cono was twirling the pine needle in his mouth. "I'll convey the news, with your wishes for the whore's safety."

The Chinese man slapped Cono's knee and stood up. He was tall for a Chinese, tall like Cono's father had been, but well built, with real shoulders, not just suit-coat padding.

"You don't look very Chinese," the man said, staring down at Cono. "But you speak Mandarin like a native. How is that?" He snapped his cigarette butt into the pine mulch.

"I watch a lot of China Central TV."

"I never watch TV. Especially not something as dull as CCTV. It leaves too little room for thinking. And doing." The man's suit pants were barely creased from the sitting. He paused before walking to the car. "It seems strange they would trust a, shall we say, ragtag foreigner like you with this small fortune and not a Kazak."

"Yes, it is a *small* fortune. As for Kazaks, even *they* tell me it's a country where nothing's nailed down. Maybe a neutral party was needed."

"Is there such a thing as neutral?"

"Then, shall we say, a buffer." Cono's voice was only slightly mocking.

"Good thinking. That's why we want the girl. To get our buffer back." The Chinese man stepped to the trunk and opened it. "It's in four cases. Four more are waiting." Cono reached for one case and the Chinese man grabbed another. They dropped them in the shade where they had been sitting, followed by the other two.

The man in the suit put his hand on the door handle and paused. "By the way, did you like my joke about the Dalai Lama?"

"I've heard it before. Next time you tell it, make it Kazakhstan instead of Tibet. But yes, I did laugh."

The man forced a smile.

"Tell me," said Cono, "how do your people trust a well-dressed man like you with this very small fortune?"

"We have so many checks and balances. It makes the system work. Not like here in this country. Maybe they could use our help."

"It seems they're already getting some help from you." Cono tore a sprig from the overhanging branch and stroked it with his fingers. "Although it is quite modest."

"The world, even this empty piece of it, is full of competition from people wanting to help. Are you saying our bid is unsatisfactory?"

"It's not alligator hands. But for pumping rights it will get only a frog's glance at a gnat while dragonflies are hovering. And as a bid for larger influence, the frog will only croak at you and swim away."

The Chinese man turned his face to avoid the bright reflections from the windows of an apartment block at the far edge of the park. "You wear those sloppy clothes, and you are very, very impolite, but you see where the future lies."

"Only one of several possible futures. It depends on who you back and whether you insult them with half-gifts."

The Chinese man let out a long sigh. "A neutral party. We could use a neutral party like you."

"Ah, but the competition …"

"Tell your boss—is that what he is?—that the bidding is not over yet, and that we have a strong interest in talking further with a man of vision, who can see the benefits of a closer relationship, both for his dear, ragged country and for himself."

Cono twitched the pine sprig in a dismissive little wave goodbye, to acknowledge that he had heard. The man got into the car without looking again at Cono, and the Mercedes slowly backed away.

In a room high in the deteriorating apartment building that overlooked the park, Katerina Rulova kept her face at the tripod-mounted binocular scope as she spoke. "Yes, it's him."

"How do you spell his name?" asked the blond-bobbed woman seated next to her writing on a notepad. They spoke in English.

"Z-h-e-n-g L-u P-e-n-g. Pronounced *Jung*. Arrived seven months ago. Previous station was Urumqi, for four years, running the campaign against Uyghur separatists, the Muslims. Infiltrated the first Xinjiang uprising and ordered the retaliatory slaughter at the second one. Reportedly he had lots of opportunity there to make use of his interrogation training."

"What else?" said the other woman.

"Your predecessor, Mr. Simmons, had a whole profile on Zheng, said he's a useful pit bull that Beijing brings in for the dirty work. He came from a rich family, elite, all well educated. During the Cultural Revolution, when Zheng was a boy, they were sent to shovel dung, and worse. His parents were paraded like pigs on hands and knees, made to eat from a trough. An ex-colleague of his, a defector, said Zheng always carries a photo taken that day, of his parents eating slop. Then they were beaten to death. Zheng's background was a drag on his career. And he had another black mark—he's only half Chinese. Mother was from some place north, Korea or Mongolia. Not pure. He couldn't advance in the party. So he became an eager tool for the government, trying to prove his worth to them, and to his China. Mr. Simmons told me ..."

"Enough psychobabble. Why has Zheng been posted here?" The blonde, Clara Hodgkins, had herself arrived in Almaty only two months previously, from Delhi. Her accent was northern Midwest American.

"He's probably here because of the oil, like most of us," Katerina said.

"And who's the other man?"

"I couldn't really see him. He was beneath the trees the whole time."

"You said they took cases out of the trunk."

"Four cases."

"And you didn't see the other guy?"

"He kept his head down, almost like he knew someone might be watching."

"Maybe he knew we picked up the phone call, at least part of it," Clara said as she stood up to look through the scope.

"Or maybe he's just smarter than average," Katerina said.

"Well, I don't see anything going on now."

"He's probably deep in the park by now. We could call someone to track him," Katerina suggested lightly. "I have some local stringers."

"Not enough time." Clara sat down. "I'd have to spend an hour just clearing it. It'll be dark soon. He'll be gone, probably is already."

Katerina looked into the scope and saw an old-model Toyota swing into the museum's driveway. The trunk popped open when it came to a stop. Cono stepped out of the shade. He loaded all four cases in the trunk, then got in the front passenger seat. The Toyota reversed and was soon shrouded by trees and out of the scope's view.

"What's happening now?" Clara said, her pen clicking on the notepad.

"Nothing," Katerina said. "It's over."

"With a little more lead time we could've hooked up a high-def camera and run an image analysis on the other man. Why don't we have the equipment up here?" Clara stood and pressed her head against the window.

"I'm told we have several rooms like this around the city," Katerina replied. "I guess the office doesn't have enough equipment to go around."

Clara sighed. "For an ugly town, the view's not bad today," she said. "Pretty clear." She looked back into the room. "Tell me more about Mr. Zheng." As her eyes adjusted to the relative darkness inside, Clara assessed with quick glances the well-cut aquamarine pantsuit that drew attention to the younger woman's breasts, waist, and hips. Her shape reminded Clara of herself ten, fifteen years ago. But Clara had never worn those absurdly high heels.

"After Mr. Simmons briefed me, he told me to make the man's acquaintance. It didn't work the first time, but the second time he invited me for a drink."

"And?"

"And we didn't talk about his time in Xinjiang, of course."

"Sheenyan?"

"The Chinese province where his last station was, where the Muslim uprisings happened."

Clara groaned. "Here I am, learning Kazak for weeks, and we're only talking Chinese. What did you find out from him?" The small golden cross dangling from a chain around her neck winked in the light as she spoke.

"He thinks Almaty is a beautiful city, with so much greenness, not at all like Xinjiang."

"And?"

"And he said he represents China's commercial interests in Kazakhstan. He was vague about how much time he would spend here—it would depend upon the progress of Chinese trading in the region."

"Did he say anything about the Muslims in Kazakhstan? Is he here to deal with them, like his last assignment?" Clara was back in her seat, scribbling on her notepad.

"He didn't mention that. Of course they're *mostly* Muslims here in Kazakhstan, except for the Russians and Koreans. But their religion is more of a tradition, only as much as they could carry on their horses in the old days, they say."

"What about those mullahs whining over the loudspeakers?"

"You hear more prayer calls around the city now than a few years ago, but not a lot more." Katerina looked out the window, down to where she had seen Cono a few minutes earlier.

"Many churches here? The big one in the park looks more like a museum."

"There are some others. The Russians still go to them, but the Russians are fewer now, and they're poorer."

"So the Christians are losing out. What else did Mr. Zheng say?" Clara's pen was hard at work on her pad.

"He wanted to take me to a hotel room, but Mr. Simmons's instructions didn't include that, so I didn't. Instead, Mr. Zheng talked about the superiority of the Chinese in all things, and how his nation would regain its past greatness and rightful position in the world. And we agreed to meet another time."

"And?"

"He was very gracious. He even said, 'Till our paths meet again'—his English was quite good."

"And did Simmons give you different instructions sometimes?" Clara's chin wrinkled as she pursed her lips.

"I'm sure he put everything in the reports," Katerina said idly, gazing out the window.

The Toyota's engine strained on a winding road that rose in the foothills beyond the southwest edge of the city. Cono told Timur about the encounter with the Chinese man, and how many flowers had been offered, but left out mention of the three million that rested on turning over Xiao Li. Timur listened intently to Cono's recounting of the well-dressed Kitai's wish to negotiate further with a man of vision.

The motor almost choked as the car mounted a final incline that ended at a gate of wide steel doors topped with razor wire. Timur yanked the parking brake and got out to unlock the chain securing the gate, then returned to the car and eased it forward to a truck landing in front of a high aluminum roll-up door. To the left, beyond the truck landing, the steps and grooves of a giant quarry pit were encased in shadows. Timur got out again and relocked the gate.

"It doesn't make money anymore," Timur said. "Rocks are too cheap. My old man was hoping to turn it into a tourist lookout like the one at Koktyube. But he's too old, and I took it from him. The equipment still works. The machines make a hell of a noise, especially the grinders. It all makes for easy burials."

Timur unlocked a sliding bar, hoisted the aluminum door high enough so he could squeeze underneath, then pulled hard on a thick chain to raise the door higher.

With the car inside the long, vaulted building, they lifted the four cases into an interior metal shed that Timur had opened. It was full of jackhammers and wire on wooden spools. Drill-bits as tall as a man were stacked against one wall.

When the shed was shut Cono said, "It's not a very princely palace to house your state treasure. Where are the porters?"

Timur brushed the dust from his hands. There was dust everywhere, even in the still air. "I have thousands of porters working for me, the whole National Security Bureau, but none of them has been to this place. When there's a big job to be done, you have to do it yourself. Every sheik knows that, even if it means driving a beat-up Toyota."

Timur flipped open a metal lid on the wall of the shed. Cono saw the digital touch panel just before Timur's body blocked it from view; Timur punched in a code, each tap making a different tone, which Cono memorized. The lid twanged shut, emitting a small cloud of dust.

"If anyone touches the treasure, they'll be surprised," Timur said.

"Looks pretty low-tech. It blows up and the flowers burn with it." Cono kissed his fingers to signal a goodbye. "But then I guess there's no better technology around here."

"I can't show you all the state secrets, can I, brother? There's a lot more."

"More places to blow up money?"

"Cono, I wonder if you have confidence in me. The place is full of tunnels from when there was a little silver down below, before the old man had to blast the big pit in search of rocks to make gravel for his Soviet bosses. The good thing was, they ignored the mine after that. But I didn't. I'll be back later without you."

"I guess you played here as a kid. Underground."

"I know the tunnels better than I know my family." Timur's gaze flickered momentarily toward the back of the building, where a horizontal double door was fixed to the crusty floor, flanked by a disused forklift and a rusting iron frame with flywheels. There was a metal box mounted to the side of the horizontal doors, like the one on the shed. The glance had lasted less than a second, but Cono took in all that Timur's eyes exposed.

"And when the money is downstairs," Cono said, "and everything goes poof above, no harm done."

"The jihadis aren't the only ones who can rig explosives. You see through too much, Cono. That's why I prefer to keep you as a friend."

"As a friend," Cono said, "as a friend." He waited a second, looking at Timur, before he raised his right hand and rubbed his ear.

The Toyota's engine screamed as Timur downshifted to check their speed on the swerving road descending toward the city.

"How's the girl?" Cono asked.

"Not eating much, but at least she hasn't scratched the eyes out of any more of my toads. They tell me she tries to come on to them, but I'm sure they overestimate themselves."

"Most men do. It's the only way they can reproduce. It's why we're all here, us humans. Overestimation."

"Humans," Timur grunted.

For a fleeting second Cono thought of Xiao Li's captivity with Timur's thugs, but he swept the image from his mind. Then the sweet smiling face of Dimira's dead daughter appeared and dissolved. Timur swung the wheel to take another tight corner. One of the city's power plants loomed on their right, its two towers jetting black smoke into a darkening sky. A skinny man was squatting outside the wall of the plant, defecating.

Timur was silent through three more curves, the brakes squealing in protest at each one. As he let the car glide down the final straight incline, the last fingers of daylight receded behind the foothills in the west.

"You said the Kitai wanted to hear more from me."

"He told me he wanted to propose something to my boss," Cono replied. "So it's a good moment to hand the ball back to you.

The Kitai bid is in, the condition for the girl to be freed. I told the Kitai that you're his man, if the price is right; I even bargained on your behalf. It's time for me to clear out."

"Cono, friend, I need your help a little longer, so I've got to keep the china doll. Just for a while." Timur kept his gaze straight ahead. "You get too attached to your women. It's always a big mistake." A black SUV sped toward them and went by, accelerating effortlessly up the grade.

They were now at the far western reach of Almaty, where the terrain stopped its headlong descent from the foothills and began to flatten out. Timur made a loop of the roundabout, headed east toward the city, and ratcheted into third gear on a two-lane street that was deserted except for a few body shops and two cows grazing on a narrow wedge of weeds.

"That girl Katerina played you too, when you were here last time, working for her and helping me on the side. She's still around, playing with the Americans. Fucking at least one of them. I could throw her out of my fine country, but with her here at least I know what I've got." Timur allowed a small smile to turn up the corners of his mouth.

"Cut the shit, Timur. You've got your money and the Kitais wagging their tongues for you. There's no reason to hold onto the girl."

A face behind the windshield of an approaching truck caught Cono's attention—a driver's face wrinkling with momentary creases of panic, his eyes darting as his flatbed accelerated. The Toyota's headlights illuminated the driver's fingers. Cono perceived the tension in them even before the driver jerked the wheel to his left. Nearly instantaneously, Cono yanked the Toyota's steering wheel, sending the car into a skid. The truck almost tipped as it veered sharply to block the pavement from curb to curb. The Toyota fantailed, its rear fender smashing into the cab of the truck.

Timur was stunned by the collision, his head drooping against the steering wheel. Cono shoved his left foot onto the pedals and gripped the shift. The Toyota lurched backward and then forward over the curb, clearing the truck's front bumper as Cono heard the first shots smacking the air and pocking into the back of the car. He spun it around the truck and rammed its nose under the belly of the flatbed, which provided a partial barrier against the shooters. Then he seized Timur's gun, rolled out of the car, and lay prone beneath the truck. From this position he could see three men hunched around an SUV on the other side of the flatbed signaling to each other and dispersing, one to the left, one to the right, the third crouching as he approached the truck head-on. To Cono's mind they were all three nearly motionless even as they skittered and dodged, firing, maneuvering for a kill. Cono felt exhilaration— the ecstatic awareness that his strange brain and body had ordained him for just such moments, by allowing him to enter a space outside of time.

His first shot, at the slick-haired man on the right, revealed that the pistol aimed high. His second shot found its mark below the man's ear. The thug to the left had almost found protection behind the truck's cab but the piercing of his temple tipped him into a dive that planted his head into the big front tire. The head rebounded and fell, its face wide with surprise.

The crouched man straight ahead clamped the trigger of his automatic rifle. Cono rolled away in time to avoid the sparks spraying off the concrete and in one motion grabbed the brake line above him and hoisted himself against the undercarriage, pressing his toes against a chassis strut. A burst from the automatic rifle raked the road beneath him. Another burst battered the truck siding near his head. He lowered himself just enough to take aim, upside down. With his last shot Cono saw the crouched man's mirrored left lens crack as it made room for the nine-millimeter hole; the attacker's tucked body rolled back and slumped to one side.

Cono slid out from beneath the truck and moved to the cab's passenger door. He could see in the side-view mirror that the driver already had his hands clasped behind his head. Cono opened the door and rose up on the step plate.

"Your friends?" Cono asked in Russian.

"Not friends," the man said, shaking his head, his nostrils flaring. "Not friends. Just money, a call." Cono pulled a cell phone from the chest pocket of the driver's patched denim jacket. "I have family. Just work," the driver said. His face was dull except for the fear; Cono saw no flickering micro-expression of contrivance. He kept the cell phone and told the driver to get out and lie down on the road.

Cono went back to the Toyota and folded Timur's long frame so he could push him into the passenger seat. Metal creaked against metal as Cono backed the car out from beneath the truck and swung it around to face their original direction, toward the city. The darkness intermittently yielded to oncoming headlights that caught the fractures in the Toyota's windshield and momentarily blinded Cono with their flashes. His head began to pound.

They were well up Satpaev Street, near the army sports club, when Timur came to and spit out saliva laced with blood.

"Where to now, Genghis?" Cono asked. "You took a bad knock, but you'll be back for more conquests after a good rest."

With slurred speech, Timur directed Cono to take the next right onto Dostyk and head up toward the mountains, to the

National Security Bureau's training barracks. It was a low fortress behind a high spiked fence.

"I have friends here," Timur mumbled as Cono supported him on the short walk to the barricaded gate.

"You have only one friend, and that friend, your friend of long years, is asking where to find the girl."

Timur hesitated, almost lapsing into a faint. Cono grabbed him with a steely grip. "Your friend needs to know."

Timur sputtered out a street name. "It's above the General," he added, unsteady against Cono's shoulder, "but you'll have to get her out yourself. Don't lose the gun, my Makarov. It's my first piece." Cono lifted Timur's arm and placed it on the shoulder of a young man in uniform who looked frightened by the burden of propping up his terrifying hero, an icon to all the elite young recruits, a hero whose forehead was smeared with blood.

7

Cono veered back down Dostyk Street in the battered car, knowing there was a risk in keeping it, but in need of the speed it provided. He cut through the city using the smaller streets, which were uniformly dark except for dimly lit intersections. He knew the General; it had been popular in Almaty four years ago, and he was surprised it was still in operation in a town where nightclubs and casinos appeared and disappeared regularly, like the flashing lights on their garish marquees. When Cono had known it, the General was a casino and disco and more—it was the luxury joint favored by Russian mafia high rollers and the most fashionably dressed working girls, of all ethnic flavors.

He stopped three blocks short of the club, backed the Toyota into a narrow side street, and walked beneath a row of oak trees until he was opposite the gray building. The General's façade was the same, except that the black plate glass was spider-webbed by cracks and a string of red lights had fallen from the marquee and was waving lazily in the slight breeze. The club was surviving, but on its way to an unrecorded demise.

Cono eyed the structure above the casino, which was part of a seamless row of pre-World War II buildings fronted by trees and broken sidewalks. The third-story windows above the General were black; the others glowed with either yellow incandescence or a fluorescent blue haze. Cono knew that the backsides of these old stone buildings—narrow, unlit alleys or car parks—had made them easy break-in targets after the collapse of Soviet state security, so the rear doors and exterior staircases were now secured by iron caging and heavy locks. He'd have to go in through the front door. He considered tossing the Makarov, but decided to keep it.

Cono crossed the street, feigning a limp. He leaned heavily on the railing as he mounted the front stairs and extended his hand toward the chubby-cheeked bouncer for help with the last step. As the oversize man gave him an indignant once-over, Cono thanked him profusely in English.

"Can I throw some dice in here?" Cono added, using the bland accent he had learned in California. "Wudya want for gettin' in?"

Chubby Cheeks held up nine fingers, for 900 tenge. Cono pulled a wad of bills from his hip pocket and gave him triple that. The bouncer opened the door and Cono limped in, smiling at the two grim black-clad security men inside. He bumped into one of the vertical risers of the metal detector, setting off its bleeping alarm. One of the guards waved his thick arm to signal Cono to pass through the detector.

"I've got metal in my bone here," Cono said in English, slapping his lame leg. "That's me*tahl*," Cono said with a sloppy Russian accent. "Me*tahl*," Cono pointed to his hip. The detector bleeped as he limped through it.

"Give me phone," said one of the guards, holding out a fleshy hand. Cono reached beneath his shirt to pluck out the cell phone he'd taken from the truck driver and handed it to the guard. The metal detector objected again. Cono struck an awkward, crippled pose.

"Come, come," barked the guard. From outside, Chubby Cheeks waved his hand to show his approval. The guard gave Cono a cursory frisking. "Okay, okay. Go make money." He gave the phone back to Cono and swept his arm toward the red velvet entrance. Cono limped forward, the Makarov's handgrip tormenting his testicles as he brushed through the curtain.

It was early. Rotating spotlights stroked a small, empty dance floor. Four croupiers wearing red satin bustiers raised their eyes briefly from the clutches of clients gathered around their green gaming tables. Cono heard the riffling of betting chips and the clatter of a roulette wheel.

To his left, at a horseshoe-shaped bar, a beefy man was cursing the barman for putting triple sec in his drink, and he smashed the glass in the barman's sink. The General hadn't lost its Russian *raket* clientele, who probably owned the whole building.

A waitress in low-cut purple-laced lingerie asked Cono what he'd like to order; he smiled and signaled that he'd visit the toilet first. His hobbling diminished as he walked up three shadowed steps at the far side of the dance floor. Past the restrooms, the back corridor was illuminated by a single wavering ultraviolet light. Cono transferred the gun to his waistband, pushed open an exit door and stepped into a dark exterior stairwell surrounded by grillwork.

He heard footsteps and laughter behind him, on the other side of the door he had just passed through. He hopped up to the second-floor landing as the drunken voices of a man and a woman rose from the yawning door below. He flitted up to the next landing, and the next, keeping ahead of the couple as they stumbled up the stairs.

"Don't pull so hard," the woman whined. Peering down through the grate of the stairs, Cono recognized the man as one of the thugs who had driven off with Xiao Li. At the third-floor landing, below Cono, a door cracked open, sending a wedge of light across the prisonlike bars of the stairwell. The laughing man grabbed the woman by the neck and thrust her through the doorway.

"Here's a fresh Uzbek, boys. Let's prime her for her night's work. Says she likes three at a go. It'll make us all penis brothers." The laughing man brayed again, this time joined by intoxicated cheers from two other men. There was a sound like that of a beer bottle skidding across a floor and hitting a wall.

"Let's make the Kitai bitch watch us. Mama Uzbek Big Tits, you like Kitai pussy?"

"You pay for three, no discount," the Uzbek woman said. "And me fucking a girl means you pay for four." She was snapping like an experienced pro, but beneath her toughness she sounded scared.

"You'll get it so good you'll be dying to give a discount."

There was a crashing sound, like a lamp falling over. The wedge of light disappeared as the door slammed shut. Russian pop music began blaring from within the apartment.

Cono stepped lightly down to the third-floor landing and onto the narrow balcony spanning the rear face of the building. All the windows of the apartment were blacked out, but there was a high, small window that had two faint lines of light, as if a coating of paint had been scratched. Alongside the window a sewer pipe ran down, joining another one that emerged from the wall. Cono planted a foot on the V formed by the two pipes, reached for the sill of the window and lifted himself up. The scratches were too thin to provide any view of the inside.

He climbed down from the V and examined a small water pipe that came out of the wall, encrusted with insulation that he quietly picked at, revealing a gap between the pipe and the hole it ran through. Yellow light began to glow on Cono's fingers as he coaxed away more of the crumbly material. He tried to peer through the hole, but couldn't see anything. He put his nose to the opening and inhaled. Mixed with the smells of an unclean bathroom and insulating foam was another barely perceptible scent, the residue of a perfume he knew well.

He pressed his ear to the hole. In the brief intervals between loud refrains being sung by a Russian pop star, Cono could make out a reedy second voice, singing, almost purring, a Chinese tune about the purity of young love.

He stepped again onto the V of the sewer pipes and rose up to the scratched window. He tapped a finger against the pane. There was a faint rattling from the insulated pipe. Cono tapped another time. The pipe jiggled rapidly. He heard a soft scratching sound at the window just in front of his nose. Another line of light appeared.

Balanced by one foot and a hand, Cono pulled out the pistol and wedged its nose into a bottom corner of the window. He pushed, grinding the barrel deeper into the wood of the frame; there was a muted pop as fine cracks arced outward from the broken corner, each crack forming a new thread of light. He plucked out shards of glass, tossing them into the black void behind him.

The small pipe below him was jangling again, rocking in its brackets. Cono quietly smashed most of the remaining glass edges with the butt of the Makarov. He felt for the window's lock; it was screwed shut. The window's frame was small, but might barely accommodate his shoulders. He lifted himself and peered over the sill.

Two recognizable fingernails, red with the tips painted white, grabbed at him in desperation. Only the instantaneous backward snap of his head saved his corneas.

"I can't save you if I'm blind," Cono whispered, just loud enough to be heard above the music wailing from the next room. The pipe jangled again.

This time Cono put his head fully through the window frame and looked down into the bathroom. Xiao Li's bloodied right wrist was handcuffed to the pipe connected to the radiator. It must have been an acrobatic feat for her to have climbed on top of the radiator and reached up with her free arm to scratch the windowpane. Clothed in the same sashed black dress with purple frills on the neckline, crouching and shaking, she was looking up at Cono with the face of a beaten child. Her mouth was opening to emit a cry.

"Silence." Cono put a finger to his lips, then reached into a slot in his vest and pulled out a coil of titanium-alloy abrading wire with a ring at each end. He wedged his arms through the window and pressed his elbows against the frame to bring his torso through. Small streaks of blood sprang up on his arms where they were cut by the spicules of glass remaining in the window.

He looped a finger into one ring of the wire and let the rest fall toward Xiao Li. "Take the end. Put it around the chain. Pull the wire back and forth with me." Xiao Li's left hand fumbled for the wire and grasped it. She tried repeatedly to wrap it around the cuff chain, but there wasn't enough play in it. After four failed attempts her eyes filled with tears and her body started to shake in an effort to keep herself from crying. "Not enough," she whispered.

By jamming his arms against the window frame and kicking his legs in the air, Cono was able to shift his torso farther inside. He extended his arm as far down as he could. Xiao Li got the wire around the cuff chain and hooked the loop with her finger. There was now enough play in the wire to allow an inch of back-and-forth, but it still wasn't enough. A woman's shrieks rose above the blasting music.

Cono pressed his palms against the interior wall and dove, landing in a handstand atop the radiator, his calves braced against the window frame. He lowered his body until his feet cleared the window and pushed off the radiator in a supple handspring that left him standing on the bathroom floor. He knelt next to Xiao Li, who touched his face with her free hand. Cono smiled and winked and went to work. His hands pumped the abrading wire, his arms a blur of movement to Xiao Li.

The music hammered in Cono's head.

Xiao Li quivered.

A drunken voice became distinguishable over the yelping and shrieking on the other side of the bathroom door. "Fuck the boss. Fuck sending me on a holiday. The Kitai bitch has waited long enough."

The cuff chain snapped.

"It's time we showed her some fun."

Cono saw the first millimeter of the doorknob's rotation, and before the door began to angle open he was standing behind it. A naked, drunken man stumbled into the bathroom; Cono heeled the door shut as he whipped the wire around the neck of the burly man, whose last vision was of the toilet where he and his friends had sat to defecate in front of Xiao Li. Cono thrust the struggling body to the floor and pressed his knee between the scapulae as the wire sawed through the soft tissue.

When the burgundy blood started to puddle on the sky-blue tiles, Cono said, "Look away." He felt the persistence of Xiao Li's gaze. "Look away!"

Xiao Li staggered to her feet and leaned against the wall beneath the window with her hands and forehead.

"Stay there." Cono ripped the wire away from the neck, curling it back into his palm. Standing over the body, he yanked one of its arms with such force that the body flipped onto its back, the hairy legs splayed like a frog's. The man seemed a mixture of Russian and Kazak. There were partly scabbed scratches on his heavy brow and over both of his cheekbones.

Xiao Li's knees gave in and she slumped against the radiator. Her head turned.

"Keep your face against the wall." Cono's voice was steely. Xiao Li turned her eyes away.

He knelt down and looped the wire around the man's genitalia. He squeezed and cut until the wrinkled mass gave way—scrotum and penis together. He lifted it all by pinching the foreskin and got to his feet. Reaching up, he grabbed the string hanging from the bathroom's light bulb and tied it tightly around the penis. Cono ducked his shoulder to avoid the dripping blood, but still two drops hit his shirtsleeve. He spun the red-tinged wire into a tight coil and slipped it back into his vest. "Penis brothers," he muttered.

Cono wiped his hands on his pants, reached above the suspended genitalia and pulled the string. The light went out. Coming from the other side of the bathroom door there was now only loud music, no yelling and laughter. "Let's go," Cono whispered. He stepped up on the radiator and shimmied out of the window. Xiao Li's grip crushed his knuckles as he pulled her out. They hugged each other long enough for Cono to feel two thumps of her heart against his chest, then he pushed her away, and the two of them stepped softly down the staircase. Xiao Li gritted her teeth as the corrugated-metal steps bit into her bare feet.

The door of steel slats at ground level was locked with deadbolts, forcing them to go back up a floor. The balcony walkway adjacent to the stairwell on the second floor had no grillwork, only a railing of horizontal bars. Xiao Li immediately grasped the top bar and lifted herself up, placing both legs on the other side of it. By holding onto the stairwell's grillwork, she climbed downward until she was stopped by barbed wire almost ten feet from the ground. She pushed off the grillwork into midair, cleared the barbed wire, and thudded onto hard dirt. She was in darkness except for her arm, illuminated by a faint bulb in the stairwell. With a frantic wave she beckoned to Cono.

Cono hopped over the railing and followed her path down. Just as his feet touched the ground, he felt it: Xiao Li's blow against his Adam's apple was first perceived by Cono as a tender brush of the skin. Immediately the sensation became an inviting pressure, then an energetic thrust, and finally a bewildering pain.

"What took you so long! Waiting for Buddha?"

Cono coughed and swallowed.

"Is Almaty such a big town?" Xiao Li punched Cono's chest with both fists. He was relieved that she still had her strength and her attitude. *At least they hadn't managed to rape her,* he thought.

"We're not clear yet." Cono grabbed Xiao Li's hand and led her into a jerking trot, her feet mincing on the gravel. They dodged parked cars, making their way along the dark alley to a gap at the end of the row of buildings in which the General was embedded. The gap opened onto tree-lined Furmanov, a busy street by Almaty standards. Still hand in hand, Cono turned them north on the sidewalk, running faster with the downward tilt of the city. Xiao Li suddenly pulled away. "And now you want me to run? With no shoes?"

Cono continued running, aiming to cross over to a dark lane. When he no longer heard Xiao Li's pitter-patting behind him, he turned and saw her facing back up the street, waving an arm, trying to flag a taxi. Taxis in Almaty were not taxis—taxis couldn't compete with the fleet of local car owners who were happy to accept a passenger headed roughly in their own direction, or a different direction, if the fare was sufficient.

A car with a broken headlight was idling next to Xiao Li as Cono sprinted back to her. Xiao Li jerked on the door until it finally opened. "After you, Mr. Always Late."

"Hotel Tsarina," she snapped to the driver in remedial Russian.

"No, make that Zelyony Bazaar, where Pushkin Street runs into it," Cono said as they tumbled into the back seat.

"After all that, you won't take me to … ?"

Cono squeezed Xiao Li's thigh so hard that there was sure to be a bruise in the morning.

"Zelyony at Pushkin," Cono repeated in Russian.

Xiao Li turned toward Cono and scowled. Then her gaze softened and she leaned toward him. Her eyes were improbably elongated upward curves; the perfect oval of her mouth was misshapen by the leftovers of smudged lipstick. Cono put a finger to his lips to signal quiet, then tried to clean off the lipstick with the cuff of his sleeve. The wayward pink gloss was erased, but a streak of deep red was left on her chin—blood from the man in

106

the bathroom. Cono rubbed it away with his fingers and wiped it on the seat in front of him.

"Move down with me so our heads don't show," he said in Mandarin. "They'll be hunting us nonstop. You're not safe in this city anymore." He slid his long frame down and placed Xiao Li's head on his shoulder. He stroked her arm until her hand met his in a tight squeeze. She let go, tapped two fingers on his wrist, and interlaced her fingers in his.

Cono thanked the driver for picking them up; the man responded in Russian that was almost as bad as Xiao Li's. "No problem, and it's not for free."

Cono switched to English and asked the driver if he was from Pakistan. "Somewhere north. Islamabad or Lahore?" he asked.

"But I was talking in Russian. How do you know?"

Cono was silent. The driver answered. It was Lahore.

Cono asked what had brought him to the gracious city of Almaty. First it was to trade textiles, the driver explained, but the Chinese competition sank prices to levels that were unbeatable. Then he tried dealing in raw leather and tanned hides. The Chinese traders could do better at that, too. "Now they're even building a railroad from China to Kazakhstan. I think I'll move the family to Tajikistan," the driver said. "It hasn't been invaded by China yet."

The car seemed to have no shock absorbers. The deep dips at several intersections tossed the back-seat couple into the air and landed them in a closer nestling. The car jerked right to avoid two Mercedes speeding up the middle of the street.

"Must be top government police, maybe *raket*," the driver said, apologizing for the jarring swerve. "What brings *you* to my fine city?"

"The women, of course."

Xiao Li jabbed a thumbnail into Cono's ribs and twisted it like a knife. Cono felt pain, then pleasure.

"And I'm here for the oil, of course," Cono said as he stroked the inside of Xiao Li's thigh and felt the envelope of money he had slipped into her purse the first night; it was strapped to her leg with rubber bands, further reassurance that she hadn't been raped.

"They're *all* after the oil. But you don't look like a business type." The driver was trying to catch a glimpse of Cono through the rearview mirror.

"After hours, you know; time for entertainment." The thumbknife again dug into Cono's ribs.

Cono had the driver stop just before they reached the bazaar. They were now six blocks from Dimira's apartment. He paid the driver twice what he asked, saying, "See you in Tajikistan."

Cono led Xiao Li on a shadowy route behind bushes, below drooping boughs of oak, and along walls of flaking paint that they could feel but barely see.

"Not even a kiss?" Xiao Li whispered from behind.

Cono turned and enveloped her with his arms. He kissed her— a long, slow, lingering kiss. The mingled scents of her perfume and her unwashed body seeped in, as did the memories of their giddy days and nights together during simpler, naïve times. As their kissing became more aggressive, Cono's hand rode firmly over the sinewy muscles of her back, across the little scar lying near her sacral dimple, and on to the utter smoothness of her thigh. Xiao Li clamped her arms around his neck and pulled herself up, wrapping her legs around him. Her mouth was at his ear. "Please, Cono," she breathed. "Please. Now."

Cono grasped her bottom and took one step to place her back against a tree. The pad of money strapped to her thigh pressed against his hip. He raised a hand to caress her face. She started humming softly the song they had sung when they'd first met, as if she were trying to further distance herself from what she had endured, to obliterate it through melody and fond remembrance. Cono hummed along with her while kissing her neck and shoulder, and reached down to free himself from his trousers. His other hand held her up and plucked away her thong. He prodded gently, and then pulled back.

"Cono, please."

Xiao Li's humming grew slightly louder as their eyes joined in the faint light from the street. She guided his hand to her ear, to make him graze it with a fingernail in the manner she had taught him, her secret for arousal and intimacy while she engaged in a career that precluded both. Humming faster, she reached down to bring him inside her, clasping his neck even more tightly. Her heels pressed against his buttocks. "*Please.*"

He tried once more. And pulled back once more. "I'm hurting you."

"*I don't care.*"

Cono lifted her away from the tree and held her until she finally put her feet on the ground. She grabbed his organ roughly.

"Try again, Cono. Come on."

"It's not our time."

"Come inside me, Cono. Why won't you give me a baby, and be with me? You saved me. You love me."

Cono sighed. He willed the mast to tilt down under her harsh grip, but it would not. He freed it from her hand and wedged it back into his pants.

"You told me we already had a child, a boy," he said gently.

Xiao Li adjusted her dress, pulling it down over the bands holding the money to her thigh.

"But we *do* have a son. And he looks like you. Isn't that why you came to save me?" Her voice had in it the same tremulousness in the higher frequencies that had always signaled to Cono that the son was an invention. An invention to seal a compact with him, to assure herself of an anchor in a sea roiling with uncertainty and degradation. He had never challenged her. After all, he reflected, the whole of humanity was anchored by inventions, contrivances, unrealities. Xiao Li lived on dreams, as most people do. She herself had told him on the telephone that by knowing she had a son, she had greater strength.

"You saved me. You love me. Say it."

Cono sat down with her next to the tree. He told her he had come to Almaty to help her because of the respect he had for her and her fearless passion for living. He had never known such unpredictability and beautiful fury and tenderness. She was unique, and part of him, a part that would not fade, no matter the distance or time.

Xiao Li was silent and brooding as he pulled her toward him. "Tough man can't say three little words? Never mind. I don't love you, either."

Cono held her close and wondered what to say. "What is love, Xiao Li? Is it words, or is it the soaring we feel inside when we see each other? Is it my coming here to Almaty when you call?"

Xiao Li turned her head away.

"Tell me what else happened at the Svezda," Cono said. "I'm sorry to ask you now, just after … being locked up like that." Cono thought of her chained and crouching next to the radiator. "I should have killed them all," he said.

He stroked her hair and the back of her neck. "On the phone you told me about the Beijing men, and Timur. Is there anything more? And why is Timur a snake?"

Xiao Li punched Cono in the chest. "And you called him your friend, your brother!"

Cono touched a finger to his lips and whispered. "What happened at the Svezda?"

"Your *brother* was nice to the Beijing men, after they almost had a fight. He said he would get rid of the body, my client. They said they would get rid of me. He laughed and told them he had done the same with girls he didn't like. When the Beijing men tried to take me with them, Mr. Timur said no. He had more men with him than they did, and the Beijing men left. Mr. Timur ordered his men out of the room. He hit me. He opened his pants. He had a gun. He made me put my mouth on him. I didn't want to. He hit me again, with the gun; it cut my neck. The whole time the alarms were going off. A hotel worker opened the door …"

Cono heard the faint snapping of a twig in the blackness somewhere across the vacant street. He put his hand over Xiao Li's mouth and whispered close to her ear. "Time to move."

The couple was slowed by Xiao Li's tender feet. As they neared Dimira's building, Cono forced her into a crouch behind a prickly hedge. He listened, scanning the street. It was dead and motionless, not even a breeze.

"You go first, in that door, quietly, and up to the second floor landing. Wait there," Cono whispered. Xiao Li slid through the door like a cat. Cono let two minutes pass, looking, listening, smelling, feeling the earth with his palm. Nothing. He glided swiftly through the entrance and up the stairs.

Cono's light rapping on the door of Dimira's apartment finally brought tentative footsteps from the other side. He spoke her name softly.

"Cono, is that you?"

"Yes, it's me. I need your help."

The locks clicked one by one. A vertical strip of orange candlelight wavered as the door cracked open. Cono put his hand through the gap. Dimira grasped it and pulled him in. Her arms wrapped around him before he could say in Russian, "I have a friend who needs your help even more than I do."

Xiao Li recognized the word *droog*, "friend," in Russian. "Friend—that is me," she said in English, slamming the door behind her.

Dimira pulled away from Cono and looked at Xiao Li with shock—at the stunningly beautiful face, the fiery eyes, the cuts on the neck and the back of one hand, the slinky black dress, the cuffed bloody wrist, the dirty bare feet with bright-pink toenails. Dimira took a step backward as Xiao Li snarled at Cono in Mandarin: "You bring me to the home of one of your concubines? After we tried to make love? Tell her that—tell her your cock was in my hand a few minutes ago!"

Cono put his arm around Xiao Li's shoulders. "Calm down. You have no reason to be angry with her. Let's all speak in English so nothing is hidden. Dimira. Xiao Li." He nodded to each of them in turn. Xiao Li glared at the sad-eyed woman.

"You are bleeding," Dimira said, looking at Xiao Li's wrist. "You are both bleeding." She pointed at the glass cuts on Cono's arms, and to the mud-colored slice through the fabric on his shoulder.

As she twisted the door locks shut, Dimira said she would get peroxide for their wounds and prepare tea. "Sit down. My home is yours."

Cono and Xiao Li sat on overlapping thin carpets as Dimira stood in the tiny kitchen. Cono pulled out the blood-tinged wire saw and used it to cut through the handcuff to release Xiao Li's wrist.

"What are we doing here, Cono?" she asked angrily in Mandarin.

Cono replied in English. "We are here because no other place in Almaty is safe for us. Dimira is a friend, a brave friend whose daughter was murdered six months ago."

"Was the daughter yours?" Xiao Li stuck to Mandarin.

"She was a lovely child, as lively as a hummingbird. She was not mine. There are pictures of her on the wall."

Xiao Li sprang up to examine the photos. As she quickly took in the dozens on the wall, Asel's dark skin assured her that Cono was not the father. Xiao Li looked at each picture a second time and finally returned to sit cross-legged next to Cono. "She was a beautiful girl," Xiao Li whispered. "Such a bright face. Such a happy smile." Xiao Li bent her head. She was crying as Dimira took her wrist and daubed a wet cloth on the raw flesh.

"This will hurt a little. It looks like you struggled." Dimira placed Xiao Li's hand on her lap. The peroxide bubbled on the wounds and dripped onto Dimira's flowered dress.

Xiao Li licked the tears that had fallen to her lips. "I am sorry. Your daughter." The tears now fell in streams. Dimira stroked the length of Xiao Li's bare arm.

"She was all that I am," Dimira said. "Even now, I feel her arms around me. Even now, I hear her laughter." Dimira rose to a kneeling position. "Here, Xiao Li, take these and clean Cono's cuts. The tea is ready."

As Xiao Li took the bottle and the cloth, she raised her head and was taken aback by the sudden sight of the ear Dimira revealed when she flicked her hair away from her face. The ear looked like a crumpled cabbage leaf. The strange sight made Xiao Li's stomach turn, and she closed her eyes and breathed deeply until the nausea passed.

From the kitchen Dimira glanced at Cono's naked upper body while Xiao Li daubed his wounds, her exhaustion making her movements slow. Dimira busied herself with the food longer than necessary, arranging piles of biscuits, apple wedges, and sausage slices on a tin tray. She added a gardenia blossom from a vase next to the refrigerator.

Cono was buttoning his shirt as Dimira delivered the tray and sat down. Her guests had no hunger at first, but soon all of the food was gone, with little said. Dimira knew from Cono's earlier visit to Almaty that he would give only sparse details of his reasons for coming to her homeland, this land of her hardships.

Dimira asked no questions but searched Cono's eyes as he explained that Xiao Li had been in the wrong place at the wrong time and now was threatened by dangerous people who couldn't ever see the beauty or smell the fragrance of a flower like the gardenia on the tray, who were tools of the gods of money and power. Xiao Li would have to leave Almaty in the morning by taking a bus across the border to Bishkek and flying from there to Urumqi in China. From Urumqi she would travel on to join relatives. If Dimira had some spare pants and a shirt and sneakers Xiao Li could wear, of course it would be an imposition, but he would be grateful. He would leave Almaty in the morning as well, because he had done what he needed to do, and it wouldn't be safe to stay longer. Cono thanked Dimira, and regretted that despite their stealth in coming to her home, he had exposed her to some degree of risk. He thanked her again.

Xiao Li was sprawled across Cono's lap, one bat of an eyelid away from sleep.

"Cono, thanking me … there is no need," Dimira said. "I feel Asel when you are here. Your presence is a gift." Dimira saw that Xiao Li's eyes were closed, her breathing deep. Dimira whispered to Cono, "If only my daughter had a father like you."

Like me? Cono thought. *Like me?* He saw in his mind the hairy legs of the man he had just killed and castrated. *There had been no choice,* he told himself.

"We must sleep," Cono said. He laid Xiao Li on the mattress that had been Asel's. He said he would lie on the floor, it was his preference, and that he hoped it wouldn't disturb Dimira if he did his exercises in the dark before sleeping.

Dimira lingered in the far corner of the room, standing next to her mattress, observing Cono's movements. She unbuttoned her blouse and let it fall from her shoulders, then stood for another minute, watching, until she blew out the last candle.

An hour later Cono's disrobed body cooled with the evaporation of his sweat. Lying on his back, he inhaled through his nostrils, his arms outstretched on the floor. He inhaled again, smelling the tea, the carbon of the extinguished candles, the sausage grease, the gardenia, the mustiness of the wool carpets, the scents of two different women. All was dark. And silent, except for the rhythmic breathing of Xiao Li and Dimira, faint whooshings that were out of sync, but which together formed a constant, slow beat. Sleep fell upon him like a blanket made of lead.

8

"Cono, wake up." Xiao Li's lips were brushing his cheek. The pungent aroma of frying onions was teasing his nose; the sputtering of eggs in a hot pan danced in his ears. Xiao Li was wearing a loose T-shirt with silk-screened latex that rubbed against his nipples as she wiggled on top of him, kissing him again and again. His hand fell to her hip and felt the slippery synthetic fabric of running pants. He reflexively squeezed her there, feeling the beginnings of his arousal.

She slipped off him. Something sharp whacked against his semi-erect member, snapping him to alertness. "Not now, Cono," Xiao Li said, waving an envelope over his startled eyes. "What's this? It's in Russian. I opened it. It was under the door. What does it say? Wake up, Cono!"

Cono felt pain in his wounded shoulder when he rolled onto his side and pulled the note from the stiff envelope. His kept his face expressionless as he read it.

"I know you will help. You are addicted to the thrill of it. The public swimming pool on Abay, 10:00 this morning. You will know me by the scar on my shoulder. Freedom is so hard to come by. For us all."

"What does it say?" Xiao Li asked again, more urgently.

"We've been discovered. You must fly, like a falcon. Go to your apartment, get your passport and only the things you absolutely need and don't waste time. Fly home."

Cono checked his watch. 9:40 a.m. If he hurried, there was just enough time to get to the swimming pool.

"And Dimira?" Xiao Li demanded. "We just leave her?"

"If I help them, Dimira will be safe."

The note was from his friend Katerina or someone pretending to be Katerina, that much was clear. Xiao Li had nothing to fear from Katerina, and neither did Dimira. But if Katerina had been able to track them, surely the Chinese or Timur's thugs at the General could have done the same.

Cono stood up and strode quickly to the kitchen. "After we leave, Dimira, take your passport and money and go straight to the school. Stay there all day. I will get word to you if you are not to return here tonight. If you don't hear from me, it's safe to come home."

Dimira nodded, a wooden spatula in her hand. "I gave Asel's sneakers to Xiao Li," she said. "Asel had big feet for her age."

As Xiao Li wolfed down breakfast, Cono reviewed the escape route he had described the night before—Xiao Li would hide among the crowd on the bus to Bishkek, then take a plane to Urumqi, and continue on to the village of some distant relatives.

"You must leave immediately, Xiao Li," Cono said. "Promise me."

"I promise, Cono. I promise."

"And I must go too." He opened the three locks on the door. Xiao Li smothered him with kisses and pressed against him, whispering that he must find her soon and hold her in his arms over a high balcony with the moon in the sky. "And you must come visit your son," she added in Mandarin. She watched with jealousy as Cono said goodbye to Dimira and pecked her on both cheeks. Then he was gone.

Eight minutes later, while Xiao Li was lacing up Asel's sneakers and Cono was two miles away, gulping blood-red pomegranate juice that had just been pressed by a boy with a pushcart off Avenue Abay, there was a gentle knock on the apartment door.

Xiao Li looked with alarm at Dimira.

"Maybe someone came from the school," Dimira said quietly in English, "to ask why I'm late." She set down the tray she was holding.

Xiao Li grabbed Dimira's arm. "No," she whispered, plucking a knife from the tray. "Don't open."

There was another knock, a little louder.

"Other door?" Xiao Li whispered. "Way to go out?" She pointed the knife around the apartment, examining the windows; the only two in the apartment looked out on the front of the building. Xiao Li tried to recall if the bathroom had a window. "Toilet?"

Dimira shook her head no.

"Don't say nothing, no one home." Xiao Li whispered. She reached to hand another knife to Dimira; it clinked against a teacup on the tray, tipping it over.

"You have gun?"

Dimira shook her head again.

There was another knock, more insistent. And a voice from the other side of the door, too quiet to understand.

Dimira edged softly to the door. She put her ear near it.

"Mr. Cono sent me." The man spoke in English with a heavy Kazak accent. "Mr. Cono said to come help you."

Xiao Li touched Dimira's shoulder and shook her head violently, holding her knife in a dagger grip. Memories of the two days in chains swept like a cyclone through her mind.

"Mr. Cono said this place is not safe anymore. He says you need to leave now, go home."

The two women exchanged glances. Xiao Li's dagger hand gradually fell to her side. Dimira put her fingers on one of the locks.

"Mr. Cono said there is not much time. He wants you to be safe."

Dimira unlocked one of the bolts. Xiao Li stifled a short gasp. Dimira's hand reached for the second lock and clicked it open. Xiao Li looked down at Dimira's quavering fingers on the third lock. She forced Dimira's hand away from it.

The door exploded open, ripping the last bolt from the jamb and sending the two women to the floor. Two large men jumped on them. Xiao Li tried to stab her attacker but the knife didn't penetrate his leather jacket; a fist smacked her in the face and she lay stunned for a moment. Then she began kicking and biting. Dimira was crushed under the weight of the heavier man as he wound duct tape around her arms and legs, and finally around her screaming mouth. From the corner of her eye, Xiao Li saw Dimira being hoisted up. She yelled in Mandarin, then in English, "Good Kazak mother! Good mother, little daughter! Don't hurt …" Then her mouth, too, was sealed with tape.

9

The public swimming pool on Avenue Abay was fronted by a large building containing volleyball and basketball courts. Almost hidden behind the flank of the utilitarian gray structure was the entrance to the pool: two small doors, one for women and one for men, with a ticket stand between them. Cono paced in a circuitous route around the sports complex before quickly walking across an open space between a large promotional tent for Marlboro cigarettes and the pool doors. He bought his ticket from a sleepy woman whose vastness spread beyond her chair and onto the wooden desk at her side. She had reason to be bored—the pool had only just opened, and there would be little traffic on this day, one of the last of the season.

Cono undressed. His blue-and-green striped boxer shorts would have to double as swimming trunks, and after more than two days on his body they would benefit from the cleansing chlorine, as would his cuts. The few other clothes he'd brought, along with some toiletries, were probably now in the lost and found of the Hotel Tsarina, along with Xiao Li's high heel. Katerina's choice of the swimming pool reassured him somewhat, even though there was no reason to view her as a threat. And yet, four years after the tontería he had performed on her behalf, there was no way to know what were her current allegiances in the mutating patchwork of interests that hid beneath the overgrown trees of Almaty. "You never know when this tree or that tree will go yellow," Timur had said. First or last or in between. But they always did, eventually. And then they waited, to foliate again in the next season. Brother Timur.

Addicted, the note had said.

Cono closed the locker in the changing room; instead of putting the key's rubber bracelet on his wrist, he hid it atop the row of lockers nearest the stairway that led up to the pool. He stood at the top of the stairs, still shaded from the morning glare. The mountains in the distance were gleaming with sun on snow. The pool deck was empty except for a gaggle of kids on the far end being taught how to dive by a woman pointing her arms as she stood on the edge, snapping at the children, who paid little attention and continued kicking water at each other. There were no buildings around the rest of the pool, only open sky; no roosts for observers or snipers. It was a good day to be alive, to have a swim. Cono waited.

A lime-green towel was the first image to invade his left eye. A bright-orange bikini followed. Long, slim arms unfurled the towel; it fluttered from Katerina's fingertips, creating a progression of ripples that instantly entranced Cono's eyes, absorbing and transporting him as each ripple was slowed by his mind and became a wave— advancing, rising, preparing to curl. *That one's mine. Paddle, hop up. Slide and torque, make it last.* He felt the spray and the breeze streaming through his hair until the last crash and tumble onto the foaming sands of his childhood.

The towel fell without a single fold onto the deck at the pool's edge, and Cono returned to the present. Katerina stretched herself out, face up, and dropped her left arm into the water, swirling it with lazy fingers. She squinted as she glanced around and then closed her eyes against the brightness.

Cono walked soundlessly to the right side of the pool and slid into the water. He swam across the bottom until he saw Katerina's fingers dangling above him, then rose slowly and bit one of them. The hand jerked away, but not before Cono gripped her wrist. Still submerged, he braced his feet against the pool's wall and pulled her into the water. She struggled ferociously on the bottom and had a thumb jabbing Cono's larynx before he brought her up. The knee hitting his groin was slowed by the water's viscosity, but her forehead, now above the water, butted against his brow with no impediment. Cono floated away, only slightly stunned. He stood and squeezed a stream of water from his clasped palms into her murderous face.

"You didn't know they have sharks in Kazakhstan?" he said, grinning.

Katerina's face slowly relaxed, and her long eyelashes blinked away the water in little flecks of airborne light. "There are good sharks and bad sharks."

"And what for you is a good shark?"

"A good shark is one that hunts for its food elsewhere." She gazed at him a moment, then smiled.

"Well, this shark says, 'Peace.'"

"Cono, thank you for coming."

He nodded. Katerina's voice had lost the lilting timbre of four years before, and her smile was less ready, less coquettish. She seemed to have an inner steadiness that had been missing before. Her body was still long and lithe, and the shape of her erect nipples just above the waterline was the same.

"'Addicted,' you wrote."

"Why else would you be here, in this messy city?"

"To help a friend. Or two," he replied, moving closer to her.

"'Better to fight for friends than countries,' you told me in Barcelona."

"But first, help yourself, I said." Cono reached for her hand, and she took it. They walked through the water to the steps at the shallow end and sat down shoulder-to-shoulder, their torsos warmed by the sun.

"So you're still here," Cono said. "You must like those mountains." He nodded toward the faraway peaks. "I don't think it's the cuisine that keeps you."

"I'm still here because freedom is hard to come by." Katerina clasped her hands together and rubbed one thumb against the other. "The Americans made promises—just do this one more thing, that one more thing, then you'll get the passport. The money was another lure, but just enough to keep me biting. And the little hints that they knew all about my family back in Ukraine …" Katerina massaged the base of her neck, near one of her scars. "I was so close, the promises were hardening, with specific dates. Then my handler was sent away, back to Washington. And now more promises. More empty promises to me, the only one they have here who knows, who has the network … that's what they call it, 'a network,' when they ass-kiss in reports to their bosses."

"A network good enough to find me," Cono said as a child belly-flopped at the other end of the pool.

"My stringers are good. Men with kids and wives and a lot to lose. And usually relatives in jail because they wrote something honest or stood up for themselves. The one who followed you keeps an eye on the Bureau's little love hotel above the General, among other popular destinations." Katerina put her hand into Cono's under the water.

"And that's how you knew I was here."

"I'm glad that you are here." She momentarily squeezed his fingers. "The stringer called in. A handsome foreigner was leading a Chinese girl out of the alley behind the General."

"Handsome foreigner. Well, thank you. So your stringer must have also seen her being dragged there in the first place, kicking and biting." Cono turned to examine Katerina's face.

"Cono, there are so many … who go in that way." Katerina half-winced. "How would we know she was a friend of yours?"

The momentary tugs of muscles beneath the soft creamy-white skin of her face confused Cono. Apprehension, certainly. Suspicion, desperation, and even ambivalence—they were there, too.

"Come on. Let's swim." Cono pressed himself against her, pushing her away from the stairs. They breaststroked to the other end. As Cono treaded water, he watched a child diver standing on the edge, her hands nervously pancaked together, head tucked between her arms.

"Fly, fly, little bird!" he called. The girl plopped headfirst into the pool and surfaced quickly, sputtering and wiping strings of black hair from her face. Cono clapped his hands in applause.

Katerina did the crawl back toward the steps; Cono swam beneath her, facing upward, kicking like a dolphin, his body covered with polygons of refracted light. When they reached the other end and sat again, he slipped the dislodged strap of Katerina's bikini back on her shoulder. Her face was serious, worried.

The Americans, she told him, were alarmed about leftover HEU—highly enriched uranium, weapons-grade. Her slang for it was high-U. Kazakhstan had been the major producer of it for the Soviet Union, mining the uranium ore and enriching it for submarine reactors and nuclear weapons. When the Soviet Union fell apart, the new lords of Kazakhstan cut a deal to let the Americans ship it out.

Katerina examined Cono's face. "But maybe you know all about this. Maybe that's why you're here."

Cono laughed and scooped water onto his hot shoulders. "I'm here for a friend, not geopolitics or radiation. Radiantly beautiful women, of course, are a different matter."

The twitching creases at the corners of Katerina's eyes relaxed. She continued. The deal, called Project Sapphire, involved an undisclosed payment—$25 million, possibly more; a modest sum because of those cash-strapped times, before the oil was discovered.

"And I'm sure the money was put to the service of the fine citizens of Kazakhstan," Cono said.

"Only fools doubt that it got divvied up at the top."

"I understand now," Cono chuckled. "The American *government* can bribe officials, but American *companies* cannot. That makes for a level playing field."

As with all deals, there was a catch, Katerina told him. The inventory numbers didn't match what was flown out on C-5 transporters to the U.S. Hundreds of pounds of high-U had remained in Kazakhstan, unaccounted for. The U.S. government had downplayed the discrepancy, saying it was a matter of who was doing the counting. Now, years later, the Americans had indications that jihadis were maneuvering to get access to it. But it wasn't clear who controlled it. Infighting at the top in Kazakhstan made things even more uncertain. Kurgat, the powerful interior minister, who had purview over everything from the oil contracts to the security service, was threatened by an ambitious rival who was courting the jihadis. The high-U would be valuable currency for a usurper.

"Sounds like the rival is a good soldier," Cono said. "Like the Russians say, a bad soldier is one who doesn't try to become a general."

"You tell me if he's a good soldier." Katerina bobbed her head, sending drops of water from the ends of her locks onto Cono's chest. "You know him—Timur Betov, the head of the National Security Bureau. Your friend."

Cono squinted in the direction of the mountains. "A drinking buddy. And a *very* good soldier. But he's not the one I came to help." He turned to look squarely at Katerina. "I came to help a woman. I'm sure jihad is the last thing on her mind. And the only reason I'm not on a long flight out of here right now is your note. And your radiance."

A small smile played on Katerina's lips, but the tension in her face remained. The communications being picked up by the Americans, she continued, suggested that the rivalry was coming to a head, that Betov already had the high-U and was under pressure to make the transfer to the jihadis quickly. He needed the jihadis to back him and get rid of the minister before the minister eliminated him. The transfer was imminent.

From prior experience, Cono doubted that the hapless CIA staff at the embassy could have picked up what Katerina knew. He guessed that she was still working her sadistic admirer, Kurgat, and that he was a pillow chatterbox.

"It's worse," Katerina said. "One of my stringers says the local police arrested two foreigners last week. They had diagrams for making a simple device, where one chunk of high-U slams into another. The foreigners were released. Pressure from high up."

"So, you think I can help you in some way," Cono said. "And preserve the interests of your good friend Mr. K at the same time? After all, even the minister of the interior needs a little help from his friends sometimes."

Katerina drew her head back and glared at him. A little too angrily, he thought.

"Cono, don't you see what they will do with the uranium?" Katerina whacked her hand on the water. "Once the jihadis have it, it's child's play to make a bomb, or bombs."

"And you think if you can stop the transfer to them, this will be the big score that makes the Americans give you your freedom. At last."

"My handler, Simmons, before he got called back … he said they couldn't deny it to me if this one thing went right." There it was again—the slight change of timbre in her voice that had earlier made Cono sense ambivalence.

"Katerina, buy your own freedom. I'll give you the money to do it."

She put her hand on Cono's knee. "But I know too much now. If I run … if it's not with their backing … they know everything about my mother, my father, my brother, my little sister."

Cono saw his own mother in his mind, teaching him to dance on the beach, her bare brown abdomen beading with sweat before his eyes. She was dead. His father too. His grandmother. There was no one else to worry about.

There was a splash and another splash as two kids dove into the pool, followed by a shout of praise from the instructor.

"And what of Mr. Kurgat?" Cono asked. "You seem to have reconciled with him. I'd make him your backup plan in case the Americans ditch you. He's a friend in the know, after all." Katerina's little finger contracted against Cono's knee for an instant, and then, as if to conceal the involuntary movement, she made her hand retreat in a titillating glide across his thigh.

"He's older now." Katerina's voice lowered. "The pills don't even work for him. He just wants me to lie naked with him. And there's no choice. It's part of my assignment, the reason the Americans hired me in the first place."

"No more biting?"

"No more biting."

"Ah, men losing the power in their dicks. When they can no longer fuck their women, they fuck the world." Cono slid down the steps to douse himself in the water, and pressed with his arms to lift himself back up. The movement caused his triceps to ripple.

"I took a chance, telling you all this." Katerina was stern. She had changed in the intervening years, but there was still truth in her voice. Either that or she was a witch of deception. "Now tell me what you were doing with Zheng Lu Peng."

Cono's eyes returned from their scan of the perimeter of the pool deck and the fence around it. "So that's his name. He didn't have the good manners to introduce himself, despite being dressed like a gentleman. I'd guess he's a fan of yours too."

Katerina waited in silence.

"It was my little assignment, to meet with him," Cono said, "in exchange for the liberty of my trapped woman friend. I was just an errand boy who happens to speak Mandarin. You're a busy woman, in so many places at the same time, listening in on so many telephones. I can see why the Americans want to keep you under their thumb. Makes me wish I was on that long flight out of here."

"I didn't tell the Americans, Cono. I didn't tell anyone you're here."

Cono searched for the telltale signals of dissimulation on Katerina's face, but her wet hair was draping her features. He leaned back and let his head sink until the water reached his earlobes. "What else?"

"Zheng Lu Peng is Beijing's new man here. I don't know what he's up to. Simmons thinks it's more than oil."

"Katerina, Katerina, you have so many worries on your shoulders. It's a good thing they are so strong."

"They aren't strong enough for this. Not alone. The big problem is the uranium. How will you ever enjoy a meal or make love again after you see the news? How would you live with yourself? Half a million people killed, no matter what city it blows up in. Thousands of little kids like those over there." Katerina pointed at three children poised to dive. "And after half a million dead, the dying continues for the ones who weren't incinerated; they die later from the radiation, like at home, in Ukraine."

Cono's forehead creased in puzzlement. "You mean the reactor that blew up."

Katerina's face flushed instantly. "Yes. Chernobyl. Two of my cousins and their families lost everything." Her rising voice was thick with anger. "One cousin's baby was born with no arms or legs. And there was a little girl who died of leukemia, daughter of my cousin Nadya, a mother of three who now has tumors growing out of her skin. In a full nuclear explosion, they'd be counted as the lucky ones, not like my sister, who ..."

Katerina stopped. "I don't think it's possible for you to understand," she said quietly, "unless you have seen it yourself."

The children at the end of the pool dove in and rose up and slapped the water, trying to find the edge. Cono saw their little fingers clawing for the lip of the deck.

"What do you want me to do?"

"You're buddies with Timur Betov; he's your friend. How that can be, I don't know. Help us get close to him, get a device or a tracker on him, so we'll be there to squelch the transfer of the uranium. Please, Cono. I need your help." Katerina held his gaze as he searched her eyes.

A long moment passed. *Friends,* Cono thought. *What is my friend Katerina not telling me?*

Despite the wringing he'd given them, Cono's boxer shorts were still uncomfortably wet as he sat in the car he'd flagged several blocks away from the bustle of Avenue Abay.

Katerina was certain the transfer was due to take place the next day, she had told him. Cono had said he'd try to help and had taken her private phone number, but he hadn't disclosed to her the location he suspected. If she were to call in the bumblers at the embassy … he'd seen that before. It smelled like a mess in the making, a mess with the highest stakes. Cono could simply walk away from the stench. And yet, maybe he had become addicted after all—addicted to being the pivot point, to being as central as that crucial joint between copulating man and woman, but with a danger that did not know the bounds of orgasm. What was more, Katerina was right about one thing—if he didn't do his utmost, and the high-U was later detonated, how would he ever live with himself?

What Katerina had said, if it was true, combined with what Cono knew, meant that Timur was arranging two wings to lift him to the top. Beijing, in its quest for control of the country, would lift one wing, and the jihadis, with their desire for the high-U, would lift the other. Cono's inadvertent presence in Almaty had provided Timur with an arm's-length way to play Zheng Lu Peng, who had said that the timetable for the oil bid had been moved up by Cono's "boss," who was obviously now dealing outside the chain-of-command. Timur's instructions to Cono, in his darkened apartment, to make the rounds as an oil-contract auction boy, were a decoy, a ruse. Only support from the Beijing sow mattered, and it had to come fast. Being seen with the Chinese during Xiao Li's rescue at the Hotel Svezda had endangered Timur's plans, Cono saw more clearly now. It had confirmed Kurgat's suspicion of Timur's intentions to cut a deal with Beijing, provoking both men to act now.

With one wing ready to soar, Timur must have revved up the jihadis. He'd probably sequestered the high-U years back, when he'd shot to the top of the Bureau. "Maybe a little thanks to you," he'd said on the phone when Cono had tracked him down from Istanbul. No doubt Timur had been waiting for his chance to use the high-U as a lever for a long time.

With both wings rising, Timur could regard the premier as irrelevant. Minister Kurgat, on the other hand, was taking potshots at Timur twice a day on average, so far.

And what winds were set to blow under Katerina's wings? The Americans were using her and her talents like fodder. They would continue to string her along; she must know this, unless she was blinded by some illusion of allegiance. On the other side, dear toothy Mr. K could offer her a sealed marble mansion among the embassies and new high-security expat enclaves strung along the boulevards up toward the mountains. She could stroke his fat belly as he promised a Western passport that would never come, and she would stare out the windows until the day arrived when Kurgat's protection of her crumbled, and he couldn't even protect himself.

And yet with that bleak horizon before her eyes, Katerina had said the first problem was the uranium. All the children dying. It came to that: women and their children. Even women and the children who did not belong to them. It was the only force in the world resisting the centrifugal destructive rage of men.

Katerina didn't add up. He could feel that she wasn't being straightforward with him, but her sense of urgency about the high-U danger was real, and Cono was relieved that beneath her slightly hardened skin, her motives seemed to extend beyond her selfish survival impulses. And what a survivor she had proven herself to be.

Cono's impromptu taxi passed an Internet café. Four blocks later he told the driver to pull into an alley and stop next to a row of garbage containers. He got out of the cab and stepped into a gap between the containers, waiting to see if anyone was following him. After several minutes he walked briskly through a maze of back alleys, eventually doubling back to the café. He wanted to see if he could find any information on the Web to confirm Katerina's story, and to reacquaint himself with HEU. He had no choice now. Do nothing when his fingers were on the fulcrum of a disaster? Impossible.

The young man minding the café was Chinese; he looked like an eager college student, with black plastic glasses riding low on his nose.

"How's business?" Cono asked in Mandarin, surprising the youth and making him smile.

"Well, there *is* business."

"Almaty a new home for you? Like it?"

"Home is always China, but we're here to stay."

"Why?"

"We can do what we want. My parents and I can stuff the piggy bank for the future. No government guy taking our operation or shutting us down. Bribes, sure, but the protection's worth it. Money's coming into the country. Game's open, like the Wild West."

"Wild West?" The expression was new to Cono.

"Wild West, you know, America in the good old days. You living in a seashell? Like in *High Noon*. You seen it?" He drew his fingers out of imagined holsters. "Bang, bang, be your own marshal. You can get it on DVD."

"Thanks, I'll look for it." Cono said, pointing back with his own finger-pistol, then raising it to his mouth and blowing over the tip.

He took a seat and began to click through links on HEU hazards. The only previous brush he'd had with high-U was a tontería for an "unnameable Western nation" hoping to detect an illicit shipment of the material on a container vessel due to pass through the Bosporus. The plug was pulled at the last minute, for undisclosed reasons, but in his apartment near Galata Tower in Istanbul, Cono still had two rather cumbersome multiple-wire proportional radiation counters, sampling gear, and a plastic suit with a rebreather, all stashed behind a panel in an empty closet.

He'd prepared himself for that assignment with the details of emission stats for various degrees of enrichment, the handling and safety procedures, the types of containment—whether the HEU was in simple ingot form, metal-oxide shavings, or beryllium pellets. But it had all faded from memory now, like the words to a song he hadn't sung since childhood, when he had stolen oranges and crackers and the occasional slippery fish only because he was hungry. Over time the stealing had extended to uncomfortable secret facts and even inconvenient people—not kidnapping exactly, but a sort of temporary relocation. Now he was hunting for uranium. He was moving up the food chain. And he was still hungry. Hungry for what? Money? No. Power? Over people? That was like having power over clams. Hungry for what? He didn't know.

The search results flashed by in a rapid series.

Sixty to seventy pounds of HEU would be more than enough to enable a primitive gun-type explosive device that could be engineered in any machine shop.

When contained in canisters, highly enriched uranium is of no immediate danger to persons nearby.

The refined ore and semi-purified metal can exist in several chemical variants and oxidative states …

Blah, blah, blah. Click, read. Click, read. Click … Cono was momentarily dazed by the flicker of the computer screen—it was an old type of CRT, probably with a vertical scan frequency that was in the sweet spot for rasping his brain. He stood up and composed himself as the painful throb deep in his head subsided.

He sat down again and searched for Project Sapphire, keeping his eyes off the screen except for short glances.

... On 21 November 1994 1278 pounds of HEU were transferred from the Ulba Metallurgy plant near Ust-Kamenogorsk to the Y-12 plant at the Oak Ridge National Laboratory in Tennessee, in a highly secret project code-named "Sapphire" ...

1300 steel canisters for shipment by two C-5 transport planes from Kazakhstan to the U.S. ...

The United States agreed to compensate Kazakhstan for the material, though the transaction was "not handled as a straight business deal" ...

The value of this quantity of HEU is difficult to ascertain, but it certainly is far less than the billions of dollars the Kazaks could have garnered by selling it on the black market ...

The U.S. Defense Secretary said they had accomplished their mission of keeping the bomb-grade material "forever out of the reach of black marketers, terrorists, or a new nuclear regime."

November 22, 1994. Reuters. "Nuclear Bomb Cache Found In Kazakhstan."

November 24, 1994. Washington Post. "Kazakhstan Site Had Lax Security."

October 24, 1996. Washington Times. "Kazakh

Uranium Shipment Was Shy Enough For Two Bombs."

November 11, 1996. Nucleonics Week. "Sapphire
HEU Is Less Than DOE First Claimed, Government
Admits."

The pain in Cono's head returned, now with greater force and centered just above his palate. He stood up, walked shakily to the bright-eyed young man behind the cash box, and paid with a trembling hand.

"You all right, man?" The youth's brow creased in concern.

"Just fine, just fine," Cono responded automatically in Mandarin. "Just fine."

The pain was excruciating. A sharp metallic taste spread across the back of his tongue, as if he were chewing on aluminum foil. He turned and focused on the glass door, which was filled with flashing zigzags of blurred light. His toes turned inward as he tried to walk, stumbling with stiff legs that didn't want to move. His feet suddenly pointed like a ballerina's, lifting him in his last lurch toward the exit. His hand was just able to swing the door partway open before his rigid body fell onto the sidewalk.

"Hey! You all right?" The Mandarin voice sounded strangely like Cono's father's, but the fuzzy face didn't match. The young man was poking a finger against Cono's carotid. Cono's jaw was so tightly clenched that he couldn't have spoken even if his mind had formed words. "Open your eyes! *Ta ma de*! Shit, are you alive?" Cono's eyes fluttered open. "Oh, man, you're scaring me. You've been out for a while. I called the embassy. You don't look so Chinese, but that's the way you talk. They'll be here any minute. Better than calling an ambulance in this town. I'll get you some water, okay? You okay? Your head okay?"

Cono's body slackened slightly. He uncurled his fingers. He could feel his arms, but barely. He tried to turn over and get his knees under him. Gradually he pushed himself up onto all fours, wobbling as he watched strings of saliva elongate from his mouth down to the concrete. Two vaguely familiar polished black shoes planted themselves on either side of his splayed hands.

"Your description of him was quite accurate, young man. Thank you for alerting the embassy. He doesn't look it, but he is one of ours. Your guess is probably right, just a seizure, or maybe food poisoning. He will be grateful to you when he regains full consciousness."

Still unable to speak, Cono felt his body being lifted and carried. The sun blanched his retinas. As he was folded into fetal position in the back seat of a car, he heard the faint whisper of Xiao Li's voice in his head, saying, "Is Almaty such a big town?" The fleeting thought of her led to a jumble of pleasurable sensations that vanished when he felt the blunt pressure of the Makarov's muzzle on his pubic bone. The wetness down there was warm. The vague thought assembled in Cono's mind that he had peed on Timur's cherished pistol. The humor of it partially assembled itself too, then faded, as did the whole of Cono's consciousness.

Zheng turned to the troubled café attendant. "And now please show me which computer our compatriot was using."

"Aren't you going to take him to a doctor? He looks pretty bad off."

"Which computer?" Zheng said tightly, forcing a smile. "Maybe we can discover some information that will allow us to inform his family."

The young man pointed to the terminal Cono had used. Zheng sat down and scrolled back through the recent queue of sites. HEU, radiation containment, enrichment stages, canister configurations, Sapphire, Kazak uranium shipments … Zheng became more puzzled and disturbed as he scanned page after page. The insulting foreigner with the dirty face in the park was much more than Zheng had surmised, not just a go-between. Now he appeared to be a threat, but from which angle? At last the clicks of the mouse arrived at a site for Romanian marriage brokers.

Zheng was already pushing the door open when the attendant said: "Hey! You have to pay." Zheng turned back and faced the upstart.

"Who owns this place?"

"My mom and dad." The attendant was blustery and perturbed. He planted his hands on his hips and stuck out his chest.

"So you are a good son. Where is your family from in China?"

"Why do you want to know? We live here now. Where are *you* from?" The young man had an accent from the south, perhaps Yunnan. His Mandarin was shabby, and it grated on Zheng's ear.

"I'm from Beijing." Zheng pulled a business card from his suit coat and held it in front of the young man's eyes.

The attendant snatched it and read. "So, big man, this isn't China," he said. "We already cough up enough cash to the *raket* for our roof here. You try to butt in on the action and they'll fuck you good." The card landed on the toe of Zheng's shoe. "Now pay up."

The only other customer in the café, a middle-aged Chinese woman wearing socks and sandals, placed a bill on the desk and eased around the two men in order to leave.

With a look of disgust, Zheng pulled a few tenge notes from his pants pocket and let them drop on the floor. As he walked out the door the attendant shouted: "Hey! You take care of that guy. And … and *fuck* Beijing!"

Zheng emitted a low growl as he turned back to the door and opened it, a fresh smile on his face.

"Tell me, young man, where is the toilet, please? Bodily functions. I'm sure you understand."

The attendant pushed his glasses back up his nose. "Pee or shit? There's no toilet paper."

"No need for toilet paper, thank you. Where is the bathroom?"

"It's back there." The young man waved his hand impatiently.

"Where exactly? Can you show me? I need to go."

The young man strode to a narrow door wedged between two computer terminals and opened it. "You have one of those prostate problems, big man?"

"You're so cruel, speaking that way. Age comes to all of us."

They were now on the threshold of a small hallway crowded with stacks of partly dismantled computers. Zheng walked ahead.

"Show me the toilet please—it's urgent."

"It's down there on the left. I'm not a tour guide. And if you're one of those perverts, you'll just have to shake it off yourself." The young man turned to go back into the shop.

Zheng rotated swiftly on his heel. His left arm encircled the young man's neck like a noose. He flicked open a knife in his right hand and swung it around, plunging it into the young man's chest just below the sternum. Zheng squeezed with both arms, so hard that his victim could not cry out.

"You are an insult. Your family too. Hear me?" Zheng probed deeply with the blade, up to the heart for two swipes. "An insult to our people, to my people, to all we have suffered through. *Quitters.*" Zheng pushed the blade all the way back to reach the descending aorta; he felt its pulsations through the knife. "Ah, there you are." One more sweep of the blade. Computer screens crashed to the floor. The young man's kicking stopped. His hands released the snarl of computer cables he'd been trying to loop backward around his assailant's head, and he slumped over.

Zheng withdrew the knife and let the boy fall to the floor, face down.

"Peasant trash," Zheng said as he spat and wiped the blade on the young man's shirt. He clicked the knife shut and slid it into the pocket with his business cards. He rolled his head right and left, tugged on his coat sleeves to make them straight again, adjusted the white trim on his breast pocket, and strolled out of the shop.

It was cool when Cono opened his eyes again, but his wrists and ankles were warm. He felt as if he were arched in a backward swan dive, looking up at a ceiling with fluorescent lights. There was a cold, hard surface under his back, and the chill of it against his shoulders and buttocks told him that he was naked. He moved, and found that his wrists and ankles were tightly bound, and that the surface underneath him was too small to support the full length of his body. His head draped off one end of what turned out to be a desk, and his legs were dangling off the other end toward the floor. He felt like a slab of meat on a butcher's block.

Something brushed against his cheek and eased with greater pressure toward the corner of his lips. A knob wedged between his teeth and into his mouth. The taste was of oil and smoke. The knob went deeper until he was choking.

"It's quite an old gun, but still very useful." Zheng's carefully cropped head was just a silhouette against the bright ceiling lights. The Makarov barrel was withdrawn with a snap, breaking off the point of one of Cono's canines.

"So sorry," Zheng cooed in Mandarin. "I don't want to hurt you." He stroked the tip of the gun against Cono's cheek. "I want to help you. I want to help you out of this mess you've gotten yourself into." Zheng's voice was cool and smooth, like the gun muzzle that caressed Cono's face.

Cono's eyes rolled, trying to register the scene; he was still dazed in the aftermath of the seizure. Zheng's features were coming into focus, but a pulsing pressure in Cono's head made it hard for him to take in anything else. He thought he could make out two more cropped-hair silhouettes, one at each side. Were there others? He opened his mouth to speak, but no sound came out.

"Ah! You are thirsty. I forget my responsibilities as a host. Please, forgive me." Zheng motioned to one of the silhouettes, who presented a glass. Zheng put down the gun, cradled Cono's head in one hand, and with the other tipped the water glass carefully so Cono could drink. "Is that better, my friend?"

Cono swallowed repeatedly, but the water came too fast. He coughed and jerked his head away from Zheng's hand.

"Thanks for the drowning," Cono said groggily in Mandarin, looking around the room. "How can I help you, my friend?"

"Let me begin by saying that you are such an *intriguing* personality. I knew it the first day we met, so at ease, so charming. I don't even know what to ask first. Maybe you can just talk to us, tell us what is on your mind, what attracts you to Almaty. You seem to have many friends here."

"I'm attracted by the women. What attracts you to Almaty?"

Zheng sighed and paced from one end of Cono's bound body to the other. He picked up the Makarov and stroked the muzzle lightly along Cono's chest, slowly down his abdomen, and then along the inside of his left thigh and all the way to his instep. "I am very, very curious about who you are working for here in Almaty. It's a simple question."

The stroke on Cono's thigh had reflexively caused his cremaster muscle to pull up the testicle on that side, and Zheng had noticed. Cono feared his genitals would be the first part of his body to suffer.

"I said I like the women here, so I don't think I'm the right one to help you," Cono said. "But I can arrange to get you laid by a horse-hung teenager working at Hotel Ratar." The angle of the light on the face to his right allowed him to perceive one of the henchmen half-smirking.

The pistol slammed against Cono's jaw.

"So you're an S&M guy," Cono said, his senses recovering. "Go ahead and suck the iguana, but don't bite *too* hard." The half-faces on both sides compressed their lips to contain either their amusement or their shock at Cono's nerve.

Zheng ignored the remark; he took off his suit coat and laid it neatly across the back of a desk chair. His white shirt was sweat-stained beneath the armpits. Cono's eyes had regained their focus, but to see anything he had to lift his head up, and his neck muscles were already feeling the strain. He saw that the white trim at the breast pocket of Zheng's suit coat wasn't a handkerchief; it looked like stiff paper, the size of a postcard.

"What's that, your torture notes?" Cono asked, his eyes on the pocket. "And I thought you were a pro."

Zheng's body tensed. The blood vessels in his forehead became engorged; it seemed that he wasn't breathing. Finally he closed his eyes and let out a long exhalation. He reached for his suit coat, carefully folded it so that the breast pocket was covered, and placed the coat on the shelf behind him.

"It's a shame," Zheng said, still recovering his breath, "that in this primitive outpost we don't have the drugs at hand to make this easier for you. But being such a reasonable and experienced man of the world, I'm sure you'll tell us what you are doing in this backward place." Zheng lit a cigarette and took a long drag, speaking as the smoke veiled his silhouette. "Who are you?"

Cono tried to find Zheng's eyes within the shadow of the face. "I'm a swimmer, like Mao in those old pictures—all that paddling around. A surfer too," Cono said. He tried to find an equivalent of *surfer dude* in Mandarin, but failed and laughed.

"Well, my dear friend, you are very far from the waves. In fact, you couldn't be more distant." Zheng filled his mouth from another glass of water and spit it out on Cono's face.

Cono let his neck muscles relax and his head tilted back over the edge of the desk. The water trickled into his hair. He was now fully alert. "You can find a wave to ride anywhere."

"A philosopher, and a bad one at that. Tell me, so that you don't suffer, what wave or waves you are surfing here in this mangy town." Zheng's voice had become soft and coaxing again. "With all these passports in your finely tailored vest, it seems you are a well-traveled man, one who must know when harm is near."

"Harm?" Cono raised his head and looked across his stretched nakedness. "I feel quite comfortable here with you, my friend, basking under your gaze."

Zheng grunted and tossed his head as a signal to his henchmen. Arms swung from both sides. Shot-filled rubber hoses slammed onto Cono's chest. The sensation of each blow was divided in time—the deflections of hairs in their follicles, the pressure on the dermis, the inward flexing of ribs near their breaking point. There was pain, but there was something else too. The blows continued in a syncopated drumbeat that reverberated against the bare walls of the room. The beat of the drum went on and on.

It stopped. Cono breathed and felt the vertebral joints in his neck popping with the weight of his head as his muscles relaxed. He was glad there was not yet any taste of blood in his throat.

"There is no harm, you are right," said Zheng, surveying the burgeoning welts arrayed like zebra stripes on Cono's torso. "It is only persuasion, for a good cause—the health of your face and other parts of your physique. The questions are very simple for an intelligent man like you. Who are you working for and what do they want? Such a sophisticated man cannot merely be collecting flowers for a Kazak who wants to be king. Why this fascination with uranium, and the American scheme? Project Sapphire—what a *gem* of a code name. Surely the Americans are trying to insert themselves into the struggles for this tin-pot dictatorship." Zheng sucked on his Dunhill. "Who is your CIA runner?"

Cono groaned. "*Now* I hurt. Putting me in that kind of company. We both know their type. Sloths that can't find the way down from their own tree." Cono breathed in again. There was no wheezing. The duo who had beaten him were experts; they knew precisely what force would snap a rib and puncture a lung. "The Americans are nothing against your breed," Cono said, "but they have the same erotic love of torture."

"You mean *our* breed." Zheng smiled just as Cono raised his head. "You're really one of us, after all." Zheng glanced at his assistants with a strained grin in search of agreement. "Part of the great Chinese diaspora, unable to resist your glorious cultural heritage." The duo gave tepid nods.

"I've known Chinese fathers who ..." Cono laughed through the pain cutting like barbed wire across his chest. "Who are losers. Who couldn't even feed their families. Good reason for a diaspora."

Zheng pressed the cigarette to his lips and inhaled deeply. His forearm ratcheted down step by step, like a tree branch that was yielding to the weight of snow. The burn of the cigarette on Cono's left nipple was stretched out in time as if it would never end. A network of involuntary neurons conducted the sensations of pain and pleasure radiating from the nipple until Cono's whole body was tingling within an electrified dermal web. The tingling reached his perineum and engulfed his organ. Cono felt the redistribution of blood with every heartbeat. He heard a snicker from the man to his right.

"Shut up!" Zheng barked.

Cono lifted his head and looked down at the rising spectacle. "Oh, Mr. Zheng, you are such a good lover." Cono pursed his lips in a kiss. Zheng was shocked equally by the sound of his own name and the response of Cono's body.

"Shut up, you pervert!" Zheng whacked the pistol against Cono's temple.

"Let me strap *you* down naked like this," Cono said. "Then you'll see what a pervert I am."

Zheng gave sharp looks to his henchmen and smashed the gun two more times.

The bars of light above Cono were multiplied in his vision. As he tried to focus and see only one of everything, he was relieved to observe that he was in an old building, with ceilings high enough that the flicker of the lights above didn't disrupt his brain. He was lucky—unless Zheng was holding that tool in reserve. Cono wondered in half-confusion if Zheng's intelligence apparatus could have somehow found its way to the medical lab in Palo Alto that housed the details of his performance anomalies. *Performance anomalies.* Cono laughed to himself at the term, at his erectness, at the years of absurdities that had delivered him, naked, precisely to this uncomfortable old desk.

"My dear Mr. Zheng," Cono said as blood leaked down from his temple into his ear. "Can I call you Lu Peng? You tell me to shut up, but I understood that you wanted me to talk. Are you a … a confused man?" Cono darted his eyes at the two other men, his neck muscles cramping as he kept his head raised. "Everyone knows torturers are after sexual pleasure, Lu Peng. I'm sure you have an erection right now. A big one. Please, show it to me, Lu Peng."

Cono heard Zheng's exhalation and saw the sweep of the gun coming in micro steps toward his face. He relaxed his neck muscles and the gun missed his head, continuing into midair. Zheng lost his balance and landed across Cono's bare chest. Zheng flailed with the gun, trying to find its mark, at the same time struggling to regain his footing. The assistant on the left tried to help his boss to his feet.

"Don't touch me!" Zheng shrieked as he shook off the henchman and stood upright, waving the gun in the air. Cono registered the micro-expressions of embarrassment flashing across Zheng's face. Cono's eyes also caught the minute creases of shame and doubt on the faces of the two assistants.

The ash and the burned skin from Cono's nipple had left a smudge on Zheng's white shirt, which all but Zheng could see.

Zheng cocked his head and grunted and pointed to where the next blows were to be delivered. He did not direct the blows at Cono's genitals, and all four of them knew why. Through his taunting, Cono had saved his most cherished parts.

The blows with the heavy hoses were mild at first, tempered by the ambivalence of the two underlings, but Zheng sensed their reticence and pointed the Makarov at each of them to reignite their vigor.

In intervals of consciousness Cono heard Zheng demanding to know who he worked for, who his CIA runner was, was he stringing for the Russians, what did he have to do with HEU and Project Sapphire, was he working with the Muslim separatists in Xinjiang, who was paying him. In his anger, Zheng sprinkled his interrogation with threats that anyone he dealt with in Almaty would have to know the punishment for noncooperation—a message that the naked mongrel would carry back, if he was allowed to survive at all. Cono responded intermittently, mechanically, by saying, "Yes, my dear Lu Peng, please suck it."

Zheng pretended to ignore Cono's refrains. "You've got no country, no one to save you. You are from nowhere," he seethed. "You are a roach soon to be squashed."

More blows to Cono's dangling head sent him into a nether land that made Zheng's voice seem distant and garbled. In his mind, Cono saw Timur at his side in the car, giving a thumbs-up. And Xiao Li's face with her bright-red lips hovering over him for a kiss and retreating as she laughed and started to sing for him. But the song was lost amid the ringing in his ears.

The swinging of the arms of the able assistants stopped with a grunt from Zheng. Cono felt his body swelling like a balloon that would soon burst. He managed to spit out most of the blood.

"Who are you working for?" Zheng began his rant again. "Why the uranium searches? Who are your jihadi contacts? Who is your American handler? You're an American stooge, aren't you? Trying to grab what isn't yours, what is the natural right of the glorious People's Republic, the kingdom of *five thousand years!*"

Cono lifted his head, and with his eyes still closed, began to sing in Mandarin.

Let us pull the oars together
The little boats cut through the waves
As the lake reflects the passing clouds ...

"Enough!" Zheng slapped Cono's face. Cono knew that all three of his tormenters would know the anthem by heart from their childhood years. They had sung it daily to belong to the elite future of their country, wearing around their necks the red ties of the Communist Party Youth Brigade, which had formed their beings and all that they would be and would ever believe, even as communism became a ghost and the party a web of corruption.

Our red ties are shining in the sun
The fish are watching us from below ...

Zheng snatched a bludgeon from one of his assistants and pummeled Cono's head, but Cono kept on singing.

I ask you, my comrades,
Who gives us the happy life?
The little boats are floating ...

Zheng struck again several times, but he was flustered, and his blows were ineffectual; he had always relied on his underlings for this. He thrust the hose back into the hand of his puzzled henchman. "Finish him off. He's worthless. Show these Kazak apes who is glorious."

The two assistants shifted their footing. Cono sensed their hesitancy and sang again.

I ask you, my comrades,
Who gives us the happy life?
The little boats are floating …

"I said finish him!"

The punishers glanced at each other, both of them disturbed by the prisoner's knowledge of the lyrics that had underpinned their careers and their devotion and their sacrifices to a crumbling ideal. By the look and sound of him, he had to be part Chinese, but …

"Kill him!"

As the two stood frozen, Zheng reached for the Makarov he had placed on a nearby shelf. He pointed it at the man on the other side of Cono's battered body, and then at Cono's head.

I ask you, my comrades …

The crackle of breaking glass behind Cono reached his ears well before the sharp pieces spread in dazzling sparkles above his face, accompanied by an arcing airborne brick that rotated just slowly enough for the imprint of the manufacturer to be seen and registered by Cono's brain: "Xinjiang Export Factory Number 2." The brick landed on his left foot and bounced to the floor just as the security alarm of the Far East Merchants Bank began to screech and wail.

Cono was hunched over and staggering at the top of the grand exterior steps that led to the bank's massive front doors. Majestic stone columns rose on each side of him, dancing in the rotating blue lights of the three police cars that had driven over the curb and were now pointed toward the pillared entrance of the bank, like fish aimed into the mouth of a shark.

Cono's shirt was only partly buttoned over his vest, his uncinched pants were loose and drooping from his hips, and he was shivering as he tried to fasten his belt. Turning, he half-expected to see Zheng and his men leering at him from behind, but he was alone, like a sole pilgrim who had climbed arduous stairs to a remote temple at night. He knelt down to pull his shoes toward him and nearly collapsed; bolts of pain shot from his forehead to his shins.

The screaming of the bank's alarm nearly drowned out the commands being barked at him from below. Cono squinted and counted half a dozen Kazak policemen moving cautiously up the marble steps, guns trained on him. Their red-rimmed blue hats, wide as platters, appeared like strange low-flying birds hovering over the men's heads in the strobing light from the police cars.

Slowly, Cono raised his hands over his head, inhaling sharply as new channels of pain coursed through his neck and shoulders and down his arms.

"Don't move! Don't move!" the officer nearest him shouted in Russian.

"Kind sir," Cono spat and choked, "I am yours for the taking." Then he slumped forward onto the cold, smooth marble.

10

The bench in the police headquarters was hard, but at least Cono's backside hadn't been bludgeoned. All the pain came from his front, as if he were a slice of steak that had been grilled on one side only. Someone had given him old newspapers so he could wipe the blood from his swollen face. He tried to breathe through the heavy fog of cigarette smoke.

"You're lucky. We're not going to hold you. Get lost." The uniformed man who had spoken turned away before Cono could lift his aching eyes.

Cono rose with difficulty and hobbled outside. He looked up and down the block: the street was empty except for the trees loitering in the darkness, waving their branches in the light breeze, and a few dented squad cars parked on each side. He turned right and walked away from the light slanting out from the police headquarters. Every step caused a streak of pain to flash down his legs. He stumbled twice when his right foot refused to lift itself and scraped the pavement, but he compensated by lifting his thigh higher, despite the cramping of his muscles.

It was time to get out of Almaty.

Cono heard coughing from the other side of the street. He froze next to a tree and watched a stout man with a broad chest angle toward him at a slow, deliberate pace. Faintly illuminated by a street lamp, he looked like countless other middle-aged Kazak men Cono had seen on the streets of Almaty, dressed in gray dungarees, sturdy black shoes, a small visored cap, and a bulky woolen jacket that seemed unnecessary in the last days of summer.

The man coughed again as he approached the curb ahead of Cono, not looking his way.

"Hard to come by." The man spoke in barely audible Russian. He coughed again. "Freedom." He stepped onto the curb and continued to walk in the same direction as Cono. The Kazak man slowed his gait so Cono could catch up and hobble at his side. His eyes were quick, and they sized up Cono in a few glances, which Cono met with his own looks, as if the two of them were playing optical ping-pong.

"I know you are injured," the man said. "But we must hurry. The Bureau will get wind of this and be here in no time."

He reached into his coat. The motion immediately caused Cono to take three excruciating steps backward. A cap appeared in the man's hand. Only a cap. It was like the one the stout man was wearing.

"Put this on. This too." In his other hand he held out a dark-blue shirt spattered with beige spots, as if it had been worn while painting a house. It was large.

Cono had trouble lifting the cap to his head. The stranger grabbed it and planted it firmly, pulling it hard over Cono's lumpy brow. The limpness of Cono's arms made putting on the shirt a struggle too. The man took Cono's wrists and plunged them into the sleeves.

"Unfortunately your build doesn't let you blend in well here." The Kazak man began to walk more briskly, and looked at his watch. Cono marched despite the pain.

"You are brave," Cono whispered. "I thank you."

"We do not have time for that."

They reached the end of the long block of old buildings and turned right onto an avenue blinking with headlights. Just as they turned right again, into an alleyway, a Mercedes with a flashing red light on its dashboard sped up the avenue, followed by two black SUVs. The stranger stepped up the pace. The alley led to a lightless courtyard that Cono estimated was at the rear of the police headquarters. They had doubled back.

"Do you want to sit down?" the man asked.

"If I did, I might never get up," Cono responded. "I'll have to watch the show on my feet. I suppose that's why you brought us back here."

The man gave a partial nod. "Do you have any wounds that should be tended to immediately?"

Cono shook his head no. "My name is Cono. Yours?"

"I am Bulat. Miss Oksana calls me Teacher." Bulat pulled a plastic water bottle from his coat. "The ones who are tortured are always thirsty, if they live." He handed the bottle to Cono, whose eyes were fixed on the yellow rear windows of the headquarters. "Later comes the hunger." Bulat placed a paper-wrapped sandwich in Cono's other hand.

Cono sucked on the bottle in urgent gulps that left water dripping down his chin. "Why are you doing this, working with Miss Oksana?" he asked, taking Oksana as one of Katerina's professional names.

Bulat hesitated. "Imagine taking orders all your life from

people far away who think they own you." He sighed, as if that was all there was to his story.

"Taking orders ..." Cono prompted.

"We were all slaves to Moscow, to their system, their crazy ideas. And then, at last, when I am still not so old, when I still have a future, the Soviet hoax falls to pieces. Imagine the joy of that— of not being beneath that big thumb. Imagine no longer being a beetle, but being a man. Can you feel what I felt?" Bulat paused, waiting for Cono to finish another drink from the bottle.

Cono swallowed. "Go on."

"So you think you are a man. You are very happy. You think you are now a citizen of a free country. And then ..." Bulat sighed. "And then it all repeats. The local bosses of the ex-Soviet empire take over, the KGB gets a new name, the Bureau, but the faces stay the same, and the Politburo is now replaced by a few clans who think they own you and that all the riches of the country are theirs. You are a beetle again."

"You look like a strong fellow," Cono said. "Did you fight against the bosses?"

There was a deep rumbling in Bulat's chest that faded gradually.

"I guess you didn't."

"No, I remained a beetle. But my brother started to fight, with words, with a small pamphlet newspaper. They took him away. I visited him once in prison. What they had done to him ..." Bulat's words faded; Cono stepped closer. "That was the last time I saw him, a few years ago. I hope he is still alive. Or maybe that he is not."

Cono bowed his head slightly. "Does he have a family?"

"I sent them to the countryside. I lost my job after the visit to the prison, so I sent my family away too, to be safe, I hope. Two boys and two girls, and my wife. On a normal night, if there were any light, I'd show you pictures, but these are not normal times, and I cannot carry their photos with me anyway."

"I hope Miss Oksana pays you for your sacrifices."

"Yes, she does."

"What was your job?" Cono feebly held the sandwich to his lips and bit into it.

"I was a math teacher, and I liked it. In truth, I like to solve puzzles, like the one you have presented today, and like the others Miss Oksana poses." His speech became more formal, like an instructor giving a lecture. He looked at his watch again and peered at the window. "I also do it because I like to please Miss Oksana. She is exceptional, as you know. She compliments my work. She is strong, and reliable. Our situations are not so dissimilar. Both of us are stuck between high walls. And we share a dissatisfaction with her employer, which is ultimately my employer."

"My father was a math teacher, of sorts," Cono said. He drank again from the bottle. "Tell me about today's puzzle."

Bulat said he had been trailing Cono with some difficulty since the meeting at the swimming pool. "I would have liked to assist you when you were lying on the sidewalk outside the computer shop, but the exposure … I'm sure you understand," Bulat said. "In addition, your sickness wasn't at all expected."

"I suppose the brick floating through the window was from you." Cono's swollen mouth formed a partial smile. "The timing was good, except that my face would have preferred an earlier rescue." Cono's hand shook as he tried to place the sandwich in his mouth again. Bulat held Cono's forearm to steady it.

"The credit goes to an insider, a Kazak employee of the bank, who told us some weeks ago how that room is used. Blood in a bank is an unexpected finding, as I am sure you would appreciate." Bulat helped Cono position the sandwich for another bite. "I wish I could say we placed listening devices in that chamber after the employee's revelation, but the Americans have diplomatic sensitivities, as I understand. Yes, the brick was my idea. Methods are simple here in my country. Besides, I always wanted to play baseball, but never had the chance. I regret that I was instructed to wait until nightfall. But, as we see, you are still alive." Bulat placed the diminishing sandwich into Cono's mouth.

As Cono chewed, he asked why the police had released him. Bulat explained that he had paid a bribe, through a friend, with a message that the Far East Merchants Bank didn't want to pursue charges. After all, nothing was stolen. No reason to stir the pot. And, anyway, where was the proof that the shoeless man they had found on the front steps had anything to do with the tripped alarm?

"Yes," Bulat added, "the captain was suspicious about the paraphernalia in your clothing, but at least you had no weapon. And the bribe was generous for his rank. I think it likely that the money came from Miss Oksana herself, not from her employer. I suppose she thinks highly of you." Bulat's eyes swept across the yellow windows. "She may also want your help."

Shouts came from the headquarters, muffled by the windows. There was a gunshot. The sound echoed against the buildings surrounding the void of darkness in which Cono and Bulat were standing. Cono looked at Bulat's face, expecting some expression, perhaps a wince, but there was none, or it was simply too dark to see it. "The police captain?"

Bulat nodded. "I hope so. My friends say he's a stooge for the regime. I was pleased to have the opportunity to set him up tonight, if indeed he was a good mark and if he's gotten his due just now when the Bureau agents found out he'd released you. But one never knows for sure, not here. It's a statistical problem."

A siren's whine drizzled over the barrier of buildings and was joined by another siren.

"The chase for you begins in earnest," Bulat said. "Best to stay put here until they lose a little steam. And perhaps I can ask *you* a few questions. Why do you do this? And what is *this*?" Bulat tried to make out Cono's face in the dimness.

"What do you mean by *this*?" Cono's knees were wobbling, and he slowly lowered himself cross-legged on the weeds and propped his forearms on his thighs. Bulat sat with his haunches on his heels.

"This ..." Bulat seemed to be searching for the proper phrasing. "Miss Oksana says that you have had experiences in these matters, and yet you don't attach yourself to any government. She told me this to reassure me, of course. It all sounds very strange. Most people get tortured because of principles or resistance against a government. You ... you seem like a puzzle piece out of place."

"This time I just came to help a friend. I'm sure you have fought for a friend before."

"Surely I have," Bulat said after a long pause. "But friends are mostly family, even if somewhat removed."

"Your clan, you mean. You fight for your clan. I have no clan."

"You don't have a family?" For the first time there were quaverings in the upper frequencies of Bulat's voice that signaled suspicion or uneasiness.

"My parents died when I was young. I was on my own when I was about nine."

"So perhaps you were like those feral children we read

about, growing up with the animals in the jungle," Bulat said with amusement.

"A bit like that. I had to make up my own rules."

"And where are you from? What kind of rules are there where your people are from, before they all died?"

How could he answer this question? His childhood had been spent in Brazil, in a series of slum towns, each one poorer than the last. After that, he'd traveled alone for years—the Middle East, Europe, and Asia, especially China.

His father's father was from Tianjin. His father's mother was a half-Gypsy from the Mezzogiorno who had tried to convince people she was an Italian duchess. His mother's mother, Antonina, had been born in St. Petersburg and had escaped the revolution only because her aristocratic parents chose to shove their youngest offspring onto a boxcar headed to Siberia under the protection of fellow White Russians. The chaos chased them all the way to Harbin, China, and then a lucky few, among them Antonina, were freighted away to Yokohama.

After years of barely surviving in Japan, Antonina left on a ship bound for South America. On board her belly grew, and she gave birth to Cono's mother in the train station of the coastal city of Guayaquil, on a bench shrouded by the only blanket she had. Antonina never spoke of the father.

Cono's parents eventually met in São Paulo. His father, tall and reedy in his youth, seemed to diminish in size with each move the family made, always north—to Rio, Porto Seguro, then Salvador, Maracaipe, and finally, Fortaleza—as he chased transient trading scams and teaching assignments, just as his own father had done, and with even less success. One day Cono was startled to notice for the first time, as his father walked through the doorway, that the man no longer had shoulders; his neck seemed merely to merge with a thin chest attached to spindly arms. Thereafter he appeared to dwindle day by day.

But Cono's mother, Isadora, had a physical vitality that never left her until her death. She found waitress and dancing jobs in most towns along the way, but they became fewer and fewer, until the small family was playing an endgame of slum poverty on the outskirts of Fortaleza. At the time, Cono had no appreciation of how poor they were, except for the hunger that seized him and led him to learn how to fish and to steal.

Bulat nudged him. "Have you fallen asleep with your eyes open?"

Cono shrugged. "I am from nowhere, really. Everywhere and nowhere."

"You are teasing me, I think." Bulat frowned.

"I couldn't tease the man who saved me with a brick. Sorry, but there's no good answer to your question."

Bulat was silent for a while. "Tell me this," he said at last, "What is your religion? I am Muslim, a Kazak version of Muslim, like my father and his father and his father. What are you?"

"I don't know much about religions." Cono ran his fingers over his chest, mapping the most damaged portions by feel. "When I was young, someone asked me if I knew Jesus. I said, 'Isn't he the one who swam for forty days and forty nights in a river called the Ganges?' "

"Really?" Bulat was intrigued. "I didn't know he did that. Forty days and forty nights … But after all, he was a prophet. Tell me though, without a religion or a family, how do you know what to fight for? What principles?"

"Principles change as fast as an octopus ripples its colors, depending upon who makes up the principles," Cono said. "It's easier to fight for friends." He planted his knees between tufts of weeds and lifted his torso. He put his palms on the outsides of his thighs and arched backward, then rounded forward, repeatedly, breathing deeply as each movement pumped lymph from his damaged body back to his heart and onward to his kidneys, cleansing him from the inside.

Between arching movements he said, "And I find women to be better friends, more reliable, like you said of Miss Oksana."

Bulat seemed glad that the subject had returned to his employer. "Miss Oksana says you have been doing *this* for a long time, and yet I see you are so young."

Cono was not accustomed to talking about himself. It always led to dead ends thrown up by precaution. But Bulat had put himself on the line that night for Cono, and he was still at risk. Cono finished his abbreviated exercises and stretched out on the ground.

"This is the only life I've ever known," he said, "taking risks for food or friends or fun."

"Fun? Risks for fun?" Bulat clasped his hands. Cono heard the rubbing of keratin, like wet dust. "How strange."

"You're a man with an education," Cono replied. "I'm not, except for the languages that stuck on me, and what I picked up from wandering and living to the next day. The thing you call *this* began to grow like a snowball. Now it's what I do.

"Yesterday," Cono continued after a moment, "yesterday I killed four men." He heard Bulat's hand snapping off a few stems of weeds. Cono was relieved that the darkness made it difficult to read the expressions on Bulat's face. The darkness itself was a reprieve, and Cono felt his brain searching for sleep.

"Four men," Bulat repeated.

"Four men. The first three were of necessity, by reflex."

"And the fourth?"

"The fourth was of necessity, and yes, there was reflex, but there was also anger, and pleasure."

"Well," Bulat said, trying to maintain a whisper, "it seems your career is progressing." Cono searched for irony or contempt in Bulat's statement but couldn't find them. "You are violent, but you are honorable in your violence," Bulat added. "Let's just hope that you can control your killing … your killing reflex."

The comment disturbed Cono and jerked him out of drowsiness. He was worried that he had told Bulat too much. He stood up slowly, less shaky now, and walked toward the dim outline of a tree. His fingers jittered as he opened his pants. He urinated, recalling what little he could of the frenzy and confusion that had ensued when the brick came through the window: The bewilderment on the trio's faces as the alarm blared. Zheng with the Makarov, hesitating, calculating the repercussions of the sound of a gunshot and the discovery of a tortured body in the bank. A knife cutting Cono's limbs free.

He could have slaughtered all of them right there. Wresting the knife away from the hand that had cut him loose had been a simple matter, as was kicking the Makarov out of Zheng's grasp. He could have left corpses there on the marble floor, but the reflex said no, or said nothing. Maybe it was still under control. Or maybe it had been short-circuited by the torture.

He had let Zheng and his men scatter and had hobbled down the grand interior staircase and into the fresh air of night, guided by his grandmother Antonina's imperious voice in his head saying, "Lift your eyes, straighten your back, let fear and pain walk away like the turtles they are."

Cono finished relieving himself against the tree. His tongue involuntarily rubbed the sharp-edged strangeness of his newly broken tooth as he sat down next to Bulat.

"You said Miss Oksana wants my help. For what?"

"I will tell you what she *should* want your help for. But perhaps I would be speaking inappropriately."

"You saved my life. You can be inappropriate."

Bulat nodded. "I have friends in the Kazak military, middle rank," he began. "They say several generals have been buying new houses—much larger houses than their outside sources of income would normally support."

"You mean graft."

"That is what I wish to say."

"Big houses."

"Yes. A month ago, Major General Baldeev, head of Special Forces, moved his family into a fancy chalet on the road that goes up to Chimbulak, the ski resort, the road where all the rich people are moving. It's not just big houses. The generals are dining and whoring with military attachés from Beijing. I need not tell you who pays for these activities. And, in the past six months the Kitais have sent enough military attachés here to start their own army."

"Sounds like the usual diplomatic schmoozing," said Cono, now wishing he could examine Bulat's face.

"You don't know how vulnerable we are. If they bite the top, they can feast on everything." Bulat pawed his hand toward Cono and grasped the younger man's wrist. He was strong for a schoolteacher. "All this talk about Beijing going after Taiwan, a little island with nothing but computer factories—they have thousands more factories in China. It's a diversion. Just look at the map. Taiwan is out in the sea. Kazakhstan is a hundred times bigger and right next door, stretching all the way to Europe. 'We're neighbors,' the Kitais say all the time. Our leaders have knuckled under to Beijing and are giving long-term leases to Kitai farmers. Those lands are ours! But do you think the Kitais will ever give them back? And now they're building a railway and a *pipeline* to connect us, boasting about being even closer neighbors." Bulat checked the volume of his speech. "They want our oil fields, and now. If they waited until the spigot is wide open, when it's gushing in a few years, then the Americans would put up a fight. If Beijing waited until then, it would be too late."

Cono was silent, thinking about the faded globe of the world his grandmother had given him for his sixth birthday. It was an old globe, long out of date. Antonina would spin it and Cono would stop it with his finger. She would explain, with her knobby hand on his shoulder, what she knew about each country or sea his finger landed on. The seas always seemed simple, but the countries, rimmed in faint lines of varied pastels, always led Antonina to tell complicated stories of how this one or that one now had a different shape, which she would trace with a long, yellowed fingernail. Some of the countries were bigger, some were smaller, and some had disappeared altogether.

"Nana, what happens when a country disappears?" he had asked. "My dear grandson, when that happens, the good people have to leave." The hand left his shoulder. He looked back and saw Nana in a chair, covering her face with her hands. He had never seen her cry before.

Bulat slapped at Cono, hitting the shoulder that had been nicked by the bullet a day and a half earlier. "Hey, Mr. Cono, are you here, in Almaty?"

Cono snapped away from his memory. "The Kitais. You don't like them, I guess."

"Would you be happy if your homeland was about to be grabbed and milked by foreigners?"

"I don't have a homeland," Cono said. "Besides, it's all in one's mind."

Bulat released his grip and patted Cono's arm. "I feel sorry for you, my friend. A kite only flies if it's tethered."

Cono reached out into the blackness, breaking stalks of weeds and releasing their bitter scent. "And Miss Oksana wants help with ..."

"Unfortunately she is buying the American paranoia about the nuclear materials and the jihadis. It is nonsense. Travel across my country and you can find uranium in many places. Biological agents too. The Russians used us very well. What do the Americans think they can do? Seal up the whole country, like meat stuffed and tied in a horse's rectum? Because of that obsession, the blind Americans will wake up one day and find we are a province of China."

Cono perceived no obfuscation in Bulat's voice, and guessed that the teacher was unaware of the high-U specifics Katerina had talked about at the swimming pool. "And the note?" He left his question open and vague, like a psychiatrist's query.

"The note?" Bulat shifted his weight off his heels and sat on the ground.

"The note I received, in a fancy envelope, at my friend's apartment. Written like poetry, in Russian."

"It wasn't from me. I'm not a poet."

"Another Almaty mystery." Cono brushed his fingers over his face, feeling where the skin had split. So Bulat hadn't been the one to leave the envelope under Dimira's door. Cono had wanted somehow to extract from him an assurance of Dimira's safety.

The note must have been left by one of Katerina's other stringers. She was compartmentalizing, of course. It occurred to Cono that he and Katerina were mirror images of each other—she had her network of men, he had his carousel of women.

Cono saw the faint light of a digital watch as Bulat held it close to his face. The greenish glow accentuated the spokelike creases radiating from the corners of Bulat's eyes into the meatiness of his broad face.

"History is running very fast in my country," Bulat said. "Time to go."

11

"It's that one, the door next to the lathe shop. Up one flight, to the back, on the right." Bulat handed two keys on a string to Cono. "Miss Oksana said you would need a rest. That is my opinion also."

Cono scanned the two-story building in a row of nearly identical dwellings across the street. The lathe shop and the floor above it were dark; about half the windows left and right were lit, in shades of yellow and amber. It was a poor district, but tidy. A pack of five dogs, as variable in size and shape as humans, trotted in a veering path toward the two men; they sniffed and growled and nipped at one another, then broke into a lope down the street, with the smallest mutt in the lead.

"So, it's a safe house for the Americans," Cono said, combing Bulat's face with his gaze.

"I've never been here before." Bulat winked. "I should think that Miss Oksana has no desire to share you with the Americans, and that she maintains these humble quarters for emergencies. She has a budget that doesn't require signatures, I suppose. But on this matter, I am in the dark."

"Goodbye then. *Rakhmet.*" Cono said thanks in Kazak as their hands met and shook, tightly.

Bulat blinked several times as he looked into Cono's swollen eyes. "I don't know why," he said, "but I am glad you are still alive."

"Thanks to you, my friend. It's a heavy responsibility, having saved someone's life. You feel an allegiance because you saved them, but it's hard to know if you did the right thing."

The stocky man walked away, slow and steady, his hands in the pockets of his bulky jacket. When the faint glow of a solitary street lamp released him, he vanished.

Climbing the stairs to the apartment brought on the pangs of the torture, but Cono made his way up with the help of a drooping railing. Inside there was a bathroom with a tub and a high shower nozzle. Cono refused to look at himself in the corroded mirror as he undressed. He turned on the shower. There was a bar of soap, but he couldn't seem to keep it in his shaking hands. He sat down, hugging his knees with his arms as the hot water pummeled his head and broad shoulders. He was thirsty and lapped up the falling droplets, each of which he felt distinctly on his outstretched tongue. His arms released his knees and his legs partly straightened as he slid down into the tub. Each drop that hit his flesh was a piercing spear and yet also a warm kiss on the endless fields of inflamed neurons. Furrowed rows and rows, acres upon acres, a wide vast terrain that soaked in the rain, drop by drop …

In his sleep, amid the patter of raindrops, Cono did not hear the intruder's soft footsteps, not even the squeak of sneakers on the tiled floor near him. He didn't feel the shift of the spray as the nozzle was turned toward the wall next to the tub.

It was a brushing sensation running up his battered left thigh that jarred him out of sleep. He opened his eyes to find his left hand already clamping a throat, just as his rigid right hand was en route to strike the philtrum of a face. But the face was Katerina's. The traveling right hand deflected itself, touching her ear as she tried to duck. He saw her fist hooking toward his brow, but he didn't try to stop it. It landed on one of Zheng's wounds. His arm, the one still attached to her throat, acted by itself, crashing down until Katerina's face landed on his knees. She bit in, just above a kneecap. Cono raised his head quickly and glanced over the edge of the tub. No one else. He loosened his grip on Katerina's neck slightly. The pressure from her jaws slackened almost imperceptibly. Cono further relaxed his grip, and her jaws loosened a little bit. Less grip on her throat, less penetration of her teeth—less and less on both sides until Katerina's mouth was free of the bleeding skin and she was sucking in air.

Cono felt her breath on his wet thigh. "I guess you like it rough," she murmured.

"We don't know each other that well," Cono replied, folding his arms across his chest and lying back. "But I see you prefer chewing on legs. Doesn't that complicate intercourse?"

She wore a gray cotton sweat suit, as if she'd just been to the gym. It absorbed the drops of water bouncing off the wall. Katerina pulled herself up and away and sat on the edge of the bathtub, dripping.

"And this is a thank-you?" she asked.

"You interrupted my dreams." Cono's eyelashes batted away the water spattering his face.

"I'm sure they were nightmares anyway." She inspected Cono's body. "You look like the meat in Zelyony market."

"Just the price of waiting until nightfall. But I thank you nonetheless for arranging to save me from the dreariness of a bank. Bulat was very kind to me."

"Bulat?"

"Teacher, then."

"Teacher." Katerina smiled as if she had just gotten some inside joke. "I know him by another name. His real one is Slem, not uncommon for men of his generation. It stands for Stalin Lenin Engels Marx. He's always making up new names for himself— wouldn't you? But he is a worthy man."

"Yes, a worthy man. What about the high-U? The transfer to the jihadis is still tomorrow?"

Katerina let her hand fall onto Cono's leg where she had first touched him. She traced her hand in a line just below the tapering ends of the welts, lightly following his thigh, his hip, up the side of his chest, along the fold of his armpit and onto his shoulder. Her fingers briefly touched the back of his neck, and then she sat erect, perched on the tub's edge.

"We know it's set for ten in the morning," she said.

"Who is 'we'? The Americans or Minister Kurgat?"

Katerina was distracted. She pulled off her top and tossed it out the doorway of the bathroom. It was followed quickly by her bra. "'We' means 'I.' At last I've got a stringer on your nasty friend Timur Betov. The stringer says your friend looks a little roughed-up, but he's on the move again. He'll lead us to the uranium, the transfer, and we'll take care of it from there." She was unlacing her shoes with one hand and untying the drawstring at her waist with the other. She shed the sweatpants and her training underwear and stood naked above Cono. "So we don't need you after all."

Katerina knelt on the floor and leaned over the edge of the

tub to caress Cono's organ with her hands and mouth, her breasts swaying with her movements.

"Don't need you …" said Cono. "Is that *we*, or *I*, don't need you?"

Katerina was in the tub, straddling Cono's hips. Her head was bent down; her hands and eyes were fixed on his hardness. "Well, maybe I do … need you … right now." She was rocking back and forth over him, in short arcs that became longer and longer as she forced the entry and brought him deeper inside.

"And where will the high-U go if you intercept it?" Cono tried to keep his breathing regular, to make it seem that he didn't want her, that he hadn't wanted to seize her from the very first moment of their encounter at the pool in Barcelona.

"I will … decide, I will … I … I …" Katerina grabbed Cono's hair with both hands and slid her tongue into his beaten mouth. Her hips pivoted with athletic force. One hand left its grip on his hair and reached down to their locked organs. Cono felt a fingernail grazing his pubis as she thrummed her clitoris. Her body was vibrating, her knees pressed by the tub's walls into Cono's welt-striped abdomen. The cascade of water bouncing off the wall prevented Cono from breathing through his nose, and his swollen lips were sealed against Katerina's. In near-asphyxiation, Cono saw in his mind Bulat checking his watch. There had been an appointed time for this, and Cono had been delivered, with a wink. The fingernail dug deeper. Her other hand was behind his neck, pressing their faces together. She was a quivering vise. Cono had to breathe, and he felt his own wave surging, about to crest. Finally he grasped her buttocks and squeezed them and spread them. He wiggled a finger into her other orifice. Her strumming intensified. The pivoting of her hips became more forceful even as it slowed, until her body became entirely immobile, like a gun hammer that had been cocked back by a thumb. Cono pushed his finger in deeper. Katerina suddenly pulled her tongue out of Cono's mouth. The hammer fired and Katerina's body shuddered violently. Cono gasped for air.

"I, I, I …" Her yelling reverberated off the tiled walls. Cono's tongue chased her hardened nipples as his member was squeezed within her. He bucked several times, each time raising her higher, and then exploded, with his back arched and Katerina collapsing upon him. Her shuddering subsided. To each of her contractions his organ responded with another pulse. Her cheek fell against his chest. She reached back to push his hand away from her rear and breathed deeply; their bodies were now entirely relaxed, except for the contractions and pulsations stretching out in time as the warm water rained down. Cono wrapped his arms around her and stroked her back in long sweeps from the nape of her neck to the far end of the curvature of her muscular rump. And the words *we don't need you* echoed in his mind.

A few miles away, in a shed in the flats beyond the tilt of the city, as Katerina and Cono were being softly pelted by their private rain, a cow was grinding her teeth on hay and watching three humans with her big black placid eyes, occasionally blinking her long lashes.

"Where will we go when we've got it loaded?" The lanky young man glared at the big-boned woman cleaning an AK-47 with an oily rag, and ground his cigarette into the dirt.

"I will tell you, once we have it."

A second young man, wearing a rectangular skullcap, twisted uneasily on a stool. "So, we are expected to follow a woman, not a man, a woman who dresses like you, like a Russian, not even covering her head, and you won't tell us what happens after we go into the devil's mouth?"

"If Allah takes you, your family will be compensated," said the woman, raising her head, the dark slots of her eyes flashing at both of them. "You should be proud to be following the path of our fallen brothers."

The lanky young man jumped to his feet. "Men don't follow women. Especially one who treats us like sheep. My family has suffered. What will they get? Where is the uranium going? Do you know how much it is worth, Tamaris?"

Tamaris picked up a rifle magazine. *He already knows too much*, she thought. "We have all suffered." She slammed the magazine into its catch. "You know they tortured my brother to death. My brother who brought me under Allah's beneficent hand. We do this for our fallen brothers and sisters, and for the return of this land to Allah's law. Not for things you buy in the market."

The watchful cow swung her head low in search of more hay, nudging against the fresh mound that the lanky man had sat on. Her head retreated with the swat of his hand.

"Almaz, Azmat, you are brave men. Warriors chosen by Allah, bless his name. He will guide us." With a solemn voice Tamaris led the three of them in prayer. Almaz, the lanky one, cut it short. He sucked on another cigarette and blew the smoke toward the imperturbable eyes of the cow. "Why has the timetable been moved up?"

Tamaris glared at the two young men. "You know about the work of our brothers in Tashkent—the bombings last week. And the uprising in Osh. What you don't know is that eight of ours, three men and five of their wives, were taken in Taraz, before they could serve as Allah's sword here in the city." Tamaris stared at Almaz. "It was the *wives* who were wearing belts of explosives when they were caught, not the men. Women who have children, like me. Have *you* worn a belt? Do you have children who will be left behind, Almaz? Do you, Azmat?" She slashed each of them with her gaze. "And now there is worry about a crackdown on our group. They have eyes everywhere. We may not have another chance. Speed is our ally."

The serene cow emitted gas in a small explosion that startled all of them.

"Azmat, check your gun and the grenades—we may need them. But don't be too eager to use them. Almaz, your gun looks like you bury it in the dirt. And your skullcap will be a liability in the morning. You will be known as Omar on our mission. Azmat, you shall be Mansour. I will be known as Nargiz." She snapped a few more commands and then her voice became softer. "In the name of Allah, the most merciful, the most compassionate, let us pray for our fallen brothers and sisters."

Cono lifted cold chicken chunks and cashews to his mouth with chopsticks, hungrily surveying the take-out dishes Katerina had left for him. They were arrayed on the bare floor of the one-room apartment: glass noodles, Sichuan beef, broccoli in oyster sauce, almond jelly, the chicken and cashews, and three American-style fortune cookies. Between bites he reached into the little pile of his vest on the floor and pulled out a bubble pack of antibiotics. He swallowed two pills. The bullet nick on his shoulder was beginning to fester. The cuts on his face would probably be next, even though he had washed them well. No matter what position he assumed, he was in pain. The curative powers of sex were formidable, he knew, even better than meditation, but they had had little effect this night.

Katerina had left him there in the warm rain. Whatever else she had said as she stepped out of the tub and vanished was overshadowed by the words that kept repeating themselves. *We don't need you.*

Cono placed a nest of noodles in his mouth, thinking that in fact, no one really needed him. Intermittently there were emergencies—panicked requests for his talents that brought him into an amusing tumble, into a game that was fun to play. Maybe he was just another Bulat, with his puzzle-solving fascination. A lesser kind of Bulat, without a clan, without an anchor, whipped by the seas. Yet Cono loved those seas of uncertainty—and his freedom as he rode upon them.

And this mission *had* been for someone who needed him. With some luck, Xiao Li would be in China, in Xinjiang, by now. Maybe there was a son there after all, but a son by someone other than Cono. A child wouldn't keep her in China; Xiao Li would be eager to get back to Almaty as soon as she guessed the heat was off. She had her career here, and despite her flashes of tenderness and romanticism, she would not be able to sustain the patience required by parenthood.

Cono devoured the broccoli. While he chewed it he fiddled with the red paper that had wrapped the chopsticks. He read the small print at the end of the wrapper: "Please try your Nice Chinese Food with Chopsticks, traditional and typical of Chinese Glorious History and Culture." It made him think of Bulat and his worries about the Kitais, but then Cono's mind turned to the uranium, imagining what would play out at the quarry, if indeed that was where Timur held his radioactive treasure, as well as the oil companies' cash that he'd been squirreling away.

If Katerina chose to surprise Timur at the quarry with a gang from the American embassy, there was a high risk they would botch it. It was likely that the only operatives on the payroll who could speak Russian or Kazak well enough to confront the jihadis with a language other than guns were Katerina and her stringers. He doubted that she would sacrifice herself or her loyal network to such a visible mess.

It was more likely that Katerina would tip her hand to Minister Kurgat, whose monitoring of jihadis had probably provided the details on when the transfer was to take place. And yet this meant that Kurgat, too, was relying on Katerina and her band to track Timur, and that he didn't have sufficient reach to trail Timur through his own means. Maybe Kurgat's power was already diminishing, or perhaps Katerina had persuaded him that she could get the job done. If Katerina served up the high-U for Kurgat, what would he do with it? Hand it over to his rival, the premier? Or destroy it—destroy a bargaining chip that he could use against the premier and his other rival, Timur, whom he was trying so earnestly to exterminate? No, Kurgat would employ the precious high-U for his own purposes, and cut his own deal with the next wave of jihadis, or keep it in the bank for the future, as Timur seemed to have done.

And what if Timur brought his own toads to the quarry? Which of them would stand by him? The young and inept recruits to the Bureau? Timur, Cono knew, was a lone and hungry wolf who could trust no one. The new Genghis, but lacking the hordes. The perfect tool for Zheng and Beijing. No, Cono thought, Timur would arrive at the quarry without his thugs, none of whom had even been trusted to see his palace.

In each scenario Cono would be a highly unwelcome presence.

He finished off the food. Only the fortune cookies remained. He sat up and removed them from their plastic wrappers. Then, with difficulty, he began to juggle them. One by one they were caught by his mouth and were crunched and eaten, slips of paper and all. Cono didn't believe in fortunes.

The quarry. Anyone who intruded in search of the HEU without Timur's consent would trigger the explosives he had wired, if Timur's talk hadn't been just a ruse. If Timur had rigged the explosives only above ground, inside the building, and the high-U was below, in the tunnels, the consequences would be mild. But if the HEU was topside, or if it was below and the tunnels had also been rigged, the explosions would send up a radioactive cloud. The cloud would be hemmed in by the sparkling high mountains, just as the industrial smog of the city was barricaded by those peaks. The plume would rise and drift a little east or a little west, but mostly north, floating over the heart of the city until the radioactive specks lost their buoyancy and settled onto the flourishing trees, onto streets and houses and flaking apartments and shops and government buildings and schools and mosques and parks and casinos, and even onto the love nest above the General.

The radiation would not kill anyone for a long time, but the chaos would, in the trampling panic of an evacuating city. A city that thereafter would have only trees and rats and insects as inhabitants.

The quarry, the metal building there, the tunnels—they were Timur's palace. He would have rigged it all. Cono replayed in his mind the tones he had heard when Timur punched in numbers on the touch pad, activating the protection on the shed. Each of the six sounds was actually a unique double-tone. The oscillations of the tones played like vibrating colors in Cono's mind. He replayed them again and knew he could call them up if he went to the quarry in the morning. He could only hope that Timur had encoded the same numbers for each access point. Timur managed well despite his vodka slurping, but given the risks, he probably played it safe and had only one series of numbers to remember.

And what would his old friend do if he was caught there, outside the quarry, and was forced at gunpoint to stand aside as whatever group Katerina had favored battered down the gate? Timur would calculate, and walk a safe distance from the impending explosions. He would stroll away as the intruders blew themselves up and sent the deadly cloud into the air. Almaty was but a small patch of a vast land that would be his. The oil fields, the chief prize, were a thousand miles away and would be untainted. His Bureau network of minions was more reliable out there anyway, and in the provinces generally. A dead Almaty and emergency martial law would only strengthen Timur's hand. He could even use the obliteration of the infidel city to further curry favor with the jihadis, saying it was his own humble act for Allah, that he had proved his credentials as a brave warrior for the caliphate.

Of course, maybe Timur hadn't put the high-U in the quarry tunnels at all. In that case, if Cono went in the morning, there was no worry of a dirty explosion. He would merely have a jolly time hoping he didn't blow himself up while he searched for absent high-U. If he survived, and there was no HEU, he would lick his many wounds, hope that Katerina's plans for freedom had worked out, and finally leave Almaty. He would leave and go to … the choices were endless.

Cono rose to his feet, hobbled to the kitchen, and dropped the remains of his meal into a plastic bin. There was a large wooden cutting block on the countertop next to the sink. It was deeply scored and indented in the middle, where a small cash register receipt was lying. Cono picked it up. On one side in faint blue Cyrillic print it said, "Golden Dragon Restaurant." Cono turned it over. Written in the same careful cursive lettering that had been on the note left beneath Dimira's door, it said, "We are always getting wet together."

Cono smiled and tore it into small pieces, which he poked into the trash bin. Katerina was as much an enigma to him as he was to her.

He found a folded blanket in a corner of the otherwise bare room and spread it out on the wooden floor. He slowly dressed himself, knowing that after a brief sleep, the simple motions of putting on clothes in the morning would be a prolonged agony. He switched off the light and reached in the dark for the miniature alarm clock in his vest. It lit up and he set it for 4 a.m. Without the alarm, there was a danger that his brain and body would bundle him in rehabilitating sleep until it was too late. In these circumstances sleep could take him down for twenty hours at a stretch, but this was not the night for it. He was going to the quarry in the morning, in time to beat the parade, he hoped. All his reasoning and second-guessing about whether to go there were buried, just as he would be buried by sleep. He was going to the quarry because his naked impulses said so, and because for his entire rootless and unmolded life he had always relied upon those impulses.

Slumber pulled him down as soon as he put the clock on the floor next to his ear, and the dreams crept in as his muscles relaxed and his breathing became slow and deep.

The crumpled old woman beckons strollers on the sidewalk. For a little money they can weigh themselves on her scale. Xiao Li takes her hand out of Cono's and puts money into the woman's palm, then steps out of her high heels and onto the scale. Barefoot Xiao Li chatters with the woman, laughs with her, thanks her, and skips away like a gazelle.

She is halted by the sound of a violin, by the sight of a long-haired man with no legs. His straight torso stands on the concrete, a violin beneath his chin. Pant legs are curled up like jelly rolls. The stroking of the bow. The troubled eyes of Xiao Li. The mournful melody. Xiao Li sits down next to the legless man. Cono sits at her side. People ignore the scrap of paper folded into a cup to receive coins. Xiao Li sings, without words, matching the mournful cries of the rosined horsehair on the wire strings. Feet shuffle by. Cono is lifted. Lifted by the vibration of the strings, by the gliding voice of Xiao Li. The strings are singing their top notes and Xiao Li's voice rises and soars; Cono is flying on wings whose feathers are buffeted by every lifting puff. The sounds are pushing him aloft higher and higher.

The rising becomes sinking. Xiao Li's voice is hovering in an extended cry that matches the last union of strings, rosin, hair. The bow is taking a long, vibrating ride across the low string. Cono feels the struggling of the wings as he is pulled down and down. He lands. The wings fold themselves. His eyes veer toward the rolled pant legs. There are tears on Xiao Li's cheeks, tears of joy or tears of tenderness or tears of pain. The legless man puts his violin aside. He leans to kiss Xiao Li on the cheek, and he is smiling, as if in love.

12

The scream of the alarm clock sent Cono's body jack-knifing into the air. Then the searing pain across his abdominal muscles and chest forced him to fall to his side in a fetal ball, shaking, struggling against the feeling that his body wouldn't work, that he couldn't possibly even stand up. He tried to make out something, anything, in the darkness, but his eyes closed in failure. He felt himself surrendering again, to the sweetness of Xiao Li's face, to the gliding lift of tones from the vibrating wire strings of his dream. *Wire. The cutting wire. The blood. The hairy legs.*

Cono groped for the alarm and put it against his face. The fumbling pressure of his fingers made it light up. At last there was something his eyes could register, but the numbers were blurred. He willed himself to bring them into focus, but the numbers kept dancing.

A sound from outdoors penetrated Cono's brain and gave him something to latch onto. It was a bird, with a song that was part whistle and part coo. He picked up the alarm again and smacked its sharp edge against the split swellings on his brow, trying to drag himself to consciousness. He pounded a fist on the wound in his shoulder and finally winced. He pounded it again, fighting the tide, swimming as hard as he could. The birdsong came again. Cono listened, then tried to imitate it. He found he couldn't purse his damaged lips, but he could mimic the whistle by forcing air through the gap between his tongue and front teeth. He made a coo come from a deeper place, far down his throat. Whistle and coo, whistle and coo. The vibrations of the newfound sound traveled through him, coaxing him away from sleep.

He was almost fully awake now, vaguely amused that he had been resuscitated by a lonely bird seeking a mate in the predawn hours.

He put the clock to his face again, and the numbers were now legible, but he was still struggling to reconstruct what must happen this day, a day that he knew would be plagued by the shortness of his sleep and by his battered body, which in its healing promised only more pain. A dread crept in, a fear that his mind would be crippled by the paucity of rest. He regretted not having gone straight to the quarry the night before to get it all over and done with, but given his physical state, no, he couldn't have managed it.

Cono started to crawl, taking account of the compromises demanded by each of his damaged muscles. He crawled until he found a window that might help him rise to his feet. His fingers grasped the sill, and the tension in his arms allowed him to pull one leg up under himself, then the other, until he was crouching. He pressed and pushed, again and again, and gradually made it to his feet.

He aimed his body toward where he remembered the kitchen was, and made it there, wavering with every step. He searched for a light switch, but decided it was too risky.

The jolts of pain seemed to diminish with each movement. He found the faucet in the little kitchen and slurped from it. He splashed water on his face; it stung at first, but then that sensation also disappeared. He felt his way out of the kitchen and traced the walls until he got to the apartment's locked door. He realized he that didn't have the keys, which he'd left in the bathroom before he slept. Surely Katerina would have taken them, and if so, was he locked in? He tested the two bolts; the locks released.

In the stairwell there was dim light from below. He saw no other way out of the building. He wondered whether Bulat, or "Slem," or one of Katerina's other stringers was watching for him, but he had no choice other than to go out the way he came in. Why was he worried about being trailed by one of Katerina's men, anyway? She and Bulat had rescued him from Zheng and his thugs. The thought of Zheng was like electricity in his brain. The past day's events and the layout of what he had to do at the quarry came back sharply, but then started to blur. Concentration, he needed concentration. *I should have meditated before falling asleep.*

Cono steadied himself with the loose railing, walked down to the ground floor, cracked open the door, and crawled out on all fours, taking care to let the door close softly. He continued his crawling for a full block along the row of small shops, surprising three rats in a garbage pile along the way. He stood up only after he'd crawled, *just like a rat,* he thought, to the next street corner. This time it was easier to get to his feet.

Cono dodged through the shadows. The streets were empty; there was little chance that a taxi was going to appear. But even at this hour there would be drivers at the Cactus, waiting for the last straggling men and women, hunters and hunted, trying to transact their business.

There was only one car on the curved driveway leading back around the Hotel Ratar to the Cactus, and it was parked just where Timur and his thugs had taken Xiao Li hostage. A stubby Russian man was sitting on the trunk of the car, smoking, waiting for passengers. Cono hustled against the pain in his thighs to get to him before an approaching couple could. He was lucky—they stopped to negotiate a price as the woman fondled the man's zipper.

Cono climbed into the car. The driver initially challenged his destination, up toward the mountains; Cono didn't mention the quarry, only saying he wanted to go about three miles past the power plant.

"Why do you want to go there?" the driver asked as he wheeled away from the Cactus.

"I love the stars. You can't see them through the haze down here. I have to go up higher, above it all, and before the sun says hello." For a few seconds Cono considered redirecting the driver to pass first by Dimira's apartment, which wasn't so far away; he wanted some certainty that she was fine. He quickly dismissed the idea. What would he find out, anyway? And if he tried to do anything more, like knocking on her door at 4:30 in the morning, he might only be putting her in further danger. And even if he did find her safe and sound, he still would have no assurance that Xiao Li had made it out of the country. *And Zheng was out there trying to track her down.* Cono grimaced. *I should have taken Xiao Li straight to Bishkek myself.*

"Don't you want a woman?" the driver asked. "I can get you a good one. Not so expensive. For the price of a few drinks, maybe a little more."

"Sorry, just the stars for me tonight." Cono sat so that his face was not visible in the rear-view mirror. "Queen Cassiopeia is up there waiting for me. She's for free. It's a long drive. I'll pay you double, and the price of a hooker."

"Stars," the driver said. "You must be a fucking astronomer."

Timur ripped the bandage off his forehead and took a slug of vodka to make himself alert. He called the Bureau's telecom surveillance desk from the fixed line of the apartment where he sat, not far from the barracks where Cono had deposited him thirty-two hours earlier. Timur snapped at the officer on the phone, demanding the latest on the series of calls they had been intercepting between the Kitai and the woman named Oksana. He listened for two minutes, then put the phone down, smiled, and grunted with disgust. "Humans."

He had been seated in the same padded lounge chair since midnight, sleeping only intermittently. He hated sleep; it was a waste of time. Besides, he had plenty to think about. He didn't know what to expect from the jihadis. He'd be doing the deal alone—no backups, no leaks. But if it went right, he might not need the Kitais to force the coup. To install himself. To be at the top at last. *Genghis.* He liked the name Cono had given him. Timur sloshed some vodka from his hip flask onto the floor. "Here's to you, Cono, brother, you naïve bastard." He took another gulp and lit a cigarette. When he'd finished the smoke and snubbed it out he took a cell phone from the side table and removed the battery before he put it in his coat pocket. There was more than one party who might be interested in tracking his movements through the mobile network.

Fifteen minutes later Timur was driving a dented Daihatsu pickup truck along empty Al Farabi Street, where the city surrendered to the slope of the foothills, heading west toward the road that would take him up to the quarry. Beneath his armpit he felt the nudge of the CZ 75 that had replaced the lost Makarov. He looked at his watch: 5:15. Yes, he was a few hours early. Why not? He knew he wasn't going to sleep anymore. He had to move some things out of the tunnels, rearrange some of his treasures. And the quarry was more a home to him than anywhere else. *My handiwork*, he thought with a flush of pride.

In the darkness several blocks behind Timur's pickup truck, another vehicle chugged along with its lights off; it was an old Lada sedan, a Zhiguli 2103, one of the last in Almaty, a sturdy vestige of the crumbled Soviet empire.

The stars were bright in the black sky as Cono lifted himself to the top of the fence adjoining the locked gate at the quarry. He had to flatten a curlicue of razor wire before he could slide his legs down the other side of the fence. One foot felt the top of a gate hinge, which supported him for a moment, and then he jumped free. But his frail legs couldn't absorb the landing and his rear end hit the ground.

He got up slowly and gazed northeast, beyond the gaping quarry pit and down toward the slanting grid of streetlights in the city below. He looked up to Cassiopeia and from her he traced with his eyes the converging arches of Andromeda. Perseus was next to her, holding the head of Medusa at a safe distance.

He heard no sounds from the building before him. The padlock on the high aluminum riser at the front was made of hardened steel as thick as two fingers. It would be a tough job for his cutting wire. Guided by the starlight, he edged around the side of the building to look for another entrance and found a small door of corrugated metal. Its padlock was much smaller. Cono reached into his vest for the looped alloy wire; one of the rings still had the feel of dried blood. He wrapped the wire around the lock and tugged back and forth. Metal rasped against metal in a soft, fast, rhythmic whine. The lock snapped free.

Cono wedged the door open just enough to enter the pitch-black vaulted space, which smelled of rust and machine grease. He waved his hand along the crusty interior wall until he found a switch, then hesitated. He didn't have a flashlight; what good would it be anyway, in a minefield like this? And after all, wasn't he awake in this hampering pre-dawn so that he could do his work before the crowd arrived? He tripped the light switch. Three incandescent bulbs beneath tin umbrellas glowed, suspended from a high I-beam running the length of the cavernous structure.

The interior shed where Cono and Timur had locked up Zheng's cash was just before him, to the right, and beyond it was a stack of cardboard boxes labeled "Dynobel Sweden," with crude stencils of an explosion and exclamation marks. Against the wall to the left was a stack of ovoid tanks, probably acetylene, Cono judged by the tubing and welding mask hanging from them. Huddled near the wall was a squad of upright gas cylinders, and parked askew next to them was a blasting machine whose drilling armature resembled an enormous probing finger.

Farther on was the forklift with two rigid arms raised high; beyond it was the rusting framework of flywheels. Between the forklift and the flywheels was the double cellar door that had caught Timur's wary gaze for a moment. On the far wall of the building were metal lockers with faded white lightning bolts painted on them. Cono could just make out the nearly vanished Russian lettering: "Danger! High Voltage!" In the far corner, diagonally across from where Cono stood, was a stairway that ascended to an enclosed platform supported by struts of angle iron.

Cono cautiously made his way to the left, scanning the floor for trip wires. Instead of going directly to the cellar doors he knew he would have to enter in search of the high-U, he went to the stairs at the far corner and climbed up to the small room that rested on stilts. Inside was a control panel with large red and black buttons and gauges that reminded him of the cockpit of an old freighter that had once taken him to the Yemeni port of Aden. The window next to the chair was protected by wire meshwork and covered with a film of dust. Cono looked out the window; below was a giant funnel-shaped bin formed by steel flanges. Full of rocks bigger than watermelons, the bin was tilted toward the mouth of a crusher, draped with heavy chains to prevent debris from being expelled from the force of the grinding. "It all makes for easy burials," Timur had said.

From this vantage point, Cono could see the starlit outlines of conveyor ramps radiating from the chute of the main crusher; without this elevation it hadn't been possible to see the full depth and expanse of the quarry crater two days earlier, when he and Timur had come. *Two days ago?* Cono thought his mind was blanking out, misleading him, so he started to retrace his steps since Xiao Li's first phone call. He cringed when his memory came to the bank and Zheng and his men. *Yesterday?* Time and events seemed to have accelerated. He tried to concentrate, but the gaps in his recall screamed out at him. His thoughts jumbled and scattered. Where was Xiao Li? *Home with her vile mother and her son. No she wasn't. She was dancing on a balcony. Singing over the edge …*

Cono banged his head against the wall of the cockpit and shook away Xiao Li and the confusion. He propped his forehead against the window and stared at the conveyor ramps that distributed the crusher's feast, delivering the fragments to sifters and onward to other ramps. Each conveyor was angled upward and supported by two tall legs, like a praying mantis, and each in its turn seemed to be preying on the tail of the next and the next until the last ramps led to piles of grit and gravel so far away they were just faint smudges at the edge of the crater.

He moved his gaze to the control panel and turned on the switch labeled "Main Crusher." The lights within the building dimmed for two seconds, then recovered as the pair of heavy wheels outside slowly came up to speed. Cono pushed several buttons at the top of the console, and the lights in the building dimmed again. From the wide expanse of the quarry came whines and moans like cats in heat as the conveyor belts started to move. Cono pushed a small lever marked "Main Crusher Feed." The pile of rocks in the bin moved forward in slow pulses, as if they rested on the back of a giant who was shrugging his shoulders. After three pulses, a mound of rocks at the narrow end of the bin fell into the draped chains.

The crusher roared for a few seconds, followed by thwacking sounds and growls, then just a loud hum. Cono saw the first of the ground-up rocks ascending the primary conveyor belt, making their way to the head of the nearest praying mantis. At the head he saw them fall into a subsidiary crusher joined to more ramps ready to carry the discharge of smaller fragments to the awaiting sieves and follow-on conveyors sprawling outward from the hub.

Cono's view was toward the east. He was disturbed by the indistinct hint of lilac in the sky above the highest tier of the quarry. Soon it would be daylight. And the noise? The quarry was far enough into the middle of nowhere that there was little risk, but Cono shut off all the controls anyway. The humming and whining faded. He checked his watch, focusing intently: 5:20. His mind had been cleared by the onslaught of sounds and the whirring rhythms from the machines. He left the cockpit and went down the stairs. Near their base he examined a door adjoining the wide ledge on which the crusher's bin was mounted. The door had no wires, no sensors, only two deadbolts. He slid them aside and opened the door. From here it was only a few paces to the crusher's bin. If the high-U was down below in the tunnels Timur had mentioned, he'd have to haul it back this way. He wondered how it was packaged, if it was here at all, and how much weight he'd have to carry with his weakened muscles.

He turned toward the horizontal double-doors set in the ground next to the skeleton of rusting flywheels. Mounted on the concrete rim around the doors was a digital touch pad identical to the one Timur had keyed his passcode into.

On the drive up from the city, Cono had tried to replay the tones of the touch pad in his mind. Some had sounded true, others … he wasn't sure of. His lack of sleep made them hard to catch, flitting away like sparrows.

He flipped open the metal lid and focused on the keypad, trying to make the array of buttons make sense in his mind. His stooped body was swaying. *Sit down. Concentrate. Pretend you are surfing.*

He knelt, his hand hovering over the buttons. He would have to touch each number on the keypad to see which tones corresponded to which number. Could Timur have wired it to blow up if the code was entered incorrectly? Cono balked. This was Timur's private fortress. No one else was allowed entry, so a wrong code would be deserving of retribution. But Timur must be well aware of his own sloppiness. No, he wouldn't have risked the embarrassment of blowing himself up.

Cono took a deep breath and exhaled. He tapped on the numbers in order; each one emitted a distinct two-frequency combination that was gratifying, pleasing in such a grim space. He got through them all. All was quiet. He took a deep breath again; now he was clearly remembering the tone sequence of the code, as clearly as he remembered the patterns on his mother's only dress.

He replayed the code in his mind again, sound by sound, and as each sound rang in his memory, he pushed its corresponding number on the keypad. Six tones, then a click.

Cono stood up and bent over the double door. He hesitated, then put his fingers around the handle. He twisted it and pulled the door up, easing it until it lay to the side. He opened the other door just as carefully.

Beneath the open doors was square pit a little more than a yard deep. A box mounted on one of the concrete walls lining the pit was connected to wires that linked a series of plastique charges molded into holes gouged out of the concrete. By the pallid yellow-gray of the molded charge ribbons, the color of a dead man's face, Cono knew it was Cold War-era Semtex, manufactured by the thousands of tons in the former Soviet bloc. Production was now tightly controlled and minuscule, but that didn't really matter, because the material had a shelf life of twenty years or more and there was plenty of it dispersed around the world. He'd used it himself. Semtex, PE4, C-4, Plastrite, Netrolit, Spring Korper, Rowanex—Cono felt slightly shameful about his familiarity with plastics, and yet seeing them here, even so amateurishly arranged, gave him a perverse comfort.

There was enough plastique lining the pit to make the whole building disappear, even without help from the nearby stacks of boxed dynamite. Any intruder trying to force his way into the heart of Timur's palace would be vaporized. So where was the heart of the sanctuary, which would have to survive such an explosion? In the left wall of the pit was an arched hole with a ladder descending into darkness.

Cono got on his hands and knees, eased himself backward into the hole, and began stepping down the ladder. After a dozen rungs he felt something brushing against his back. He froze. The brushing stopped.

"How convenient," he said out loud.

Slowly, he reached back and felt a string between his shoulder blades. He pulled it and a bulb lit up above his head. He felt a smile stretching his swollen face. *Timur must be afraid of the dark.*

13

The temperature dropped as he climbed deeper into the heart of Timur's hideout, and Cono became aware of a faint, unpleasant smell. Something metallic, perhaps. Or something rotting. When his feet hit the ground, he turned to see the dim outlines of a chamber as big as a modest living room, but with a ceiling of granite so low that it would graze his head if he stood all the way up.

Bolted into one of the rock walls were two chains ending in steel cuffs. Next to the chains was a military cot with a blanket heaped on it, and beside the cot a pile of decaying melon rinds, gnawed mutton ribs, crumpled wax paper, and empty bottles of Moskovskaya vodka. Lying on the ground near the bottles was a trophy. Cono picked it up. It was heavy, with the figure of a man delivering a karate kick atop a block of beveled marble. Cono read the Russian words engraved on it: "Timur Betov. Champion. High School Middleweight Division, Karate. Soviet Republic of Kazakhstan." When he looked again at the kicking figure, he noticed that it was encrusted with dried blood. He let the prize drop onto the hard dirt at his feet.

There was a pile of clothes in a corner on the other side of the chamber. Cono probed it with his foot. Women's clothes: summer dresses, bras, panties. A few bracelets partly buried in the dust.

A wave of revulsion coursed through Cono. He shook it off.

Against the wall were layers of heavy canvas draped over a stack of suitcases. Cono tugged at the fabric, gradually exposing the four cases of money Zheng had delivered and at least a dozen others. Timur must have brought Zheng's cases down from the shed earlier in the day, despite his injuries from the car wreck. Cono lifted three of the other cases. They were all heavy.

From a corner of the chamber a tunnel telescoped away into the shadows. Cono entered it, reaching into the blackness until he found a string and switched on a light. Three yards in, a military-issue tarp with bricks on top of it covered a row of circular shapes. Cono tossed the bricks aside and pulled up the tarp. Six canisters were lined up along the jagged wall. Each was about three feet high, resembling a small oil drum painted yellow, and had protruding circular ribs around the midsection for added strength. With a closer look, Cono could see on several of the canisters the faint outlines of triangular radiation symbols that had been painted over.

He crouched forward and lifted the nearest one. Holding it in his arms, he backed out of the tunnel and eased it onto the floor of the main chamber, running his finger around the top rim and wiping away a layer of fine dust. The rim was encircled by a metal band secured by a hinged clamp. The clamp had a loop of narrow-gauge wire running through it, the ends of which were pressed into a lead seal. Cono pulled on the clamp, severing the wire. He pried away the metal band and started to lift away the top. But he stopped. Closing his eyes, he tried to reassemble the information from his recent Internet searches:

> HEU poses no immediate radiation threat to the
> handler, but inhaled or ingested particles of
> metal or metal oxide, depending on quantity and
> purity, can be lethal.

He took off his shirt and tied it around his head so his mouth and nose were covered, then pulled a canvas off the stack of money cases and wrapped it around his right hand, like a mitt. With his left hand he slowly raised the lid of the canister. Under it was a disk of fiberboard. Beneath the fiberboard, wood shavings. *Very high tech.* Cono slowly massaged the shavings with his mitted hand and pressed downward. One fingertip hit something solid. Gradually he felt the contours of the object and got his hand around it. He was panting as it emerged. The ingot was surprisingly heavy, like a barbell that weighed twice what he'd guess based on size. It was about a foot long and hexagonal in cross-section; it wasn't painted, yet it didn't look like metal—there was no shine to it. It had the color of an old bruise.

> HEU as a metal or metal alloy, when exposed to
> air over time, forms a skin of oxidation that
> has a black or purple appearance.

Cono put the ingot back in the canister. He looked at his watch: 5:40. He replaced the fiberboard, put the circular band around the lid, and clamped it shut. Then he lifted the canister, resting it against his hip. He guessed it weighed about 50 pounds, at least half of it due to the ingot. Six ingots at about 30 pounds each: 180 pounds of HEU.

> Even with primitive engineering capabilities a
> simple gun-and-target configuration like that

in Hiroshima's Little Boy can be constructed
with as few as 70 pounds of 90% enriched ura-
nium-235.

Cono was sweating under the weight as his struggling brain did the division. *Enough for two and a half devices. How much was Timur planning to trade to the jihadis?* He saw Katerina's angry face as she smashed her hand against the water, the child divers playing in the far end of the pool.

He held onto the ladder with his free hand, squeezing upward through the hole. At the top he readjusted the load and carried it out of the pit toward the door next to the stairs to the cockpit. Only then did he let it drop. As he sucked for air through the shirt protecting his nose and mouth, he realized he didn't need it anymore. He put the shirt back on and climbed the stairs to the control room.

Soon the belts were whining again, and the engine of the main crusher was humming. Cono returned to ground level, hoisted the canister, and carried it through the door leading to the rock-filled receiving bin. At the edge of the great tilted funnel he raised the container over his head and looked up at the fading punctures in the heavens that were the stars. With a loud grunt he heaved the canister into the curtain of chains guarding the mouth of the crusher.

The gobbling sound was different this time. First a series of clunks, then a searing train of screams accompanied by sparks dancing behind the chains. The screams became shorter and shorter until the steady hungry hum resumed. In less than a minute, more screams came from the subsidiary crushers, but at a higher pitch, and they ended almost as soon as Cono heard them.

He went back up to the cockpit and pressed the feed lever until the crusher was chewing furiously on hunks of ancient earth that would join and mix with distributed bits of the uranium that had been so painstakingly extracted and refined. "Dust to dust," Cono said out loud.

Enough. He shut off the crusher feed, keeping the other machinery running, and went back down to the hole to get another canister.

He could see his task clearly now, and with any luck he'd be well out of the quarry before any of the other party guests arrived. Let them thrash it out among themselves, fight over who betrayed whom or didn't come through. He was done with corrupt Almaty. Done with Timur and his deadly machinations, done with Katerina working on behalf of the greedy Americans, done with Zheng working on behalf of the greedy Chinese. He was done. Thirty more minutes and he'd be out of here forever.

He had just climbed out of the pit with his second load when he saw a shadow at the door leading to the crusher. He shifted the canister to hold it in front of him with both hands, his fingers gripping the raised ribs in the middle. Then, eyes steady on the door, he crabbed sideways until the suspended armature of the drilling machine allowed him some protection from whoever might be outside.

"Welcome to the palace, brother." Timur strode through the doorway with a pistol in hand.

Cono held the canister like a shield, uncomfortably aware of the weight taxing his arms and back. "The last time I saw you, my friend," he said, moving farther to the left, "I had just saved your life. So you've come to thank me?"

"Enough of your bullshit, Cono." Timur swept his arm from one side of the hanging armature to the other, searching for a clear shot. "Now you're working for the jihadis? Who the fuck *are* you working for? The Americans? Ah, yes, for the Americans."

"Brother, there are times when one must work for charity, harvest some karma. You could use some yourself." Cono managed a smile despite the tension throughout his body from holding the canister.

"Fuck the karma. The tart was just a trick, right? An excuse to get you here, get you into my pants, fuck up my plans."

"I came to help her. That's all. It's you who made me stay." Cono adjusted his stance to each slight angling of the gun barrel. The container was leaden in his arms.

Timur registered his former friend's exhaustion. He'd seen Cono in only two modes over the years since they'd met: focused, speedy, and lethal; and laughing, boisterous, joking around. This was a new mode: tired. Tired, uncertain, and off his game.

Timur smiled. *Welcome to the real world.*

"Put it down, swifty. No need to fight anymore. The tart is finished. Your Ukrainian bitch turned her over to the Kitai, along with some other local girl. We've been listening in. The deal's been brewing for a few days. The bitch must have been very happy when you sprung your whore; you finally gave her something to trade. The Kitai made her big promises. Protection, family, yeah, yeah. She must be desperate. Like you right about now."

Cono's hold on the canister weakened for an instant, but a surge of disgust brought strength back to his arms. "The Chinese man is making promises to many people," he said, raising his voice above the hum of the crusher. "I'm glad I was able to make him see you as you are, an able puppet."

Timur smiled, and as he did so Cono saw the final tension of his finger on the trigger. Cono took a step back, preparing to dive to the side, but before he could dodge, a loud clap resounded within the steel-sheeted confines of the building. The force from the canister in front of his chest slammed Cono backward, but he kept his footing and felt no penetration. The bullet must have hit the ingot inside.

There was a flash on the drilling armature as another bullet ricocheted near Cono's ear. Then another clap and a whizzing sound on the other side of his head. Cono lunged out from behind the drilling machine and hurled the canister at Timur. A shot went off as Timur was hit just below the chin by the container and fell backward.

Timur was down, firing off two wild shots as Cono came toward him. But now, a few steps away, a glance at Timur's eyes told Cono his aim was confident this time. Cono dove back behind the drilling machine. The shot hit Cono's shoe, twisting his foot in midair. Cono rolled and hit the base of one of the standing gas cylinders. Timur was on his feet now, walking slowly around the driller.

"You were such a good friend," Timur said. "All your talk about shutting two eyes. And all the while you were just working for the Americans. Cultivating me, as they say. Here, get your rocks off on this."

Cono was already scrambling on all fours when the bullet grazed his left thigh. He skittered behind the troop of cylinders before the next two shots pinged off the steel casings; he wedged into a small space between them, near the wall. Hidden behind the cylinders, Cono could make out Timur's movements through the narrow gaps.

"So, admit it," Timur barked.

Cono remained silent.

"And your Kitai whore. She sure is good at sucking dick. You hear that, Cono? Even better than Gula and Petra. Remember them, Cono? Yes, sure you do. Back in the good times. You must have been working on me even then. Your American friends spotted me as a star and sent you my way. Such a friendly, fun guy you were." The gun appeared in another gap between the cylinders as Timur sidestepped slowly.

"Hey, Cono, your tart wasn't as good as the ones I bring here. You saw the leashes downstairs, I'm sure. They suck better when they know they're slaves, when they hear the machines."

Cono heard Timur's steps advancing around the barrier of cylinders.

"Are you keeping two eyes shut now, Cono? You're a connoisseur. You should try it that way some time. Chain your favorite tart in a cave. Feed her every three days. Make her hungry for you. Maybe you've done it already. Friends. Brothers. Peas in a pod. Fruits in the same crate."

Timur had almost made it to the edge of the group of cylinders, to the space against the wall that Cono had crawled through.

"Come on out. I'd like to offer a talented friend like you a high position in my kingdom. Minister of Pimps would suit you."

Cono was on his rump, his feet poised against the two cylinders nearest the wall. A slice of Timur's face suddenly appeared between the tops of the cylinders. Cono slammed his feet against the heavy steel. The cylinders crashed against Timur, one of them momentarily pinning him to the ground. Cono pounced. His forearm smashed into the downed man's larynx as the gun in Timur's hand exploded with a stray shot. Timur tried to twist away, but was trapped on both sides by the cylinders. Cono wrenched the pistol from him, crammed the gun muzzle into his mouth, and pressed hard until Timur was gagging.

"Hear this while you're alive," Cono said. "I am a free man. No one owns me. Not the Americans, not the Kitais, not the jihadis, not you." Timur was writhing, choking on the barrel, trying to breathe. One hand was grasping for Cono's throat; the other was trying to maneuver so he could extract the gun wedged into his belt.

Cono thought of Zheng and the Makarov he had forced into Cono's mouth. "Brother, how did it come to this?" He pushed the barrel deeper, until Timur convulsed again and again and passed out, oozing vomit from his mouth. Cono kept the gun planted between Timur's lips as he reached beneath Timur's back and withdrew the second gun. In this position Cono's face was against Timur's ear, as if they were exchanging intimacies.

The vomit stank of stomach acid and alcohol. Cono pulled the gun muzzle away and grasped Timur's face by the chin, turning his head to the side. His old friend was still breathing, faintly.

Why not kill him now? For some reason, or for no reason, the reflex said no.

Cono stood up and wedged the two pistols into his belt. With hose from the acetylene tanks he tied Timur's ankles, then his wrists, and finally made two loops around his face, pushing the hose into Timur's open mouth before tying it off in a bulky knot. Maybe within a few minutes' time, Cono would have an inspiration as to how to finish him off. *The machines, perhaps. Easy burials ...*

The hum of the crusher returned to Cono's ears as he rounded the troop of cylinders. He brushed a hand against his grazed thigh: very little blood. The shoe that had been hit was missing only part of the sole beneath the toe. Cono rolled the yellow canister that had shielded him. There was a clean bullet hole on one side, in the midsection, but no exit hole. *Saved by high-U.* Cono was too mentally exhausted for the irony to register.

The guns pressing against his abdomen would be a nuisance while carrying the canisters, so he placed them near the stairs to the cockpit. Bending over to pick up the canister seemed an impossible task—the fight with Timur had drained what strength he had left.

For a moment Cono lost track of where he was and why. He stopped suddenly, motionless except for his eyes, which swept the cavernous building. The rapid thudding of his heart told him that he was in danger, but he couldn't grasp the source of it. He squatted and lowered his head between his legs. Gradually, the extra blood flow to his brain relieved the dizziness and helped him make sense of what he saw. Now he recognized the yellow barrel in front of him, the drilling armature, the pit wired with explosives. He began to hoist the canister that had saved his life, when the import of Timur's words came back to him in a rush. Katerina had turned. Xiao Li and Dimira were in Zheng's hands.

Cono had to find them.

He felt for one of his mobile phones. He punched in the number Katerina had given him at the pool. He called again and again, with no answer. What if Timur had been lying? But why? It served him no purpose, except to ridicule Cono for the trust he had put in Katerina. He tried the number three more times. Nothing.

Cono looked again at the canister and ran his hand over the clean hole the bullet had made. Why was he going on with this? He could leave the quarry *now*. Why risk more? What did he care if someone put the uranium to use?

He hadn't learned from schools or religions or books why so many dead people would be such a bad thing. They died every day by the thousands. When he'd lived by himself as a boy in the forest, death was everywhere. He had killed to fill his empty stomach countless times—birds and coatis, young capybaras and tapirs, a monkey once. He'd felt their squirming in his hands, their bites, the fast beating of their hearts, the subtle step-by-step crunching of cartilage as he broke their necks and looked into their eyes. He ate them raw when the rains made a fire impossible, their blood and juices smearing his nakedness. Wasn't death the way of this world?

Besides, maybe the people who wanted the high-U so badly had a rationale that was simply beyond his crude knowledge. He felt trapped by his ignorance. Trapped and angered.

Back in California, Todd the mathematician had told him that the Americans had dropped nuclear bombs on Japan to save millions of Japanese lives, but Cono had no way of knowing if it was true, unlike people who had been to school. Muktar the painter—he had been a loner but a good friend, and he had chosen to join the religious fanatics, those with a twisted purpose in a wasteland of no purpose. Could Cono say he was a bad man? And Katerina, who had railed about the terrible tragedy of a uranium detonation—she had given him that high-minded sermon at the same time that she was selling him out and condemning his friends to a beast, to Zheng. Why go on with this?

He could stop now, try to find Xiao Li and Dimira; they wouldn't last long in Zheng's hands. He could leave the whole stinking high-U mess to forces he couldn't control anyway. He was one man diving in the sea on an empty tank, trying to wrestle with a giant octopus a hundred feet below the surface.

Octopus. What about an octopus? The disorienting whorl of sleeplessness was surrounding him again. Cono's mother appeared in a half-dream and took his hand—a little hand like one of the hands clutching the edge of the swimming pool, shining with water droplets on skin. His hand in hers, the breeze lifting spray from the waves that were tossing themselves onto the beach …

Cono shook himself. His mother faded away. He picked up a piece of scrap rebar lying in the dirt and pummeled his injured shoulder with it. As he looked down at the circular rim of the canister between his knees, the arguments and rationales vanished. An impulse took over. He picked up the canister.

Raising it above his head was a struggle, and the mouth of the crusher was blurry. His body swayed under the load, but finally he heaved it into the air. The canister barely reached the top of the mound of stones in the bin, but it tipped forward and began rolling down to the mouth; it disappeared. The clomps and screams and sparks jolted Cono.

Like a robot, he climbed the stairs to the control room and pressed the feed lever until another mouthful of stones was greeted by the crusher. Through the cockpit window he saw a wide tinge of pinkish gray on the slanting horizon. *Four more to carry. Four, right?*

He returned to the square pit and eased down the ladder into the tunnel chamber. He tried not to waste time staring at the chains and the pile of clothes. *Just think of the next load, and the next.*

He had made it up with the third canister to the pit and was hunched over, changing arms for the carry, when he saw three pairs of legs above him.

"*Who are you?*" The question was fired at him in Russian, and he looked up into the dark eye of an AK-47 an arm's length away.

"I am a trusted servant, preparing a delivery," Cono said, standing up slowly and looking at his wristwatch. "You're early. But I'm glad you're here. They're heavy."

"Tell me now!" shouted the woman holding the gun. "Who are you?" She searched the vaulted space with darting eyes, never quite meeting Cono's gaze.

"My name is Dmitry," Cono said. "And I'm a servant who isn't afraid of radioactivity, unlike my boss, who pays me well." He looked at the men on either side of the woman. "You two look strong. Help me with this."

Cono lifted the canister up from the pit, feigning to almost fall over. One of the men helped to grapple with it. Two guns were still trained on Cono.

"Thanks. It's heavier than it looks."

"You're not from here," the woman said.

"My boss prefers to import his workers. Says it's hard to find good help. And he says I'm expendable if I don't deliver on time." Cono began to climb out of the pit.

"Stay there. Shoot him if he moves." The woman reached into a backpack at her feet and pulled out a little metal box with a handgrip and a nozzle. She passed it over and around the canister. The Geiger counter clicked slowly, then faster. When it reached the middle of the canister it trilled like a cicada.

The two young men shuffled a few steps away when they heard the sound.

"Keep your guns on him!" the woman shouted.

"I hope this is what you're looking for," Cono said, "because it's a lot of work."

"What's that noise outside?"

"The generator. Keeps the lights on. Can I come up now?" Cono put a hand on the rim of the pit. "The boss said it was dangerous work, but I didn't expect *this*."

"Let him up. Then make him sit."

"Is here okay?" Cono leaned against the rusted flywheel frame. The young men shifted their footing to keep him in their aim. He saw the stack of boxed explosives out of the corner of his eye and worried that he'd chosen the wrong spot.

The woman put the Geiger counter in the backpack and looked warily at Cono, swinging her weapon until it was pointed at his chest. "Where is the other canister?"

Cono finally saw her eyes straight on. There was something familiar about them—their wide spacing, the extra flesh beneath the eyebrows that pushed the lids down, the broad and protruding forehead above them. Even the way the small muscles at the sides of her eye sockets tugged nervously beneath the skin.

"The other one's down in the tunnel." Cono raised an arm in a dramatic gesture and pointed his index finger down at the tunnel entrance. The guns trained on him had summoned what few reserves Cono had left in his brain, but he couldn't tell if he was giving a cunning performance, or merely acting semi-giddy with fatigue.

"Omar, go down behind him. Not too close. Bring it up. Mansour, back to the door, keep watch." The woman stared at Cono. "Anyone outside could have seen that the gate was open. It's an amateur job. It stinks."

"You're the professionals." Cono waved his hands in the air somewhat ridiculously. "I don't even get a gun. But tell Omar to be careful. My boss is paranoid." He pointed to the wires and charges on the walls of the pit. "And no shooting, please." Cono gestured carelessly toward the boxed dynamite to his left. "It scares me."

"He talks too much," the woman said to the others. "You two, do as I said."

"We should give him to Allah." Omar pointed his pistol at Cono's head. "We know where the stuff is now, Tamaris. We weren't told he'd be here. And why is his face smashed up? We should send him *now*."

"That is not the plan," Tamaris said with a steely look at Omar, who had used her real name, against orders. "It would spoil the rest of the deal."

"The rest of the deal? Tell us about the deal!"

Tamaris pointed her gun at Omar. "Go down and get it. Mansour, guard the door."

Mansour looked back over his shoulder as he marched to the same door by which Cono had entered the building. The plastique-rigged shed next to it would be another hazard if there were any shooting.

Cono eased himself into the pit and backed into the hole. "Careful with your head, Omar."

14

Omar pointed his gun below him as he descended the ladder after Cono. Cono's feet hit the floor and he stepped back to make way. When Omar reached the floor, Cono swept his arm toward the canvas, the cot, and the chains.

"Cozy, isn't it?"

"Shut up. Where is it?"

"This way. My boss hid it well." Cono stooped to enter the tunnel. He lifted the tarp, exposing one of the yellow barrels. Omar was at his shoulder.

"But it looks like there are more than they said."

"Let's see."

Omar's attention was momentarily fixed on the tarp as Cono raised it with one hand. In the instant of distraction Cono whipped his free hand against Omar's forearm. The pistol clattered against the rock wall. Cono's other fist was crushing Omar's temple before Cono could stop it. The young man's head was hammered against the tunnel wall. His lifeless body slumped next to the nearest canister.

Just a boy. Cono reached down and scraped up a handful of dust and gravel. Standing, he extended his arm over the young man's body and let the dust and gravel fall; it was the same gesture he'd seen his mother make at the burial of a neighbor boy who had died in a knife fight. With his eyes, Cono followed an individual quartzite grain as it left his hand, was nudged by other grains in midair, hit Omar's shirt, and then bounced onto a button on his chest.

"Kiss the next world for me," Cono whispered.

He picked up the pistol and climbed the ladder. As his head emerged at the top, he immediately saw Tamaris's rifle trained on him. Cono placed the pistol out of view on the second rung of the ladder before he crawled into the pit and crouched, looking back down the hole.

"He said he could do it himself," Cono said. "He said I was weak like a woman."

Tamaris's attention was divided between Cono and the door where Mansour stood guard.

"Almost, Omar. Almost. The tunnel is tight," Cono said as he backed away from the hole in the direction of Tamaris, seeing out of the corner of his eye the point of the gun turning toward him, closer now, within reach.

In a sweep of his arm Cono grabbed the barrel of the AK with such force that Tamaris was hurled into the pit beside him, the gun now in his hands. Tamaris was lying on her side.

"Don't yell," Cono said quietly. "Your Omar is in his heaven." He stood over her, searching for signs of other weapons. "Save your life and Mansour's by doing what I say."

Tamaris grunted as she kicked a foot toward Cono's shin. He raised his leg in time for her to miss. Now she was prone, the nub of the gun pressing into her back.

"I didn't like killing your trigger-happy friend. I don't want to kill you." Cono was whispering and glancing toward the door where Mansour was standing just outside.

"You can kill me now," Tamaris said. "Deliver me to Allah. But you are too weak to do it."

She screamed.

Cono's foot was strangely slow as he put it on the back of her neck. Then her mouth was pressed into the dirt, her arms and legs flailing. Cono saw Mansour running from the door toward them. Cono pulled Tamaris up by her collar and stood her in front of him.

"Kill him, Azmat!" she shouted, trying to twist away. Cono slammed her body against the edge of the pit, bending her forward over its edge. He jammed the rifle muzzle into her back, so Mansour—Azmat—could see. Azmat was now sprinting, the pistol jostling in his inexperienced, upraised hand.

"Kill him!"

Azmat halted about fifteen yards away, his eyes fixed on Tamaris and the gun between her shoulder blades. Even with her chin pressed against the floor, Tamaris could see Azmat's mouth moving with muttered prayers.

"Don't pray—shoot!"

Cono leaned hard on the rifle. "Azmat," he said, "put the gun down. Put it down and you'll both live. I have nothing against you."

Azmat aimed the gun at Cono, his arm shaking. He didn't even know to brace the weapon with his other hand.

"*La ilaha illa Allah; Muhammad rasul Allah.*" Cono recited the Arabic affirmation of Allah and his prophet in a loud, clear voice, and the confusion in Azmat's face intensified. The gun wobbled. *Just a boy, another boy.*

"He's playing with you, Azmat. Kill him before he kills us both!" Tamaris was wriggling, trying to reach behind to grab the rifle.

Cono saw the sudden firmness in Azmat's hand and lurched to the right as the young man's trigger clicked; the discharged bullet cracked the air and plunked into the wall of the pit behind Cono and Tamaris, a few inches from one of Timur's plastique charges.

Cono shifted to the right until his hip hit the edge of the pit. From this angle there was only a slight gap between the Azmat's extended pistol and the wired shed farther back.

As Azmat took new aim at Cono, Cono fired a burst of four rounds from the AK. One of the shots made a tinging sound on the metal roof of the shed. The three others passed through Azmat's wrist and forearm. The pistol fell. Azmat's arm was still extended, his hand hanging from tendons as blood spurted.

Tamaris lunged at Cono, but his knee met her chest before her hands could strike him. He hit her with the rifle butt, sending her to her knees.

He unbuckled his belt and yanked it from its loops. "Get up. Put a tourniquet on his arm. Quick!" Cono whipped her head with the belt. "He'll die if you don't. And you will too."

Tamaris turned her face upward with a look of scorn. "Death is nothing." She climbed out of the pit with the belt in hand.

She was a few paces away from Cono when Azmat, still standing, put his remaining hand to his ghostly white face; Cono saw that there was something in his fist, that he was using his teeth to pull the safety pin out of a hand grenade. As the pin came free, Cono leaped out of the pit, taking aim. But the hand holding the grenade, feebly squeezing the safety lever, was now in a direct line with the explosive-rigged shed. Cono eased the pressure of his finger on the trigger.

"Azmat, lie down. She's coming. Lie down, we'll help you."

Azmat's frightened eyes wavered until they fixed on the boxes of dynamite near the pit. Cono connected Azmat's gaze with the stack of boxes.

"Go to him!" Cono shouted at Tamaris. She, too, saw Azmat staring at the dynamite; he was going to destroy her mission.

"Azmat, lie down," she said. "I'm coming. We'll stop the bleeding from your arm. Lie down and rest, Azmat."

"No, Tamaris, stay away." Azmat was still standing, but tilting. "I am ready."

Cono moved to find an angle for a shot that wouldn't hit the shed.

"Allahu Akbar!" Azmat swung his arm in a broad arc, launching the grenade toward the boxes of dynamite just as his body toppled over.

To Cono's eyes the grenade was a blur at first, tumbling against the glow of the suspended umbrella lights. His legs felt sluggish as the AK fell against his ankle. *Just another bird to catch in flight.* The bird disappeared for an instant. Cono was running as it reappeared in the light, flying downward in a perfect arc. He dove and twisted in mid-air. Pressure on two of his fingertips. The closing of his fist. Nothing. A tap on his chest followed by another at his groin. His empty hand went down and found the metal bulb. *Make it fly, make it fly.*

Cono crashed to the ground, rolled, and eyed the open door to the crusher. His arm seemed not to be his. It accelerated like a jai alai wicker.

The grenade exploded as it passed through the doorway. Cono felt the compression of the air and heard shrapnel striking metal all around him. When he looked up, the doorway was a jagged, cloudy aperture filled with the pink of morning.

He felt a hard point against his neck as he tried to get his legs under him. His belt landed next to him with a slap.

"*You* put on the tourniquet." Tamaris sensed his disorientation and planted her hiking boot on his rear, shoving him back onto the ground. "Crawl to him."

The building creaked as a damaged beam shifted. Cono began crawling with the belt in one hand, watching her parallel steps from the corner of his eye. She was staying beyond his reach this time.

"You'd be dead already," Tamaris said, "but I need a mule."

Cono reached the puddle of bloody grit next to Azmat. The young man was whispering more prayers. Cono looped the belt around the arm and and cinched it.

"Get me something to prop up his legs, to keep blood in his head. The yellow barrel—roll it over here."

Tamaris was watching Azmat's severed wrist; the tourniquet had stopped the pulsations of blood. "You've done enough for him."

"He has to go to a hospital right now. And get me something for his legs!"

Azmat was no longer praying. Cono pressed a finger against his neck. *Tump ... tump ...*

"You are killing your friend unless we get help."

"I said we've done enough for him!"

Cono looked at the blanched, narrow face of Azmat. His eyes were half-open, the lids fluttering as if he were dreaming.

"Get up," Tamaris said. "Go down and bring up the other one. Move away from him."

When Cono had backed away, Tamaris bent over and reached into the pocket of Azmat's sweatshirt and pulled out another grenade. "If you're not back up in two minutes, I'll drop this into your grave."

Cono stood up slowly and wiped the blood on his trousers. "Azmat, you are still in this world. Hear me, Azmat. What pain you must feel in your heart, knowing your comrade is your murderess."

"*You* are the one who murdered him!" Tamaris pointed the rifle at Cono's head. "Two minutes."

As he turned, Cono eyed the gun that had fallen from Azmat's hand, but it was several steps away. He moved toward the pit, with Tamaris's aim keenly on the middle of his back.

A metallic banging sound rang out.

Tamaris pulled the AK to her shoulder, ready to shoot, but not knowing where. "What is it?" she hissed.

"The grenade damaged the building," Cono said. "It's unstable."

Another banging noise. Tamaris looked up to the hanging lights. They were not moving. "You have friends here. Bring them out."

When Cono hesitated, Tamaris tilted her gun slightly upward. "Your death rides a fast camel." She squeezed off a short burst that riffled the air above Cono's head.

"Okay." As Cono turned in the direction of the cylinders he could faintly make out Timur's head, still strapped with hoses. Tamaris had also seen the blur of a person and was following Cono.

"Bring him out!"

Timur tried to kick Cono as he approached, but Cono maneuvered behind him and grasped his still-tied hands. He gripped

Timur's belt, holding him from behind, and forced him to take two steps forward.

Tamaris edged closer. Timur was squirming against Cono's grip, trying to speak through the hose tied across his slavering mouth, the air wheezing in and out of his nostrils.

When she was close enough to make out Timur's face, Tamaris let out a howl of laughter.

"Here you are, our future leader! Drooling and strung up like a marionette." Tamaris smiled. It was a wide grin, all upper teeth with the gums showing. The grin, too, struck Cono as familiar. "Let this moment be like Allah's sword, sharp in your memory. Remember who now pulls your strings, and who will slit your throat and kick your head across the dirt like you did to my brother Muktar, Allah be praised for making him a martyr." She nodded sharply toward Cono. "Take the hose out of the bastard's mouth."

A guttural sound escaped from Cono. "*He killed Muktar? The painter, my friend?*" Cono squeezed his arms so tightly into Timur's belly that Timur couldn't breathe.

Tamaris's eyes flickered with surprise and settled back into a hard stare.

"I thought I saw him in your face," Cono said.

"You are lying."

"I have one of Muktar's paintings—human forms eating each other. He gave it to me."

There was a flash of recognition on Tamaris's face, and a softening that disappeared as quickly as Cono's eyes registered it. "You knew Muktar?"

"Yes and no. Distant. I'm sure you know."

"I know. Now take the hose off."

Cono stared at the back of Timur's head and redoubled his suffocating squeeze. "This man took Muktar's life? It is your duty to avenge your brother. This man spits on you and on Muktar's grave."

Timur tried to stomp on Cono's foot and lunge away, but his movements were sluggish and his chest was heaving for air.

"Yes, he deserves it," Tamaris said. "But Allah has a different plan. Free his mouth."

"This man's tongue is silver," Cono said.

"*Your* tongue is silver! Take it off. Let him speak!" Tamaris released two shots into the wall just above the men's heads.

Cono whispered into Timur's ear as he pushed him closer to Tamaris and her gun. "Brother, you live or die by what you say now …"

Another burst from the rifle, over the two men's shoulders. All three were close now.

"Okay, I'm taking off the hose." Cono kept one hand firmly on Timur's wrists and belt; with the other hand he tugged one loop of hose out of Timur's mouth and pulled it away. He loosened the other loop as well and started to remove it.

Timur coughed and spat. "He is *C, I, …*"

Cono's forearm clamped Timur's trachea shut as he lifted and launched Timur's body and his own onto Tamaris. She fired, but Timur's crashing chest deflected the rifle.

Even with the weight of two large men on top of her, Tamaris managed to wedge her hand behind her back and pull out a knife. Timur was kicking and trying to roll out of Cono's grip.

The flash of Tamaris's blade came at Cono from the side before he could stop it. It just missed his ribs and instead plunged into the side of Timur's chest. Cono grabbed Tamaris's fist and pulled the knife out; his arm was weakening as he tried to resist her repeated jabbing toward his neck. The blade nicked his chin. Cono's arm regained its strength and he slammed her hand against the floor. Over Timur's right shoulder Cono saw Tamaris's other hand ratchet toward her head, holding the grenade she had taken from Azmat.

"Don't," Cono said.

Cono heard her teeth gnashing against the ring, trying to pull the pin out.

"For Muktar, don't."

Her teeth raked the steel ring again.

Cono wasn't aware of the tensing of his hand around the fist that held the knife, nor of the ease of the blade's entry into Tamaris's ear canal, until the stillness of the three overlapping bodies invited the distant humming of the crusher. Then there was a soft thump on the other side of Tamaris's head; the grenade, still in her hand, had fallen from her teeth. The pin was in place.

Cono rolled to the side of the mound of bodies like a great cat that had just brought down prey after a long chase. He saw that he still held the knife in Tamaris's head. He let go and looked at her open eyes; they were already acquiring a glaze, like windowpanes frosting over in winter. Timur's head was slumped over her shoulder, the two pressed together as if they were lovers exhausted after the throes of sex.

He heard a burbling and put his hand on Timur's back. Yes, he was breathing, barely. *Friend.* The friend who had brutalized Xiao Li. The friend who had murdered Muktar. The friend who was so eager to murder Cono.

Cono waited to feel the killing reflex he had confessed to Bulat. He replayed the abuse of Xiao Li in his mind, to amplify his rage. And the chains in the chamber below, the women Timur had starved as his slave-prostitutes. *Take the knife out of Tamaris's ear. Put it where it is due.*

The reflex remained mute. Maybe, Cono thought, he had been hypnotized by his own talk of fruits in the crate, closing two eyes. *Friendship of youth. Peas in a pod.*

The reflex wasn't responding.

Cono got on his knees next to the two bodies. He reached into his vest and pulled out a coin. With a flick of his thumb the coin became two disks attached to each other by a circular joint. Cono held the disks like a scalpel as he lifted Timur's head to see his face.

The edge of one disk was as sharp as a razor blade. With it Cono sliced downward from the corner of Timur's left eye and then upward, carving out a piece of skin in the shape of a long teardrop. Blood quickly streamed from it. Cono turned Timur's head to expose his other eye. He carved another tear, longer and deeper this time, wiping the shred of skin on Timur's black hair.

Cono rolled his index finger in the blood oozing from Timur's tear-cut, then put the red finger into Tamaris's gaping mouth. He placed the same finger in the blood dripping from Tamaris's penetrated ear, and then put the finger between Timur's lips. Finally, Cono scored his forearm with the coin until it seeped red. With his own blood he painted a C first on Tamaris's forehead, then on Timur's.

"So you will remember me in the next life," Cono breathed, "and not forget each other." He wiped his finger clean on Timur's shirt.

Cono's head reeled as he stood up; he stumbled over the hoses, trying to get away as fast as he could from the bodies. *Xiao*

Li. Dimira. Zheng. He grabbed the welding mask hanging on one of the tanks and trudged toward Azmat, trying to guess where Zheng might have taken his captives. Maybe he should have given Xiao Li another mobile phone, so she could alert him if there was a problem, but it could have been a liability if she'd used it incautiously. Or so he told himself.

Cono lifted Azmat's ankles and propped them up on the welding mask. The boy was in shock, but his chest was still rising and falling with shallow breaths. Cono gathered up Azmat's fallen pistol and went back to the two bodies. He pulled the AK from between them and unwrapped the grenade from Tamaris's fingers.

He carried the weapons to the base of the cockpit stairs where he'd laid Timur's handguns. Here, next to the door leading to the quarry, the crusher seemed horribly loud and demanding. *Where are Xiao Li and Dimira?* He felt like a hunter without a spear, naked with stupidity.

The humming machine beckoned him. It would take only fifteen minutes or so to get rid of the rest of the canisters. *Only three or four more. Which was it?* Or he could stretch out on this floor, just for a little while … He closed his eyes and staggered to the door to the quarry, bracing himself against its bent frame. He felt warmth and opened his eyes. The sun, a red sphere on the horizon, was blinding. He turned his head back to the interior, blinking, trying to form images. He saw Azmat on the floor. There was another boy below, killed by two knuckles on Cono's right hand. And somewhere behind the cylinders was the boys' brave, dead leader.

Dying for a lump of metal in a barrel. What foolishness. He laughed, still holding himself against the doorframe. He could prove their foolishness by tossing the rest of the lumps into the hungry mouth. He laughed again, and again; it kept him alert as he hoisted the canister lying on the floor and carried it to the crusher, where he lobbed it into the feed bin.

He climbed into the pit to go down for another one. As he entered the hole he stepped on the gun he'd left on the second rung of the ladder.

"Your mind is mush, Cono," he yelled as he wedged the gun into his waistband and went down, laughing hysterically.

The sight of the dead young man in the tunnel silenced his laughter. Cono pulled him away by the ankles to clear the space next to the high-U.

He brought up the fourth and fifth canisters. "Yes, I *am* a mule, yes I *am* a mule," he repeated to himself. Tamaris's words formed a rhythm that kept Cono marching as he delivered each yellow barrel to its death. His hysteria broke free each time he pressed the crusher feed lever and shouted, "Dust to dust!" toward the sunrise shimmering in the distance.

The last canister seemed the lightest of all as he lugged it up the ladder, and he found it easy to thrust it onto the diminished pile of rocks in the feed bin. He felt his cheeks flushing as he came down the steps from the cockpit. *More! More! What else can I return to the earth?* Midway down the stairs, he stopped.

"Timur! My BROTHER!" he yelled. "Dust to dust!" He almost tripped as he leaped off the stairs in eagerness.

But while he was airborne, he heard above the drone of the crusher a creak, like a distant hinge coming to life. As he landed at the foot of the stairs, Cono seized the AK and spun.

It was Bulat. Same clothes, same cap. He had just walked through the little door next to the interior shed.

Cono looked for others behind the intruder. There were none. "So, Teacher, speak to the class."

Bulat steadily shuffled forward, looking left at Tamaris and Timur, and then at Azmat, lying to the right.

"Stop there."

Bulat stood still, surveying the parts of the building that hadn't been visible from the doorway, then his gaze veered back to Cono. "You seem to have recovered quickly since our last meeting."

"Take off the jacket and cap and throw them in front of you."

Bulat complied, saying, "I assure you I have no weapons."

"Assurances are as dependable as alley cats lately. Take off your shirt and pants and throw them down too. Then take five steps backward and turn around. A full circle. Arms in the air."

"This is quite, quite irregular."

"This is an irregular place."

"I assure you …"

"I assure you I am very impatient. And not normal in the head."

Bulat removed his shirt and tossed it. He had a hard time getting his pant legs over his shoes.

"The shoes too."

When the trousers and shoes joined the pile, Bulat, wearing only baggy gray briefs, a sleeveless undershirt, and drooping brown socks, stepped backward and turned around. He was a short block of a man, with legs like tree stumps.

Cono approached the clothes and began to step on them to feel for weapons.

"My phone. Don't break it. It's in the coat."

Cono found it and put it in his pocket.

"Now I am *sure* you are a very capable man," Bulat said, "just as Miss Oksana told me. It has been quite a spectacle."

"How long have you been here?"

"I came shortly after the head of the Bureau arrived."

"You saw everything?"

"All that I could see from that little door when it wasn't being guarded."

"And you didn't help me?"

"It was hard to make sense of it all. A puzzle with so many missing pieces. And, from what I could see, you seemed to need no help from an unarmed man."

Cono let the AK rest at his hip. "I could be one of the corpses here."

"With such a complicated picture, how could I know that was a bad thing?"

Cono raised the rifle to his shoulder again. "Do you think it would be a bad thing if I put you down right now?" Cono had been standing still for too long. The lack of vigorous movement, which the canister toting had afforded, was allowing weariness to reinvade his body.

"For me, a very bad thing indeed," Bulat said. "For you, I'm not sure. But a man, especially a naked man, deserves to know why he is to be killed by someone he helped such a short time before."

"Get dressed."

Bulat gathered up his clothes.

"Tell me, Slem, where is Miss Oksana?"

"I don't know. And please, Bulat is a much better name."

"Why are you here, Bulat?"

"I relieved another man who works for Miss Oksana. He was keeping watch on the Bureau chief, for what purpose I wasn't informed. As I arrived the other man got a message from Miss

Oksana. She told him not to bother with the surveillance—I like that word, 'surveillance.' The other man left with surprising haste; perhaps he was happy to get some sleep." Bulat continued talking as he buttoned his shirt. "But I had already slept for several hours. What was I to do? Go home and play chess against myself? My family is in the countryside; I am all alone. And I was right—chess is nothing compared to the drama I have witnessed here." Bulat put on his cap.

"That's enough. Do you know that Oksana has turned over two women, my friends, to a Beijing agent, who will surely kill them?"

"I heard the Bureau chief shouting something about a tart a short time ago, and a Kitai. Regrettably, I could not understand all that he said."

Cono moved slightly so he could see Bulat more clearly in the sunlight glowing from the doorway behind him. The broad Kazak face lacked any momentary ripples of lies.

"I don't know about these women," Bulat said. "Why would Miss Oksana put your friends in danger? I thought Miss Oksana was your friend too. I am confused. What Beijing agent?"

"Your Miss Oksana couldn't get what she needed from the Americans, so she cut a deal with the Kitai, the ringleader of Beijing's grab for your country—the torturer you saved me from. That's why she called off the surveillance of the Bureau chief, who came here to trade with the jihadis to get their support. She called off the chase because the Bureau chief was soon to be Beijing's man too."

Creases appeared in the wide slab of Bulat's forehead. "Miss Oksana? No. There must be another explanation. Perhaps she just took my advice that the jihadis were a distraction from the bigger problem."

Cono pulled out Bulat's mobile and handed it to him. "Call her."

"Oh, no. We never communicate by phone."

Cono planted the butt of the AK in his shoulder and aimed.

"That number is only for the most extreme of circumstances."

"Look around. There's another dead man down in the tunnel. Do you want me to cut an equation into your forehead?"

"Miss Oksana going over to the Kitais? After all my warnings about Beijing taking my country? It cannot be so," Bulat asserted, but a telltale vertical wrinkle of doubt formed between his eyebrows.

"Call her."

Bulat carefully punched in a number by memory. "It's ringing." Bulat held the phone to his ear for a dozen rings. The wrinkle on his forehead grew deeper. "No answer," he said softly.

"Call again."

"She told me if circumstances ever became extreme, she would respond immediately," he said slowly, as if explaining a theorem to a student. "She said my good service demanded that of her." He punched in the number again and listened, his head bent down.

"Hallo. Miss Oksana. Yes, it's Slem. It's an emergency …"

Cono grabbed the phone. "Where are they?"

"Cono, you sound like you've lost your cool." Katerina's voice was even. "You see? You *are* addicted."

"Where are my friends?"

There was a momentary silence. "You mean the Chinese street whore? Why bother? A woman like that is always asking for trouble."

"And what were *you* when you first came to Almaty?"

227

Silence.

"And what are you now?"

Silence.

"And the other woman you gave to Zheng, a mother," Cono said. "Children—you were so worried about them. A million dead."

Cono heard Katerina draw in a breath. "You mean the one with the ugly ears," she said. "We know her kid is dead anyway. Just get out, Cono."

"Why did you turn? Have you been hedging your bets all along? Where are the two women?"

"Listen. Simmons's replacement doesn't like my *style*. She called me a liability. You know what that means, Cono? It means my family is fucked unless I find another way, and my bones will be found someday in an acid vat at a tannery in Chimkent. So, Mr. Free to Go Anywhere Anytime, see reality and get the fuck out of town." There were three clicks. The connection went dead.

"Well?" Bulat looked alarmed by the anger in Cono's face.

"It's true. She's working for Beijing. In hopes of freedom."

"Beijing? Freedom?" Bulat started to laugh, but stopped himself. He shook his head. "Oil and water."

15

Cono redialed the number Bulat had entered and saw that it was not the same one Katerina had given him at the swimming pool. It rang, but there was no answer. He kept his eyes on Bulat as he dialed six more times, with the same result. He also again tried the number Katerina had given him at the pool, relieved that he could still retrieve it from his own memory. Three times, no answer.

"So, Teacher, where would Oksana take two women so she could hand them over as hostages?" Cono felt out of breath, and sucked in air. "Does she have other safe houses, places that are only hers, not the Americans'?"

"I am not aware of any except the place I took you." Bulat rubbed his chin. "I am sorry to say this, but you look very weary. Perhaps you should sit down and rest."

"It'll have to wait." Cono tried to think through the fog that was drifting into his head. "The note. The one you said you didn't leave under my friend Dimira's door. Who was the stringer who left it?"

"I'm afraid I don't know about the note or who might have

left it. Miss Oksana says it's better if we don't have contact with each other. It's the way it's done in this business."

"But you must have a telephone number for at least one of them." Cono scrolled through the memory of Bulat's mobile. There were no numbers listed. He went to Calls Received: None. Unanswered Incoming Calls: None. Calls Made: Only the multiple attempts to call Katerina. "You have it memorized." Cono searched Bulat's face. "Give me another number."

"I assure you, I have no number for the others. I don't even have names for them. And I don't want to know them." Bulat's voice was steady.

"Help me think. Where, how, to find Oksana and Zheng and the women." Cono walked over to the backpack lying next to the pit and took out the Geiger counter. Beneath it, wrapped in a wad of cloth diapers, were three Russian RGD-5 grenades. There was a ring of keys, and nothing else. Cono carried the bag to the base of the control-room stairs and put the harvest of four pistols and Tamaris's grenade into it.

"Think!"

"Yes, I am trying to think," said Bulat, now standing over Azmat. "What about this young man, whose arm you tied?"

"You should take him to a hospital. But I won't let you. I need your help."

"To do what?"

"Help me think, goddamn it! I can't think straight!"

Bulat looked at Cono's face and then at the AK. He was concerned that the hysterical behavior he'd seen just before entering the building was now returning, but this time Cono had a rifle in his hands, not a canister. Cono took a few steps and stood outside the doorway, in the brightness of a cloudless morning.

The damn machines are still on. He went up to the control room and turned off all the switches. As he came down the stairs he felt a vibration against his thigh. It was Bulat's cell phone.

Cono yanked it out of his pocket. He pushed the Receive button and listened to a faint buzz. When he reached the bottom of the stairs and stood in the sunshine at the doorway, the signal cleared up. "Yes?"

"My dear Cono. I have another joke for you. The Dalai Lama wants a hooker. He's a man, after all. He rings up the Chinese consulate, because he's heard they can find the best. The operator gives him a name and a number. He asks how he can be sure she's the best. The operator says, because her lovers are all willing to die to get more of her. The Lama says, she's the one for me, no problem—I get reincarnated anyway!"

Zheng's laughter was so loud that Cono had to move the phone away.

Cono brought it back to his ear. "I'm not laughing this time."

"You are so honest, always so sincere, my friend. *The small boats are floating on the lake, the red ties are shining, tell me my comrades*, all that Communist Youth Brigade rubbish. Pity that your sincerity had such a nostalgic effect on my two bank assistants. They are now trying to row themselves out of the bottom of a lake."

"Yes, a pity."

"My dear Cono, you were such a raconteur on our first two meetings. Loosen up. We should have another conversation, for old times' sake. It looks to be a pretty day. The sun's rays are already warming the cuts made by the hand of man in the always-forgiving earth …"

Hearing those words Cono dove into the building as the

sheet metal above the door ripped open. The cracking peal from a high-powered rifle followed less than a second later.

Cono kept the phone to his head as he dug his heels into the floor, thrusting himself backward from the doorway.

"Are you still there, my poorly dressed friend? You see that my new assistants are not so sentimental. That was just an invitation. To our next conversation. I hear you gasping for air. There is lots of air up here on the mountainside. We're all wondering why you chose this vacant place to enjoy the sunrise; but indeed the view is sublime."

"And?"

"And, if you want your two, shall we say, attractive friends back, you should visit me on this gorgeous lookout above the quarry."

"You can have them."

"Your lovely friend Katerina doesn't think you are so nonchalant about them. I respect the ploy. But after all, you came such a long distance on your white horse to help them."

"And my horse is ready to trot back to the stables." Cono got to his feet and edged toward the doorway where he'd been seen by the sniper.

"But really," Zheng said, "you wouldn't want to leave your girlfriends hanging like that. After all your trouble, a hero like you."

Cono looked out beyond the edge of the doorframe, still holding the phone to his ear. More than a hundred yards away, on the upper rim of the quarry that was cut into the slope leading to the mountains, were three figures—Xiao Li, Dimira, and between them, Zheng, in a silver suit, his right arm around Xiao Li's shoulders and his other hand holding a cell phone. The women had gags in their mouths and their wrists were tied in front of them. Their necks seemed thick. Cono realized why when he saw two ropes extending from the women to the rear bumper of a black SUV thirty yards up the slope—their necks were thickened by nooses. The three were standing atop a giant, rounded block of granite that had resisted the blasting that cut the highest tier of the quarry. The garnet-colored stone was the size of a four-story house; the plateau, on which the three were perched, sloped slightly downward and then to a near-vertical drop until it merged with the first ledge of the quarry. It looked like the forehead of an enormous cranium.

The neat white stripe protruding from Zheng's breast pocket blushed with the color of morning, as did his smile. Dimira was in jeans and a tight green sweater; Xiao Li, on the far side of Zheng, had on the same running pants from the previous day, but her top was different—she was wearing a bulky red pullover. She was trying to shrug off Zheng's arm, but he held her firmly.

"I'm sure you can see the situation," Zheng said. "We'll throw down another rope for you, to make it easy for you to have the conversation I desire." Zheng turned and nodded. A man with a rifle strapped on his shoulder tossed a rope over the near face of the granite block. As the rope fell and tensed, Cono saw that it also was connected to the SUV.

"Come out, my friend," Zheng said. "Take a stroll on this beautiful morning, over to the rope, and let us renew our acquaintance."

"It looks like a long walk."

"Don't worry, my assistant with the keen aim knows I am *most* eager to see you up close and alive."

"It's true, I did enjoy our last meeting. I'm coming." Cono clicked off the phone and retreated from the doorway.

Bulat was hidden on his hands and knees behind the drilling machine, peering up through the doorway at the three distant figures. "That fancy Kitai is risking a lot to chase you like this, in a foreign country," he said. "I think the word for it is vendetta. Have you killed a member of his family?"

"He just wants to finish the job you saved me from at the bank."

"Then perhaps you need help again. If what you say about Miss Oksana going over to Beijing is true …"

"It's true," Cono said. "And she must have had someone trailing me after I left her safe house; no one knew I was coming up to the quarry."

"The women are special to you?"

"Yes. He wants to hang them both, and eliminate me at the same time, close up."

"He is ambitious. I guess one needs to be that way to take over a country."

"Bulat, here's your chance to take care of your country. And to help me take care of my friends."

"And your friend Miss Oksana?" Bulat asked.

"You can put her in her grave."

"But she is, or was, your friend as well. You said friends were worth fighting for, more than principles."

"We can talk friendship and its seasons another time." Cono ripped open the backpack and handed Bulat two grenades and two of the pistols. "Do you know how to use these?"

"I had my military service. But we only practiced with dummies. Calm down," Bulat added. "We have an advantage. Even if they know that I'm here, they wouldn't think I am helping you. They might even think I'm already dead, thanks to you. I'll go out the front gate. They can't see that side."

"Unless Zheng has someone guarding it."

"That is a risk. I'll go out the gate, then circle around and get above their position. There's enough brush up there to conceal me. Do you have another mobile phone?"

Cono plucked the last two from his vest, thinking that they must have been crushed already. The first one was cracked along its entire face. The second one was partly broken. Cono switched it on; it was working.

"Put my cell phone's number into your phone," Bulat said.

Cono tried to enter the numbers Bulat recited, but he was having trouble focusing on the display.

"Give it to me." Bulat took the phone in his fleshy hand and entered the digits. "My phone's number is under C, for Cono. Now we test it." Bulat pushed the Memory button and pressed Call. The phone in Cono's pants pocket vibrated.

"Okay, it works," said Cono, reaching into his pocket. "Here's your phone. Thanks." Cono held out his hand to make the exchange.

"That won't do," Bulat said as he looked at Cono's unfocused eyes. "You must keep *my* phone because that is the one the Kitai called you on. No doubt he got the number from Miss Oksana. And now I will put your number into my phone, the phone you will keep." Bulat called up the number of Cono's phone from its memory and entered the number on the other mobile.

"I put the number under T, for Teacher. You see?" Bulat held the phone up to Cono's wandering pupils. "You see, I *am* thinking for you."

Cono began to sway, and Bulat, frightened, slapped him on the face. Cono regained some focus.

"Bulat, hit me again. I'm fading. Hit me. Hard. In the face."

Bulat put a hand on Cono's shoulder to steady him, confused by Cono's request.

"Hit me ..."

Bulat rammed his fist into the swelling above Cono's nose. Cono's head snapped back; the split in his skin was reopened and bleeding. The blood seeped into Cono's eyes and stung. He rubbed it away. "Not bad, for a math teacher."

Bulat saw that Cono's eyes were no longer wandering.

A sudden twang of ripping steel was followed by another reverberating clap from the high-powered rifle.

"Have to hurry," Cono said. "I'll call you from below when I need you to make a move." Cono picked up the AK that he had dropped, and nodded in the direction of the pit with the tunnel entrance. "Bulat, down the hole over there, you will find money for your fight. But take care about the explosives."

Bulat was looking nervously at his watch. "From where the Kitai and the women are standing, if you get directly below, he won't be able to see you," he said. "We have a three-dimensional puzzle—very satisfying."

Cono stepped sideways toward the door, holding the AK in his hands; the two pistols and two grenades were wedged into his pants.

"Wait," said Bulat, reaching delicately for the AK. "If he sees you with this ..."

Cono moved the pistols and grenades to the back of his waistband and handed the rifle to Bulat.

"The safety's off, so be careful."

Bulat took it, and, for the first time, Cono saw the plodding man move swiftly.

16

Cono stepped into the blaze of the morning sun. He squinted against the light, keeping his gaze on the three figures atop the granite block. Xiao Li's body became rigid as he marched into plain view on the ledge next to the crusher. She seemed to be making signals with one of her tied hands, but the harshness of the glare and the distance made them impossible to read. Zheng held his arm firmly around Xiao Li, and grabbed Dimira by the waist when he saw Cono emerge. His smile was a bright slash of white against the mottled brown backdrop of the mountainside.

Cono walked along the curving terrace of cut earth. The movement helped clear his mind. Zheng wanted Cono. He wanted him alive, to have the pleasure of killing him up close. Before the execution, he lusted for another chance to prove his supremacy, both to himself and to his assistants, who would propagate the story of the revenge Zheng had exacted on the insulting stranger. Cono imagined the unbecoming stories that had been seeded through the whispers of the two thugs who had been at the bank, before they were condemned to the lake by Zheng, and he understood that he was Zheng's only ticket to self-rehabilitation.

Xiao Li and Dimira. For Zheng, they were just honey for the flytrap. Once he had Cono, he would extinguish them no matter what. The only question was how.

Cono saw Zheng slap Xiao Li on the face. She was struggling, trying to pull the gag out of her mouth. Dimira was tugging at the rope around her neck, as if she couldn't breathe. Cono started running, planting his feet in the old grooves left by heavy machinery. Rounding the wide curve of the quarry pit, he looked up and saw the fury in Zheng's eyes as he tried to restrain Xiao Li. Cono stopped. He was about fifty yards away and well below them. His gaze rested on the woman who had sung with such carefree abandon when they'd first met. Xiao Li stopped struggling and stood straight. She looked toward Cono, then, without moving her head, looked down at her hands. With her right index finger she marked her thigh in Chinese characters; Zheng, standing slightly behind her, did not see the signal. Xiao Li's finger was moving quickly, but Cono's eyes tracked it in millimeter steps. *Bomb on me. Bomb on me.*

Cono felt his heart contract in three powerful, anguished strokes. *Zheng wants me to watch her die.* Zheng jerked his head, and a rifle barrel on the slope above their perch caught the light with an eel-like gleam. There was a loud smacking and thudding sound, and another. Two clouds of dust rose a few inches in front of Cono's toes.

"Don't stop so far away," Zheng barked. "I'll strain my voice."

Cono advanced at a quick pace. With each step along the curving ledge, Xiao Li, on the far side of Zheng, became more occluded by the arcing top of the great specimen of granite. Zheng had his arms around the necks of both women, who stood rigidly.

Cono stopped again. Looking up, he could see most of Dimira, the top half of Zheng, and Xiao Li's head.

"Master Zheng," Cono shouted, loud enough to be sure the rifleman also heard him, "I am your servant. I give myself up to you. I'm sure you and your comrades don't want to harm innocent women, one of whom is of your own glorious race. Let them go, and I'll come up on the rope."

"Hahaha!" Zheng swayed exuberantly on his roost, his arms locked on the two women. He kissed each of them on the head and laughed again—a bounding, histrionic laugh that filled the crater and echoed off its walls of cleaved stone.

Zheng's face turned downward to stare directly at Cono. The pearly teeth had disappeared behind taut lips.

"Innocent? *Who* is innocent?"

Zheng swung his arms forward, pushing both women onto the downward slant of the granite. Xiao Li and Dimira fell until the ropes tensed, stopping their bodies only three yards from Zheng. They were still on the hump of the rounded block, where the surface prevented gravity from taking them into the freefall of a lynching. Clutching the nooses with their bound hands, Xiao Li and Dimira were halfway to being hanged. Their attempts to scream were stifled by the choking.

"Grab onto the rope, my dear Cono." Zheng's voice was half-growl, half-command. "We'll pull you up at the same time we pull the women to safety. Have you heard of linked destinies?" Zheng shrieked with laughter.

"I'll take the rope," Cono shouted back. He ran to the base of the granite block where the rope was slung. In this position, shielded by the arc of granite, Zheng couldn't see him. Cono looped the rope around his chest and tugged. "Okay, pull me up!" He could just make out the sounds of strangulation above him.

"Pull me up!"

"Relax, my friend." Zheng's voice from above was riddled with happiness. "They have a little more time. Let's enjoy it."

Wedging himself into the vertical crease between the granite and the quarry wall, Cono withdrew the mobile phone from his pocket and called Bulat.

"Are you close?" Cono whispered.

"Close enough to throw a grenade at the sniper."

Cono saw that the phone's battery warning light was blinking. He quickly calculated the time it would take for Bulat's grenade to do its job—two seconds to prime it and throw, then a four-to-five-second delay. An eternity.

"Time is now. Throw it."

Cono began counting. *One.* He unwound the rope from his chest and took one of the pistols from his waistband. *Two.* He scanned the route around the broad base of the granite block to Xiao Li's side, where he could get a better shot at her rope. *Three. Three? Was he misjudging the duration of a second?* He saw that there was no protection for a run to the other side; he would be fully exposed to the sniper. Both women must be nearing asphyxiation, but he would have to choose. *Three? Four?* Time was being distended in his mind, making him wholly uncertain of his count. He tried to link the counting to his pounding heartbeat, something real. *Four.* He knew he'd be able to see Dimira and immediately have a shot if he backed away from the wall, but the sniper was just above. In his mind he saw the nooses tightening on the women's necks. *Where's Bulat's grenade?* Cono wondered if only two seconds had passed, or if twenty had gone by. *Five, maybe six.*

He abandoned the count and jacked his legs three steps backward from the base of the granite, far enough to see Dimira's limp body and the top of Zheng's head, rotating in search of Cono. Xiao Li was hidden by the bulge of granite. Higher up, Cono caught an instantaneous glimpse of the sniper lining up his sights.

The blast from Bulat's grenade clapped and echoed just as Cono braced the handgun and triggered twice. The rope behind Dimira's neck became a braid of just a few filaments. It snapped under her weight.

Cono's legs took control of him. He lunged to the base of the rock to break her fall. As he raised his arms and ducked his head, he heard the skidding sound of Dimira's jeans. Then he felt the crush of her weight on the back of his neck. It spread over his shoulders and into his spine, and his legs gave way.

They lay in a shocked pile for a second. Cono pulled the rope off her neck and yanked the gag out of her mouth. Dimira was gasping, but she seemed unhurt by the fall. There was no time to cut the cord around her wrists.

"He put a bomb on her!"

Cono pulled the second pistol from the back of his waistband and handed it to Dimira. "Use it if you need to."

Two gunshots rang from above. Cono edged away from the base of the block. He saw Zheng's head and arm; Zheng was on his belly atop the bald rock, trying to shoot downward at a target he couldn't see.

Cono sprinted around the broad base of the granite as one of Zheng's bullets whizzed over his head. When he got to the far side of the block, he backed away from the wall for an instant. From this angle all he could were see Xiao Li's legs. One of her feet, still in Asel's pink sneaker, was slowly kicking, trying to find purchase on the rock surface. Cono saw Zheng, too, just next to her. He had crawled farther down the top slope of the rock, and was close to the point where it became nearly vertical. Zheng saw Cono and fired, but missed as Cono dove back toward the wall.

The phone in Cono's pocket vibrated. Cono seized it.

"I'm close to the driver," Bulat said. "He's getting out. I take him now?"

Another shot from above puffed into the dirt a yard away from Cono's feet.

"No. Wait! She'll hang if the car rolls down ..."

The phone went dead. Cono didn't know if Bulat had heard.

Cono pivoted away from the wall, his gun raised, trying to get far enough from the rock to see Xiao Li and the rope around her neck. Zheng slammed his arm across Xiao Li's legs and poised the pistol for a shot at Cono, who was now in full view. Xiao Li kicked, sending Zheng's arm upward and his bullet into the air above Almaty.

Then Bulat's second grenade smacked and boomed.

Xiao Li started to slide, jerkily at first, then more smoothly, toward the drop-off that would snap her neck.

Cono could see the rope now. He saw Xiao Li's tied hands latch onto Zheng's suit coat. He saw her contorted face and the wide unblinkingness of her beautiful eyes. Cono fired three times as fast as the trigger could move. The rope above Xiao Li's head frayed a little more with each slicing bullet, but it stubbornly held her by the neck as her body became nearly vertical. Cono triggered three more times, but there were only two bullets left in the magazine. The last strands of the rope gave way; Xiao Li and Zheng accelerated in gravity's grip. As they slid, Xiao Li was frantically trying to climb onto Zheng's back to make his body absorb the fall. Zheng was trying to do the same, wrestling her with one arm as he plunged headfirst. They disappeared from Cono's view behind the hump of granite.

Cono heard their bodies thudding in unison as he ran around the base of the boulder, then he saw them both struggling to get up. Xiao Li was nearest to him, but still more than ten yards away. One of her legs was broken, the cracked femur making a bulge in her running pants. Zheng had somersaulted and landed on his back.

Zheng still had the gun in his hand. He fired wildly several times at Cono from behind Xiao Li, nearly hitting her. He had something in his other hand. Xiao Li's eyes passed from the thing in Zheng's hand to Cono's stare. She waved an arm to signal him to stay back and shook her still-gagged face to say no, her eyes magnified by her tears.

Cono saw Zheng's thumb fumbling on the small box in his hand. Xiao Li crawled toward Zheng.

A shot rang out. Dimira was standing farther back on the ledge, beyond Xiao Li and Zheng, wobbling with fright, the gun in her tied hands. Zheng screamed in pain and coughed up blood. He raised his hand to his face, his eyes fixed on the little box. Xiao Li's eyes were on the box too.

"No, Xiao Li!" Cono lunged toward her. "Come away! Dimira, shoot him again!"

Dimira raised the gun with her shaky hands.

Xiao Li saw there was no time for that. With her one good leg she sprang away from Cono's approach and dove toward Zheng, her arms outstretched to try to grab the box.

A flash of white light exploded. Cono saw Xiao Li's body separate at the waist as the shock wave lifted him and sent him flying backward. He kept looking as he flew. The part of Xiao Li that had been in the red sweater was flying too, breaking into smaller parts that rained into the expanse of the crater. The rest of her was smearing against the granite face.

Now all he could see was the sky, and instantly that disappeared too.

"Cono, please. Wake up. *Please.*" The string of words, and the sobs, were barely perceptible through the ringing in his ears. Cono tried to open his eyes, but they wouldn't budge. The sobbing continued, louder now, and he felt a warm moisture on his cheeks. A hand wedged behind his head, lifting it off the stone he had struck; the shock of pain where a finger pressed the point of impact finally lifted his eyelids.

All was white for a few seconds. Then there was Dimira's face. Round. The full cheeks. The wide, trembling lips. The dark, hollowed eyes. Red flecks everywhere.

"You *are* alive!" Her sobbing intensified and seemed to move through her whole body as she leaned over to kiss his cheeks, wet with her tears. Then, slowly, gently, she cradled his head in her lap, dabbed away the moisture, and began to pick out the pieces of gravel that had impregnated his face.

"Xiao Li. Where is she?" Cono felt the sensation return to his limbs again and tried to curl onto his side. Then the images reappeared in his mind. The separation of her body, her legs flying into the rock. *A gift—his mother had called his fast brain a gift. A gift? To witness such horror in slow motion? To see it replayed, frame by excruciating frame, for the rest of his life?* Other images appeared. Xiao Li, in his dream, singing with the man with no legs. The man leaning to kiss her. To kiss her goodbye.

Cono's cheeks were wet again, this time with tears of his own that slowly leaked into the wounds on his face. *Don't cry, don't cry,* his grandmother Antonina was saying. *The salt of tears lets nothing grow in the garden.*

He pressed his hands against the earth to lift himself up. Through the ringing in his ears, he heard another voice.

Dimira must have heard it too. She looked up, immediately grasping the pistol with which she had shot Zheng. As a head appeared above them on the crest of the granite block, she took aim.

"No!" Cono shouted. "It's a friend."

"Come over to the rope!" Bulat called out. "I'll pull you up. Come around to the other side."

With Dimira's help, Cono struggled to his feet. She was still shaking, but had been far enough away from the explosion that she had only been smattered with grit and blood. Together they walked along the ledge toward the hole that had been Zheng. Pieces of flesh and silver fabric adhered to the ground around the depression.

"Don't look at the mess," Cono told Dimira as they stepped around the debris. "Don't look or it will be with you forever." But Cono kept his own eyes open. Xiao Li's left lower leg was lying against the granite face, with Asel's sneaker still snug on the foot.

You have my shoe? Cono grimaced at the sound of Xiao Li's words in his head.

He bent down and pulled the pink sneaker off her foot. Near it Cono saw a small piece of paper lying in the dirt. He picked it up. It was a torn black-and-white photo, somewhat fuzzy, of a man and woman kneeling, with placards hanging from their necks. Cono turned it over. The writing was in classical Chinese calligraphy: "Always in the service of your memory. Your devoted son, Lu Peng." Cono read again the words "Your devoted son." He looked over at the indentation in the ground left by the explosion, thinking he would tear up the photo and throw it to the breeze, but he couldn't. Cono read the message another time, folded the picture and slid it into one of the pockets of his vest.

His eyes returned to the face of rock before him, a collage in blood and body tissue. "Don't look, Dimira," he repeated. "Instead, look up to the bright blueness of the sky. And when we get to the top, look to the clean white snow of the mountain peaks."

17

"Hurry up!" Bulat said from above. "With all this noise we won't be alone for long."

Cono looped the rope around Dimira's waist and thighs and knotted it. "Dimira first. Then both of you can pull me up."

Dimira braced her feet against the rock and rose quickly. Cono heard Bulat's grunts and Dimira soon disappeared as she approached the top.

The rope came down again. Cono wedged the sneaker into his vest and rose in fits and starts. He looked over his shoulder at the broad quarry crater, infested by the praying mantis machines, all quiet, the heat of the sun creating liquid mirages over the cones of ground-up rock. The tops of some of the cones sparkled in the sunlight—reflections from bits of digested canister metal and the chopped-up innards of the high-U itself, which in a few more days would be glazed by oxidation and made dull like the rest of the quarry's contents. He looked at the building that held the two dead jihadis and the other near death. And lying on top of Muktar's sister was Timur. Cono imagined him still breathing in his palace. *I should have made sure it was his end.* Cono fingered the knot in the rope, thinking to drop back down and run along the ledge, back through the broken door, behind the cylinders, to take the knife out of Tamaris's brain and slide it into Timur's.

"You are much heavier than you look." Bulat was panting as Cono reached the gradual slope where he was able to partly support himself. The rope was digging into Bulat's waist and Dimira was tugging from behind. "I am sorry about the girl, your brave woman," Bulat said. "Your friend here says she saved you both."

"Yes." Cono refused to think more about Xiao Li. "Dimira is not safe here anymore. And you, Bulat, you don't have much time to go down, load up the money, and get away. You have your own fight to prepare for." Cono scrabbled up to the plateau of the bald rock, then looked down to survey the edges of the quarry, the building, and the road leading up to it. "Dimira, do you have a friend who has keys to your apartment, who can remove the things you can't lose, just in case?" Dimira nodded yes. "Bulat, the phone on me is dead. Let her call on the other one."

Dimira's voice on the phone was shaky at first, but she composed herself. She asked her friend first to take all the photos from the wall, and Asel's paintings; then an envelope of money and a passport and her teaching certificates from beneath the carpet in the corner near her bed. Finally, she asked for some of Asel's clothes. "Yes," she said, "I have my identity card. Yes, that's all. Thank you."

Dimira handed the phone back to Cono. "You're not safe here either," she said. "There are trails, up into the mountains. Kyrgyzstan. There's no border—just the mountains. It's still warm enough up there, barely. Then down to the road at Lake Issyk-Kul. All in three days, maybe. We should leave now."

Bulat's face creased as he looked at Dimira, Cono, and again at Dimira. "He will need a big rest when you're up in the Tian Shan," he said. "Otherwise you'll have to think for him."

Dimira grabbed Cono's arm. "No time, Cono," she said. The words echoed in his mind, but with the voice of Xiao Li: *No time, Cono.*

"She is correct." Bulat was looking at his watch. "No time."

Dimira and Cono were a hundred yards up the rise, winding between spiny scrub and outcroppings of stone untouched by the hand of man when Bulat yelled, "Miss Dimira, remember—we will need you back in Kazakhstan!"

18

The air of the thinning atmosphere was cooler, but the sun was hot on their necks when Dimira and Cono spoke for the first time.

"Did they hurt you?"

Dimira, marching ahead, stopped without turning around.

"No." She seemed about to say more, but instead resumed the climb.

The rhythm of their inhalations and exhalations formed a soothing patterned overlay that calmed Cono's mind. Breathe in, step, breathe out, step, breathe in. The alternating sound and tension in his legs were the only things keeping Cono from collapsing on the mountainside.

He knew they would be chased eventually, and he worried about the coming pursuit, but the carnage they had left below had given them some lead time, and besides, the steepness of the terrain made a faster ascent impossible. They marched under the cover of sparse pines when they could, but Cono scanned the sky, thinking that they were too exposed.

After several hours they reached a ridgeline and stopped to rest. Below them, spanning a canyon, was a dam made of dirt and concrete. Half a mile wide, it had been built in Soviet times to hold back the floods and colossal mudslides that the mountains sometimes unleashed on the city. Beyond the dam was the hazy, tilted sprawl of Almaty, its quilt-work of low buildings and trees tinged with the colors of autumn. The city frayed at its edges into the grayness of the empty, flat expanse that blended with the far reaches of the sky. The horizon was a blur.

Cono had to keep moving. Dimira sensed his weariness, but they both knew that stopping to rest would be unsafe, so they turned to face the mountain peaks again. After another hour they reached the base of a steep rise; far to the right was a depression filled with trees that merged with a dense, narrow forest trailing up a ravine like a green highway leading to the next shelf of the mountain.

Dimira saw Cono's gaze turning toward the spruce and pine trees. "In case there are helicopters," she said.

"Yes."

The blanket of needles beneath the pines crunched softly underfoot as they made their way through the trees, which shrouded a fast-running stream. When they came to the stream, they knelt. Before they drank, Cono dipped a finger into the water and flicked drops up into the air. "To the skies." He dipped and flicked again, this time sending drops to his side. "To the winds." He wet his finger again and let the drops fall to the ground. "To the earth and sea." He dipped his finger a final time and placed a drop on Dimira's forehead, then one on his own. "And to their child, Xiao Li."

They cupped their hands and drank from the stream. Dimira turned her head away when she saw the rubber toe of Asel's sneaker protruding from a pouch in Cono's vest. Cono realized what she had seen and handed her the shoe.

They sat cross-legged in silence for several minutes.

"I should ask you now, and get it out of the way," Cono said. "What happened after I left your apartment? How did they get you and Xiao Li?"

"Xiao Li ..." Dimira choked as she said the name. "... was getting ready to leave. She told me what they had done to her, chained up for two days. She was tired. She was sad that you were gone." Dimira lowered her eyes.

Cono said nothing. The word "sad" floated in the still air.

"Go on, please."

"You'd only been gone a few minutes. There was a knock at the door. The man said that Mr. Cono had sent him to help us. Xiao Li didn't want to open the door, but the man kept saying he was sent by you to make us safe, and that there wasn't much time." Dimira splashed water on her face. "Cono, I was the one who unlocked the door."

Cono put a hand on her shoulder and squeezed.

"Two men broke the door down," she said. "I hadn't opened the last lock. I didn't think ... I didn't know ... I ..."

"They would have broken down the door anyway."

"Xiao Li fought so hard. She yelled at them. She screamed that I was a good Kazak mother with a little daughter and not to hurt me." Dimira was sobbing now.

"I know it's hard," Cono said. "But I must know. Because I am to blame."

"They took us to some sort of warehouse. We had tape all around us, on our mouths, too. It was hard to breathe. They left us there all day and all night. All we could do was twist our fingers together, and look at each other, until the lights went out."

"And this morning?"

"They put us into a car." Dimira paused, trying to calm herself. "There were three Kitai men—the ones who brought us to the quarry. The ones who are dead now. The boss man kept laughing. It was a scary laugh."

"Did you see a white woman—a Ukrainian? You must have."

"There was a woman, a beautiful, tall, nervous woman." Dimira's breathing was steadier now. "We were in the car, driving up from the city. It stopped in back of Hotel Khan and she got in. She sat right next to me. The Kitai boss told her not to talk. She was sweating. When we stopped above the quarry, we all got out. She talked on a telephone, but I was too far away to hear. When they started putting the ropes on our necks, she shouted at the boss. She said it wasn't the plan. She told him to take off the ropes. He laughed at her. She said she wouldn't be part of it and walked away, back down the road we had come on. She was cursing at him in Russian and English with the crudest words. She said, 'You don't know what kind of man you are fucking with.' The boss man kept laughing. A gun went off. I thought they were shooting at us. Then I thought they were shooting at her. But the man with the rifle—he was pointing it down toward the quarry."

"He was sending me an invitation to come out of the building." Cono put his hand on Dimira's shoulder again and looked into her eyes. "You have suffered because of me. And your road will be rough, because of me. I am sorry."

Dimira's hollowed brown eyes filled with tears again. "Xiao Li … she was so strong. I think …" Dimira swallowed. "I think if I hadn't shot the gun …"

"No!" Cono shook her. "He was going to kill us all. You had no choice. Look at me. You had no choice."

A distant whomping halted their conversation. The sound

grew louder and was joined by two harsh, continuous whistles. Dimira scrambled beneath a thick juniper tree, with Cono on her heels. They huddled against the trunk and looked up. Two military-green helicopters passed over them, so low that the prop wash shook all the trees around them. Cono motioned for Dimira to give him the pistol that had been glued to her hand during the climb.

"Just in case," he yelled over the deafening noise.

The whistles of the engines shifted to a lower tone as the copters rose up the mountainside. Only a few minutes passed before the popping of blades against the air again destroyed the trickling sound of the nearby stream. The copters were higher this time, and their noise receded quickly as they veered down the mountain.

The search seemed half-hearted. Maybe Zheng's embassy had pressured a reluctant Kazak military to find the murderers of their diplomatic personnel. Cono imagined Bulat saying: "We are most fortunate that Beijing does not have its own helicopters in my city. Yet."

Or maybe the Bureau had localized the cell phone calls made from the quarry and found their leader's corpse on top of a dead woman, and then followed up with a perfunctory reconnaissance.

Or perhaps Katerina had fled back to the Americans and claimed credit for the foiling of the jihadis and the destruction of the high-U, which duly provoked the Americans to pressure the Kazak military to make a sweep for any jihadis who might have escaped.

Cono wondered what options Katerina had left. She probably had another card yet to be played, a new role, perhaps with the Russians. Such a superb actor. For all her worries about her family back home in Ukraine, she could have left the drama behind long ago. But she liked the stage. "Addicted," she had written. Cono tried to hate her, to form feelings of what people called revenge, but they didn't come. The only time he'd had a fully formed thought of revenge was when he'd wanted to kill his father. But he never got the chance.

"They've been gone awhile," Dimira said. "I don't think they're coming back. We can go on."

Sitting out the copters' search had opened the floodgates of Cono's fatigue, and Dimira's words seemed dreamlike.

"Dimira, I need to rest." He saw her worried eyes only hazily. "It will be cold. We'll make the leaves into a pile." Cono was having trouble even forming words.

They crawled away from the juniper to a stand of ash and pushed the crackling leaves into a mound. Although it was still daylight, they were already in the shadow of the mountain spur. They crawled into the pile, sweeping more leaves over themselves. They lay with their arms wrapped around each other. Dimira winced at a pain in her chest; she guessed she had broken a rib in the fall at the quarry, but she'd said nothing to Cono about it. She moved slightly, to a more comfortable position, with Cono's face next to hers. She kissed Cono's lips, but he had already passed into a sleep that not even dreams could enter.

19

Cono slept until the morning sun had breached the spine of the mountains to the east. From the angle of the light filtering through the branches above him, he guessed he'd been out for fourteen hours.

"Your friend Bulat was right. You needed sleep." Dimira was washing mushrooms and wolfberries and wild walnuts in the stream and placing them on a slab of slate.

"Yes, he was right about many things." Cono picked a piece of leaf from his eyelid and observed Dimira. "Looks like you know the fruits of the forest."

"This is the way I lived with my baby, for almost a year, before I found work."

"I also lived like this, in the wild, for a long time when I was little," Cono said. "I miss it. I miss being wild."

They ate, washed their faces and moved on, up the mountain. There was much ground to cover on this day.

The climb was painful for Cono at first, but gradually the pumping of his legs became pleasurable and made him want to climb faster. Dimira, too, seemed rejuvenated, only occasionally pressing her hand against her ribs and suggesting a stop to admire the view and catch their breath. They followed the ascending avenue of trees hugging the stream until it met a cascade falling over a cliff. Bathed by the spray, they pulled themselves up, searching for grips and footholds that could bear their weight.

At the top of the cliff an immense bowl of meadow spread before them, and the whiteness of the far peaks flashed in the sunlight. Two startled marmots raced away, their fur rippling with gold and amber. Dimira and Cono walked quickly across the meadow, accelerating their pace with each step. When Dimira broke into a halting run, her arms outstretched as if she wanted to hug the entire landscape, Cono ran after her.

They stopped to drink from one of the strands of a stream weaving through the far side of the meadow, and splashed the cold water at each other until they were shivering.

The trail rising out of the meadow became steep. The thinner air begged more of their lungs. The larch and pine and fir became sparse and eventually disappeared. In a few more hours they reached the pass that would carry them over the snow-topped Zailiysky Alatau range and send them down toward the valley of Chong-Kemin, one more mountain range away from Lake Issyk-Kul. They were nearly in Kyrgyzstan now, but any notion of boundaries here, with summits in every direction, was absurd.

Once they were over the pass, the trail downward became a steep path of scree that shifted beneath their feet. In the air in front of them a long-legged buzzard glided slowly from one current to another.

"Cono, I think Xiao Li loved you." Dimira was walking in the lead, so Cono barely heard what she'd said.

"We had much in common," he replied. "And I admired her. I respected her."

"What do you have in common? She was Chinese. You are … something else."

"She grew up without rules. She had to make her own rules, mold her own life, carve her own dignity, out of nothing."

"Like you?"

"Like me. But she was better."

"She told me she had a son in China. Your son."

The scree beneath Cono's feet gave way. He rode the sliding rocks as if he were surfing, nearly bumping Dimira as he passed her, coasting to a stop several yards down the slope.

Cono turned his head back toward Dimira. "Maybe the idea of a child kept her going, gave her something solid. Without that idea, she was all alone."

"But she had you."

"I hadn't seen her in four years. But we spoke."

"But she still had you. In her thoughts."

"I don't know if I was any more real to her than her idea of a child. But even with the distance of time and place, she was very real to me. I …" His voice cracked and he stopped himself.

Their silence resumed. Cono's mind became absorbed by each placement of his feet—on lichen-covered small boulders, between lumps of prickly scrub, on friable stones that might or might not crumble beneath his weight. He wondered if, on that night in Almaty when they tried to make love against the tree, Xiao Li had made an innocent slip in asking him to give her a baby. She hadn't said *another* baby, she'd said *a* baby. But then again, how many hours had she been tormented in the rooms above the General? Could he, Cono, have kept his own mind straight through all that terror? He felt himself shriveling up in wrinkles of dread—dread that in disbelieving her, he had been just another one of the beasts in the salty garden of Xiao Li's life. Maybe there was a son. Maybe it was his.

Cono felt the scree sliding beneath him again; he tried to jump to a firm piece of earth, but lost his balance and toppled over, sledding on his back until he careened into a boulder. Dimira came down to him, easily navigating the loose rocks, and helped him get to his feet.

They had almost reached the valley. A man on a horse surrounded by sheep was waving at them from below. He wore a white-and-black peaked felt hat, and even at this distance they could see that he was smiling.

"Better to come down that way," he yelled in a Kyrgyz-Kazak dialect, pointing to their left. "It's easier."

The valley was in the mountains' shadow as the Kyrgyz *chaban*, a herder, approached them on his stout horse, the sheep following without looking up from their meal of end-of-summer grasses. Cono searched the lush open valley. It spread out in front of them like a vast, undulating lawn, empty except for the whitish dome of a yurt perhaps a mile away, in the direction of the river that must lie at the bottom of the valley. The sky was still a brilliant, unblemished blue.

In a mixture of Kyrgyz, Kazak and Russian, the chaban asked if they were lost. "You don't have packs," he said. "No warm clothes. Don't you know it's cold up here at night? And why does your head look like a cracked melon?" His ruddy face was smiling all the while; he was intrigued and amused by the strange visitors to his borderless meadow, which he would abandon soon, taking his livestock down from the mountains before winter selfishly took back the Tian Shan until the next spring. The chaban invited them to his yurt to eat and spend the night. Dimira and Cono had been hiking for nearly twelve hours, and the chill of evening was already reddening their ears; the two of them exchanged glances and accepted his offer.

"He seems like a happy man," Dimira said softly in English as they walked among the sheep, the herder weaving his horse back and forth at the rear of the flock.

"Yes, he has freedom in his face."

The warmth was instant as they ducked their heads beneath the birchwood mantle of the yurt's doorway. Human humidity mixed with the smoke of burning dung drifting up to the hole at the center of the domed felt roof. The chaban's wife was seated on the floor next to a stack of saddles and harnesses, squeezing two fingers along lengths of sheep intestines until the semidigested green mush emerged and plopped into a small vat. She nodded, smiled, and said, "Welcome to this home."

The herder, who called himself Nurbek, took off his hat and made them sit on the tiny red bench beneath ancestors' photos at the far side of the circular walls. He proudly offered them vodka in tiny cups; he poured for his wife as well. They all took the drink in one gulp.

"How many children do you have?" Nurbek's eyes were wide with curiosity.

Dimira and Cono passed glances at each other.

"Don't worry, you look healthy. It will come. I have four. Three sons and a daughter. And if they eat well, maybe some grandchildren in the spring." Nurbek's cheeks were flushing red from the vodka. "So keep trying!" He poured again.

Two hours later, after a meal of mutton, rice, and knots of bread fried to the hardness of marbles, all eaten with their fingers, and more vodka, they were singing: old sobby Russian tunes; a hymn to Manas, the Kyrgyz warrior hero; the ballad of the mountain-god Khan Tengri; "Only Fools Rush In," the way Elvis sang it. Cono followed as best he could, but Dimira knew all the songs by heart, and her voice was so enchanting to Nurbek that he grabbed her by the wrist to make her stand up for a duo performance of a song by Viktor Tsoi, a Russian rocker from the seventies. Nurbek swiveled Dimira by her hands as Mirgul, his wife, clapped to make a rhythm for their dance. Nurbek grabbed Cono's hand, and he in turn pulled Mirgul up from the floor. Cono put on the happiest face he could muster as he thought of how boisterously Xiao Li would be singing along and dancing. The four twirled and twisted until Nurbek banged out the song's climax with his throaty voice.

They were all laughing as Nurbek pulled away a tasseled and embroidered burgundy curtain revealing a bed less than a yard wide, snug against the wall of the yurt. "Here is where you two will sleep tonight," he chuckled with delight. "It worked for my wife and me. And don't worry—we won't hear anything."

The kerosene lanterns went out. Cono and Dimira adjusted their bodies to fit the cramped space as their hosts rustled the carpets and blankets that they would sleep on. Nurbek began humming a song, but was shushed by his wife. Cono had taken off his shirt and vest; otherwise he and Dimira were dressed except for their shoes. Two heavy wool blankets covered them. In the confines of the bed there was no choice but for Dimira to lie partly on

Cono's chest. Her breath passed over his neck. Outside the yurt, sheep and goats and horses stomped and bleated and snorted and farted. The rails of their temporary corrals creaked with their movements until they'd found their places for the night.

Dimira stroked Cono's arm and put her mouth close to his ear. She slid her leg up to his thighs, passing over the rows of bruises from the bludgeons at the bank, but her movements elicited no pain. The pressure of her embrace and her smell and the closeness of her lips, her breath in his ear, her subtle rocking and intermittent light squeezes—Cono was dismayed that even in the immediate aftermath of the tragedy, he was becoming aroused.

Their mouths searched for each other in the darkness. They kissed, lightly at first, as Dimira tried not to press on the most swollen parts of his lips. Their tongues played games until their kissing lost all restraint. Cono's hardness became an ache. He reached for the small of Dimira's waist. But as he touched her there, he saw Xiao Li's body separating, stage by stage. He felt the pulsations in the hardness diminishing. He guided Dimira's hand to the mound trapped in his pants. He wanted her to feel it, to know how much he desired her, before the images in his mind destroyed it.

He whispered, "Dimira. I want, but I can't."

Dimira said nothing. She nestled her lips next to his neck and stroked his hair for a long time, until her hand faltered and came to rest on his collarbone. Then she floated off into her dreams as Cono did into his.

Mama. Mama in her good dress. Mama crying. She cries more when the hand hits her again. Her face opens up. Pours red. No, no, no. I love you. The fist again. Grab Papa's legs. Hold them tight. Hit them. Bite them. Make him stop. Lifted by the legs. Chairs falling. Puta, puta. Smack of the fist. Mama make him stop. Puta. No, no, I love you. Falling. Pressed between her knees and his knees. No air. Kicking from both sides. Mama. Papa. No more air. The pressure leaves. Crawling along her legs, to her waist, her breasts, her shoulders. Mama. The warmth of the liquid on his cheek and hers. Her open eyes. Her stillness. Mama! The loud noise. The ringing. The crushing of his back. The smell of his father's armpit. Squirming. Squirming out of the heaviness. Papa! His father's face. Broken open. Mama get up! The heaviness of Papa's body. Pull it away. Let her breathe. Mama! The thing in Papa's hand. The stare of Mama's eyes, her beautiful eyes. Mama! The stillness of her eyes.

Cono awoke shouting: "No! I can't breathe!" But his shouts were those of dreams, mumbled and barely audible. His eyes opened to the blackness and he felt a warm hand caressing his sweating cheek. The weight on top of him was Dimira. The steady breathing and the soothing hand were hers. Gradually his hyperventilating subsided. The sounds of agitated hooves against the earth outside slowly diminished as well. Cono wrapped his arms around Dimira's reassuring solidity and fell back down the endless chute of sleep.

20

Morning came before dawn. Mirgul was stoking the tin hearth and Nurbek was outside releasing the sheep and goats for a day of grazing when Dimira and Cono knelt at the door and put on their shoes. Cono went outside to look at the last stars before they would be forced to surrender to the sun.

Soon Mirgul served breakfast—the same meal they'd had for dinner, except for the goat's milk poured into the cups that had held vodka the night before.

"Thank you for the warmth of your home, and for your kindness," Cono said as they finished eating.

"And for the dancing," said Dimira, smiling at Mirgul and then at Nurbek.

Mirgul handed a dried horsemeat sausage wrapped in cloth to Dimira, along with a large, coarse shawl. Dimira thanked her again and held her leathery hands tightly. When all four were outside the yurt, Nurbek said, "You won't have to walk today. My horses will get you down to Issyk-Kul a lot faster. But don't let them stop to eat too much. Hunger keeps them going."

"You are too kind," Dimira protested. "Thank you, but we won't be coming back this way."

"Don't worry," Nurbek said as he cinched the saddle on one of the stocky mares. "Just leave them with my friend Kuban at Ornyok town on the edge of the lake. Not hard to find him—he has the only gas station in town. The horses are his competition. *Friendly* competition." Nurbek grinned.

During the first hour of grinding against the saddles, Cono and Dimira wondered if they wouldn't be better off hiking. But they both knew that with the horses they might be able to turn two days of nonstop marching, and one dangerously cold night, into a single long day of riding. Their gluteal muscles gradually became inured to the rhythmic pain. The alternating squeaks of stressed leather mesmerized Cono; it was a pleasing sound, a soothing pulse.

Just before the sun's morning rays spilled into the valley, they forded the Chong-Kemin River at a wide bend that was shallow except for the last ten yards, where the water reached up to their stirrups. Dimira expertly dug her heels into her mount and forced a swift crossing. Cono's horse veered with the flow of water, and only with vicious kicking and tugging was Cono able to reach the other side, well downstream.

"You've done this before," he shouted.

"Growing up in Balkhash," Dimira replied. "We had no bicycles, but there were plenty of horses."

After five hours of steadily rising out of the valley, when the sun was just shy of its zenith, they reached the top of the last pass before the descent to the lake. Dimira and Cono halted the horses and stood side by side. Stretched out miles away, and a mile lower in altitude, was the mineral-blue surface of Lake Issyk-Kul, so deep and saline that it never froze under the lock of winter. To the east, at the end of the long axis of the lake, shielded by an army of progressively higher mountains, was the white pyramidal summit of Khan Tengri, King of the Sky, on whose shoulders the borders of Kazakhstan, Kyrgyzstan and China met.

The placid lake was immense, beautiful, cradled by mountains all around. The last vacationers of summer were probably sunning themselves on the beaches of its north shore, Cono thought. But even here, near the roof of the world, beauty and tranquility had their secrets. At the far eastern rim of the lake, near a town called Koy-Sary, was a naval base that had been Moscow's principal site for submarine research and testing of high-speed torpedoes. The military complex had been huge, a treasured research polygon on which the Soviet navy relied heavily during its Cold War underwater competition with the U.S.

As they sat in their saddles, enjoying the respite from constant movement, Cono privately recalled the details of the tontería that had acquainted him with Koy-Sary. The base had been winding down after the Soviet collapse. But even years later, many of the Russian engineers were still living there, tethered by families, many of them married to Kyrgyz women, all of them worried that their only future career was to drive a taxi in Novosibirsk or wait tables in Tomsk, if they could find even that work. They were brilliant Ph.D.'s educated in institutes of excellence that Cono could only imagine, reduced from party-coddled high status to a life of scratching for the survival of their children.

Cono's task had been to recruit them to new career opportunities. He was new to this kind of career himself. He had sympathy for their plight, he was caring and convincing in his conversation, and even more convincing with the cash he handed over to the ones he selected—an advance from their future employer. When they asked who that employer might be, Cono gave them only a telephone number in Bishkek, the capital, as he had been instructed to do.

Cono didn't know how many of the dozens of engineers and scientists he had discreetly met with had been successfully delivered to his client. He didn't even know at the time who the ultimate client was—it had all been arranged through an intermediary, a talkatively unrevealing man from Pakistan who fiddled with his big ring as they spoke.

Although there were only a few entities—countries or corporations—that could fit the bill, a year passed before Cono acquired any certainty about who that entity was. The big-ringed Pakistani had called him, interested in his services for another tontería. He sounded like he'd been drinking.

"The Beijing boys and I are very happy with the caliber of your work."

"Caliber?" The English word was new to Cono.

"The quaaality of what you deliver, the eeease of doing business with you."

Working for Beijing; an eeeasy servant. A tool for guys like Zheng, giving them a kick-start for the Chinese navy, and anything else they wanted. Looking back on it now, he could see that the tontería was flagrant prostitution. But weren't most of his missions just that? And yet some deep hunger kept him at it, kept him running, like the horses. Why? It was absurd, this addiction. As absurd as submarines in the Tian Shan.

But this time, Cono had failed. Xiao Li was dead, and he would be forever haunted by her. But at least on this mission he hadn't been prostituting himself. That would end now, on this day. No more tonterías for the thrills they gave him, or the amusement, or the feelings of indispensability. He would have to be driven by his own purposes, by his own rules, not the whimsies of anonymous pimps or friends unworthy of trust.

Friends. Trust. Were they at all connected?

Dimira's horse whinnied; it was eager to descend. To hold it back, she had to pull hard and wheel it around until she came to Cono's side again. Cono pulled back tightly on the reins of his mare, too, which also saw the lake and wanted to get on with it and get fed.

"What was your dream last night about?" Dimira asked.

Cono was taken by surprise. He continued smiling, at all the absurdity and at the magnificent landscape before him, but his thoughts were diverted by her question.

"Tell me," she said. "Was it about Xiao Li?"

The horses whinnied and snorted.

"Tell me."

Dimira and Cono gripped their reins. Dimira's mare rose up and tried to buck, until Dimira's sure hands and soothing purr made it come back to all fours, quivering.

"My father killed my mother when I was a kid," Cono said, facing not toward Dimira but toward the panorama before him. "He thought she was fucking a man to make money. I think she was. We were poor. I didn't try hard enough to stop him. Then he shot himself. I dream about it often."

A breeze from below, a warm and perfumed breeze born of the distant lake and carrying the scents of miles of trees and fallen summer flowers, touched the nostrils of the horses. They reared up and scored the air with their hooves. Their riders looked into each other's eyes and eased the reins, and the horses galloped back onto the trail.

The descent seemed endless. Cono leaned back in his saddle as his horse braced its front legs against the steepness. They passed inclined fields strewn with boulders, and splashed over streambeds of smooth, flat rocks. Three argali sheep with thick, helical horns eyed them shrewdly from a high outcropping; they clapped their hooves against the rock to gain a perch higher still, then stared down again at the invaders.

Dimira and Cono reached the tree line and were swallowed by the forest. After several hours in the shade of firs and tall pines, they emerged onto a ridge that exposed the lake to their view once again. From here they could see the road that followed the water's edge, no more than an hour away. The sun was flirting with the lesser range of mountains to the west of Issyk-Kul, in the direction of Bishkek. They dismounted and plucked wild apples and bit into them with mashing sounds that revealed the fruit's dryness. They fed two apples to each horse as well.

"When we get down to the lake, it'll be safer for you to travel without me," Cono said.

"I know that."

"I'll take the horses to Nurbek's friend. So no one will see you with a foreigner. You can take a minibus to Bishkek and stay there for a while. With your Kazak ID, you'll …"

"I know, I can cross back and forth freely."

"You may have to stay a long time, to be safe. I'll send you money. I have some cash on me now. You'll be able to buy a new place. But your work?"

"I will ask for a medical leave," Dimira said. "Some of the

teachers will be happy I'm away. And without Asel, what do I have there anyway, in Almaty?"

Cono was uncomfortable with what seemed to be her nonchalance. "Dimira, I think you will be out of danger in a few months. Maybe you are even now, but I was wrong last time, very wrong. It's hard to know. Maybe there's another Zheng in the wings who will try to get some leverage from you. Or maybe no one was in control of Zheng, and the only men from their embassy who knew about you are the dead ones. Maybe Katerina, the Ukrainian, or the man she had follow me to your apartment will find some way to use you. Maybe the Bureau will have some way of knowing about you. I don't know. Maybe it's best if you go somewhere far away. I'll get the visas for you. You won't need to worry about money. Maybe …"

Dimira clasped Cono's head with both hands and pressed her cheek against his. "Maybe I'll stay around here, in my homeland, and hope you come back."

21

The Burj Al Arab Hotel in Dubai rises from a manmade island in the Persian Gulf like the great white spinnaker of a yacht about to crash into the mainland. More than fifty stories up, near the top of its mast, looking like the flat disk of a radar scanner, a helipad juts out. Just behind it is a wing, a white airfoil broad enough to give the illusion that it could lift the monumental vessel into the air before it was wrecked against the shore. Within the contours of the wing is a restaurant decorated in glass, polished chrome, and vibrant overhead panels of blue and green.

Cono is seated there, alone. Outside the broad sweep of floor-to-ceiling windows, the sun is lost in the haze of the gulf as it sinks down for the night. Cono looks across the table at his reflection in the curved glass partition running along the top of the banquette. The wounds inflicted by Zheng have healed shut; the swelling is long gone, but Cono's tongue still involuntarily rubs against the cracked canine. He ignores his seafood salad as he reads again the computer-printed phone message from the hotel's operator: "Don't try to call again. Nice jumping with you, but it's over. —

Annika." Cono rips the message into tiny pieces and sprinkles them into the ashtray. He thinks of the Swede as if she were a ghost from a previous life, a life he had tried to regain by leaving many fruitless messages for her. He picks up the prior day's *Herald Tribune*. On page five there is something about Kazakhstan. Cono spears a shrimp with his fork, bites into it, and reads.

> The government of Kazakhstan unexpectedly announced yesterday the dismissal of its prime minister, Mr. Zautbek Dukayev, along with several other ministers, notably Mr. Nartay Kurgat, minister of the interior, widely viewed by analysts as the most powerful member of the regime. The premier of the republic, Mr. Ural Gukdov, said in a prepared statement that the changes were in keeping with a more representative government.
>
> Mr. Timur Betov, former chief of the Bureau for National Security, was named as the new prime minister. He was described by Premier Gukdov as "a brave man who nearly lost his life for the sake of the nation's security in the fight against religious radicalism." In a separate statement, Mr. Betov stressed the need for economic development of the country, the efficient exploitation of its oil and gas resources for the benefit of the people of Kazakhstan, and a permanent security pact with the country's neighbor and largest trading partner, the People's Republic of China.
>
> Mr. Betov praised the "fatherly" guidance of his country by Premier Gukdov, who has been mentioned in connection with an action before a U.S. federal court alleging violations of the U.S. Foreign Corrupt Practices Act in a

case dubbed "Kazakhgate," concerning the sale of rights to the country's abundant oil fields. The new prime minister gave no timetable for the naming of a cabinet. None of the former ministers could be reached for comment.

There is a photo accompanying the article. Timur is standing on a podium flanked by the premier and numerous other Kazak men, some in official poses, others, in the back, milling about. Cono looks closely at Timur's face. The scars shaped like tears are there. In time, Cono is sure, Timur will have them erased by plastic surgery.

Cono thinks of a gnarled old woman he met at Zelyony Bazaar on his first visit to Almaty. She was talkative and short, waving flies away from her apples with a knitted orange scarf. Cono was asking her about Kazakhstan and how the new nation's future looked, explaining that it was his first time in the country. "In *my* country," she said, "when we think about the future, we shake."

The old woman vanishes from Cono's thoughts as he catches sight of the singer from Hong Kong who is about to start her number. When she passes him she smiles and says hello, as she has done on each of the previous three evenings. Cono's eyes linger on her as she adjusts the microphone, then he returns to his salad. He picks up a shrimp tail that has fallen on the newspaper and looks at the photo again. A shape in it seems familiar. It's faint, like the edge of a shadow, caught between two men near the back. It is a woman in profile, from her breasts to the top of her head. *Katerina.*

Cono folds up the newspaper. He tries not to think of Xiao Li, swallowing hard against her memory and his sorrow. Instead he sees Timur, imagining him with red tears cut into his face, pointing down at the sprawl of Almaty. *You never know when this tree or that tree will turn its colors. But come spring ...*

Author's Note

"Savoring of the hot taste of life" (Chapter 1) derives from the poem *Black Marigolds* as translated from Sanskrit by E. Powys Mathers. Initial reports on the genetic basis of what the author calls human performance anomalies (Chapter 5) include the following:

> Red-blood-cell over-production: de la Chapelle et al. *Proceedings of the National Academy of Sciences USA* 1993;

> Muscle hypertrophy: Schuelke et al. *New England Journal of Medicine* 2004; and

> Pain insensitivity: Cox et al. *Nature* 2006.

Dr. Oliver Sacks notes the reaction times of Tourette's patients (Chapter 5) and other aspects of human time perception in *The New Yorker*, 23 August 2004. *Incognito: The Hidden Life of the Brain* (by Dr. David Eagleman, 2011) reviews surprising elements of brain function relevant to Cono, including awareness. The interpretation and time-parsing of facial "micro-expressions" (Chapter 6 and elsewhere) have been pioneered by Dr. Paul Ekman. The devastation of the Cultural Revolution (Chapter 6) is chronicled in *Mao's Last Revolution* (by Roderick MacFarquhar and Michael Schoenhals, 2006); the Cultural Revolution's brutality extended to cannibalism, as documented in *Scarlet Memorial: Tales of Cannibalism in Modern China* (by Zheng Yi, 1996). "Let us pull the oars together" and other lines sung by Cono during his torture (Chapter 9) are inspired in part by Qiao Yu's Chinese lyrics for the 1955 song *Let Us Sway Twin Oars*. CIA ineptitude (Chapter 9 and elsewhere) has a literature all its own; see, for example, Tim Weiner's *Legacy of Ashes: The History of the CIA* (2007). News items relating to Project Sapphire (Chapter 9) are from the Nuclear Threat Initiative, *Air Force Magazine* (August, 1995), *Reuters, The Washington Post, The Washington Times*, and *Nucleonics Week*. The word "Kazak" has been used throughout, rather than "Kazakh" (a Russian-derived convention) or "Kazakhstani" (a neologism) for simplicity and consistency with the original transliteration, "Qazaq."

About the Author

VICTOR ROBERT LEE lives on the road in Asia and writes under a pseudonym. *Performance Anomalies* is his first novel.